NIGHT ABERRATIONS

JD NELSON

To Nels, always Nels

CHAPTER ONE

I woke to the sound of sirens. Jumping to unsteady feet, I hesitated, not knowing what to do first. Should I run? Should I hide? Should I see a therapist?

Half-asleep and clutching at the pain in my chest, I stumbled across the room to turn off the siren, also known as the alarm clock, and dragged myself back under my warm blanket. I briefly considered throwing the clock across the room; it tricked me three days in a row with that siren routine, after all, but I couldn't. I couldn't do anything to hurt it. That black plastic shell held a lot more than just wires and circuit boards. It contained hundreds of memories of my father. I remembered my father laughing at me for keeping 'human hours' when he came in to tuck me into bed at night, him yelling at the top of his lungs for me to turn the clock off as I slept right through the alarm, and who could forget the times my father threatened to throw it in the trash after he had to come in to turn it off himself?

I guess the fact I didn't technically need to sleep made my super lame excuses even, uh … lame-ier, but I wanted to be human more than anything. I felt like a human. I was as normal as an almost twenty-year-old girl could possibly be.

My parents, however, were not normal. My parents didn't sleep, they did magic all the time, they didn't use contractions and spoke in a thick, almost indecipherable accent that none of my friends could understand, and they were also those parents. You know, the ones all the human parents whispered about behind their backs at the school bake sale. They couldn't help but stick out like a sore thumb in the sea of soccer moms and dads in polo shirts with the odd way they dressed. I secretly called their look, 'bohemian medieval'. Nothing else could accurately describe it. My mother usually wore a long, thick dress of dark grey, adorned, sometimes with intricate embroidery, sometimes with a leather bodice. That get-up combined with her head of shimmering silver

1

hair and matching eyes, she looked like a Valkyrie heading off to the battlefields. My father's wardrobe didn't do anything to lessen the level of embarrassment I dealt with on a day-to-day basis either. Once I saw the movie, The Princess Bride, he always reminded me of the farm boy, Westley. He was never without a worn pair of pants made of some soft leather and a billowy, roughhewn shirt. Add blond hair and blue eyes, and you could see how I, and every single person in the neighborhood, could make the comparison. I honestly couldn't tell you how many times I'd been asked if I had been abducted by aliens and forced to live with them in the biggest, most obvious house in our little suburb of Fairmeadows. It was clear I was nothing like them.

And would never be, now that they were gone.

With tears leaking down my temples into my hair, I whispered to the glowing red numbers mocking me from across the room. "You win again, Mr. Clock, but I've got my eyes on you."

It was dark when I woke next. Sitting up stiffly, I let my eyes adjust to the dimly lit room. Nothing seemed amiss as far as I could tell. The dirty laundry was still stacked against the wall (along with the empty aspirin and water bottles), and the voicemail button was still blinking at me like a demented strobe light. Yet, there was something different. I could feel it. The hairs on my arms were sticking straight up, and there was a familiar good feeling throughout the house … a sensation I hadn't felt since my parent's murders. I closed my eyes and took a deep breath, only to open them wide a second later when I realized what I was feeling. It was a magical signature. Thank God.

Quickly, I carefully climbed out of bed and padded to the bathroom to try to make myself presentable. It wouldn't be easy. I couldn't do anything about the emaciated way my body and face looked, but maybe I could manage to style my long, white-blonde curls into something that didn't look like small woodland creatures were living in it. Maybe.

It was a little disappointing, although not surprising, to see I had gotten sicker. That's the thing with magic withdrawal. You die a slow, horrible death. And you look like shit through the entire process. I expected as much. I knew there'd be a point when I'd have to make myself stop looking in the mirror, and that point came a couple of days ago when I discovered my skin had jaundiced and my cheeks had become hollow. I made a vow, then and there, that though I might be dying, I would not document every change I underwent as I made my mad dash to the grave. Nope. I would come to terms with my demise the only way I could—by ignoring it and pretending it wasn't happening.

As I left the bathroom, I knew I should have been more than a little afraid to find out who was in my home. As hopeful for a savior as I was, a magical signature didn't necessarily equate a good creature, and whoever it was could be my parent's killer, and subsequently, my killer. But really, the damage was done. What could they do? Kill me faster?

The magical signature led me all the way to the living room, but it was completely worth the slow shuffle down the hall. I nearly cried when I saw my Uncle Soren flipping through an old photo album, looking precisely as he had in the thirty-year-old photos he held. Soren Vidar wasn't really my uncle; he was my father's oldest friend, and I'd never met him formally, but he was the only person that my parents had ever mentioned from their former life on Álfheim, so, of course, I was fascinated by his mysteriousness from the moment I laid eyes on him.

Starting when I was only seventeen, I would stare at his pictures, sometimes for entire days, transfixed by my own imagination. Tall and fierce, he was almost beautiful with the hawkish severity he exuded. But, by far, my favorite of his features were his unusual white hair and red eyes. Those unique traits didn't scare me like they would a human woman. To me, he was the perfect embodiment of an Ásgardian male, even if, in every picture, he seemed detached, unfriendly, and determined to avoid the camera. None of that mattered to me. I felt a connection with

3

him through those pictures, a strong one. For the last three years, he has literally been the male of my dreams, and now, he was here in my living room when I looked like an extra for Night of the Living Dead. Just perfect.

"Hello, Uncle Soren," I said, making my presence known and trying like hell to ignore the way my heart raced with a mixture of dread and nervousness.

His deeply accented voice was as hard and as cold as steel as he said, "I am not your uncle."

"Sorry," I replied, crushed at his lack of interest. "That's the name my parents gave you." I held onto the wall for support as I moved to rest on the couch. I couldn't believe that after three years of adoration, he hadn't even spared me a glance.

"I see…" he began, then stopped, his stern look morphing into horror as he took in my frail condition with shock and surprise. "Emelie," he said, in a genuinely distressed voice. "What has happened to you?"

"Well, as you can probably guess, I'm dying."

In less than a second, Soren sat next to me, his massive form looming over my petite frame. He put his cold hand to my blazing hot forehead, and I sighed in appreciation. It felt like heaven. "Magic withdrawal? How can this be possible?"

"Without my parents, I have no one here to draw from," I murmured, eyes closed and utterly relaxed as I enjoyed the first bit of relief I'd had in a week.

"Then you have never been to the Norselands?"

Opening my eyes, I chuckled and gestured to myself. Obviously not. The worlds of the Yggdrasil were a dangerous place. Far too dangerous for a light elf that somehow never got her magic. Of course, the ridiculous irony in that was that I could give my magic a sort of 'jumpstart' if I went to the Norselands. Believe me when I say I was tempted to go after I buried my parents, but in the end, I just couldn't risk becoming a slave to its ruler, the Alfather. I'd rather die.

Sighing heavily, my Soren stood. "Your body is already shutting down. We must work quickly if you are to survive." He gingerly lifted me into his arms, marching me back the way I'd come to lay me on the bed. Why? I had no idea.

Noticing my 'what the hell' look, Soren smiled at me in what I'm sure he thought was a reassuring way. But it was far from it. There was no sympathy in his eyes for me. He didn't really care that I was dying. He was just duty-bound to save me. I couldn't believe I'd ever had romantic thoughts about this male. In my dreams, Soren had been sexy and affectionate. In reality, he was still sexy—definitely still sexy, but so cold as he joined me on my small bed and motioned for me to move closer to him.

I hesitated. I was beyond nervous to be in the same room as Soren, let alone the same bed. I'd never been alone with a male before, especially one I envisioned myself having young with.

Narrowing his crimson eyes with vexation and impatience, he admonished me. "Emelie, do not fear me. We need to be skin to skin for the healing magic to work. The more skin, the better. I promise you. I will not hurt you."

Mute, I nodded, nestling into his side and laying my cheek on his newly exposed chest. Almost instantly, I felt my strength start to return. Smiling, I tried to lift my head away from him, but he held me firmly in place.

"Not yet, Emelie," he insisted. "You are still quite unwell."

"How did you do that?" I whispered, in complete awe of his power.

"I am Soren Vidar of Ásgard, the son of Odin and Grid. I am one of the first." He spoke simply and matter-of-factly as if that should explain everything.

I stiffened against him. "You don't mean the Odin, do you?"

Soren furrowed his brows. "Please relax, little one. You are safe with me. I do not serve my father. Indeed, there are a great many creatures in the Norselands that refuse to be ruled by The Alfather. Your father and I have … had long been together in the rebellion against him."

While he continued to inspire trepidation in me, I had little choice other than to believe him. If he was Odin's offspring, he could crush a little elf like me without a second thought, and honestly, it was almost impossible to distrust him while the slight tingling where our skin touched was so soothing and familiar. It was almost reminiscent of my mother's magic. I closed my eyes and calmed myself by concentrating on the tranquility of his magic still coursing through my veins.

"Your mother was very powerful," he said, in answer to my thoughts. "Her magic rivaled my own."

"What?" His proclamation startled me. I'd forgotten there were those who could read your mind. Elves didn't possess that talent. Damn it. Why hadn't my parents ever taught me to block telepaths, and what did he mean my mother was very powerful? She was a light elf.

"I can teach you how to prevent entry into your mind," Soren said, interrupting my internal deliberation. "But first, I must address one thing."

"What's that?" I asked, my voice wavering. I was terrified to hear what he was about to say.

His soft answer was spoken with obvious reluctance. "Emelie, your mother was not a light elf."

Negotiating myself out of his grasp, I sat up. "What do you mean? Of course, she was, just like my father and I."

"You are only half-light elf. Your mother was a Norn." Frustrated, he continued, "They should not have kept a secret of this magnitude from their own child. I warned them of the implications their decision would have in the future."

My mind swam as I attempted to process this information. My sweet mother a Norn? No way. Norns were old females, cloaked in white and mad with power … the ultimate power to create fate.

Soren cast a pitying look in my direction.

I squinted at him. "There's something else, isn't there?"

"Yes." He sighed; burden evident in his countenance. "Your parents arranged your mating before you were born. You are weeks away from being a queen." He paused, seemingly indifferent to my speechlessness. "Emelie, you are cold. Come into the living room. I'll light the fireplace and tell you anything you ask of me."

CHAPTER TWO

I gaped at Soren's bluntness long after he had left the room, but eventually followed him and stood arms-crossed in front of the newly ignited fireplace. As soon as he settled onto the couch, I burst out with, "Who is this man … is he a man … how do you know this?" My mind was caught in a whirlwind of terror, causing my words to come out in one jumbled sentence.

Soren leaned up and pulled me down to sit on the couch with him. "Calm down, little one. Let me explain things fully before you start your hysterics."

Hysterics? Oh, man. I just knew he was about to tell me I'd be mating a troll king and having little troll babies under a bridge somewhere.

"You are endearingly neurotic, Emelie. I never know what you will think next."

"That is not a compliment," I said, laughing at the wink he gave me. It looked so absurdly out of place on his wintry face.

He smirked. "Are you so sure?"

I raised my brows, perplexed by the change in his demeanor. "Pretty positive."

"Well then, I will make it up to you by telling you the story of your parent's mating. I doubt they told you the version I am about to."

"They didn't tell me anything! But wait a second before you start." I shifted to dangle my bare feet in front of the fire and fluffed the throw pillow to put it behind my back. Judging by the last ten minutes of revelations, this was sure to be a good one. "Okay. And … go."

Eyes intent on the fire, Soren began. "Your parents were not meant to be. Your father was once betrothed to Princess Viveka Väsen of Svartálfaheim—the land of the dark elves. Their mating was supposed to be the union that connected the divided races of elves. However, there was another who loved your father—your mother, Wist."

"I can't imagine my father ending up with a dark elf instead of my mother. They were so perfect for one another." I shook my head as if it would rid my mind of this new thought. My parents hadn't spared me from the frightening tales of the dark elves and their mad king either. I knew as enemies of the light elves, they couldn't be trusted.

Soren made a sound of disgust. "Your mother started a war by changing Anders's fate and aligning it with her own, Emelie. War isn't romantic. Elves by the hundreds have died because of her selfishness.

"But she wouldn't have done all that if she knew the cost. I know she wouldn't."

He put a pale hand on my shoulder. "She knew, little one. How could she not? Norns create futures by placing two of the most suitable mates together, and she was chosen as their Norn. Viveka may not have been what she desired for your father, but there was a purpose behind it. It was what was meant to be. Not to mention, Viveka and Anders were happy with the match until she meddled with their future which, by the way, is the prime reason Norns are forbidden to interfere with the fates they cast.

"So, she just stole him and ran?"

She and Anders went into hiding the day they mated. Even I, his best friend, was not told. It hurt me at the time, not to be worthy of their trust, but I understand now why everything had to be done in secret. It was to protect you, to protect your future from the ones they double-crossed."

"That's incredible," I marveled. Hearing about my parent's secret double life was amazing. It was like something out of a movie. Of course, it would be even more amazing if they hadn't screwed my future ten ways to Sunday. "So, how did you find them out?"

"Anders called me. He knew I could be trusted. He knew I do not believe in the mockery that is Odin's fate system today. The inhabitants of the Norselands should be able to live their own lives, make their own mistakes, and be able to love the one who is meant for them. Not be at the mercy of a wicked Norn who is money or power hungry enough to break a fate for their own personal gains. Times have changed, and we must convince him of that or break free of his rule." He tucked my hair behind my ear. "Your father knew I could never betray you."

What a sweet and poignant thing to say. I took his hand in mine and held it to my heart in a traditional elven gesture of thanks, then ignored the look of distaste that flashed across his face at my touch. "Thank you, Soren."

He examined our intertwined fingers with a frown but started speaking again without removing his hand from my feather-light grip. "Anders contacted me almost nine months after they left when you were born. They wanted you to be raised in a normal family, safe from the risks they brought upon you. I helped them come to Midgard, and they settled in California as humans in secret. No one, but I, knew your location."

"Risks? Because of the death sentence?"

Ignoring my question, he continued, "The dark elves declared war against the light elves, despite your mother arranging for you to take Anders's place. Until it is time for you to mate, the fighting will continue. They want what they were promised, a union between the purest of their races."

"How can I be pure if I'm only half-light elf?"

"They consider you to be one of the purest of all the light elves. Your father was among the oldest of his race."

"And I'm supposed to take his place? Me? Unite the elves? The same elves who have been fighting for twenty years for no reason? Oh, that will not end well. Nope. It has dismal failure written all over it."

"Yes, Emelie. The same elves." He sighed heavily. "It is unfair for them to have put this on your shoulders. It must seem like an impossible task to you. This, I understand. But what you must understand is that most are ready to end this battle. They will welcome you. Remember, they have awaited your arrival for two long decades."

I sat back dejected and a little more than pissed that I'd never be able to experience falling in love. My whole damn future was already mapped out for me. Thanks a lot, Mom and Dad.

"I know who killed your parents," Soren declared, effectively pulling me out of my sorrow and into ass-kicking mode.

I let go of his hand and stood up. "What? Who?" No matter what my parents had done, they were my parents. Someone would pay for their death. I would make sure of it.

He frowned again. "Several hundred years ago, the citizens of the realm of Vanaheim wanted to honor their god, Freyr, with a being in his image. The experiment went horribly awry. The abomination they created escaped, almost killing Freyr in the process. It has been wreaking havoc upon the Norselands ever since. There is little doubt it was behind the attack. And there is no doubt my father is involved in some way. This is not something he would ignore. Did you know he once gave the elves to Freyr as a gift?"

I shook my head. I think I would remember something like that.

"Ages ago, they were his to do as he pleased. The elves eventually rebelled against Freyr's depraved ways and won their freedom, but amid all the chaos, broke into the two factions that you have today. The doppelgänger is insanely obsessed with controlling them. From what we have learned, the creature believes he is Freyr. He is convinced that if you do not unite the elves with your mating, he has a chance of lording over them once again."

"Does that mean this thing is looking for me?" My mind raced with frantic scenarios. All of them ending with my untimely death.

"I shall endeavor to find that out as soon as I return to Ásgard."

I was skeptical. "How are you going to do that?"

"I will ask my father."

He sounded so sure of himself. Like he was doing something as simple as taking his father to brunch on a sunny Sunday morning instead of asking him to divulge his devious master plan. "Um ... isn't that a bit dangerous, Soren?"

Arching a brow, he mused, "Is it my dexterity you doubt?"

I cringed. Did I just insult his masculinity? "No, of course, I don't. But isn't Odin like Superman or something?"

Laughing, he disregarded my worrisome concern with a flick of his hand. "Or something. I will be fine."

Okay. Clearly, he could handle it. "How will you know where to find him?"

An alarming smile crossed his lips for a moment. It looked almost unnatural on his face. "That is the easiest part of it all. Do not distress yourself. Remember, I have yet to tell you about your intended."

I flopped back down on the couch and feigned overly enthusiastic interest. "Oh yes, my intended, tell me all about him!"

"Emelie, you should take this very seriously. No one has ever escaped the fates your mother has cast."

My stomach sank. "Oh."

His expression softened. "Have hope, Emelie. We still have time before your birthday. Together, we will do everything we can to avoid your forced mating and unite the elves once more. Do not forget, you are half Norn. It is certain your abilities will surface as soon as you are near the portal in Uppsala, and who knows, you might have the ability to change your own fate. We can experiment tomorrow. Until then, you must be very careful that you do not bring attention to yourself. No one, not even Kristian, can know about your Norn half. You are one hundred percent light elf if anyone pries. Do you understand?"

"Yes," I said reluctantly. "Is Kristian the one I'm fated to?"

"King Kristian Väsen is your fated mate." He looked irked like he hated even saying his name.

"The king!" I screeched, feeling faint. "I'm to mate the mad king?"

"You are."

Cue the panic attack. I laid my head on the back of the couch and stared at the ceiling. "What is he like? Are the stories about him being an evil underling for Odin true?"

He looked thoughtful. "His reputation is well deserved from what I have heard. However, I have never met him in person. I could not say whether all the rumors I have heard are true."

I looked at him hopefully. "What rumors? What do you know about him?"

He looked everywhere, except directly at me. He was hiding something. Something big. "Uncle Soren!"

"I am reluctant to tell you. It is most unsettling. As is you calling me uncle, by the way."

"Soren, if I cannot get out of mating him, I'll need to know what I'm up against. You must tell me this. I don't want to go in blind."

"Emelie," He took my hand, hesitant to speak.

"Go on, Soren," I urged. My heart was beating out of my chest. What could be that terrible?

Sighing, he continued, "It is rumored Kristian only takes his females by force. I have heard from a very reliable source that the females he invites to Väsen Castle are put into a harem and never heard from again. They are supposedly kept as slaves for his sick fantasies until he tires of them and has them replaced."

In a voice, far calmer than I thought I would be able to manage, I asked, "Are you telling me my mother sold me out to a slave-driving rapist?"

"Alleged rapist, I suppose."

Seriously? I just couldn't catch a break. First, my parents, and now, this? "Well, that's just … awesome. I guess I need to add learning Jujitsu to my list of things to do this week."

"I will assist you in self-defense training myself," he assured me.

I froze in fear. The Jujitsu crack had been a joke. Did he really think I'd have to defend myself physically? "This is unbelievable," I said, hot tears springing to my eyes. "How could my mother do this to me?"

"She was in love, Emelie, and sometimes love causes irrational judgments to be made. Although I must admit, it is entirely possible your mother knew Kristian is not guilty of the offenses laid against him. He was once known as the best of the King's sons."

"I wish there was a way to find out what he's really like."

"You could find out from the male himself. He is sure to be lurking outside the house."

"Come again?" I asked, pinching the bridge of my nose. I didn't think I could take much more of this.

"King Väsen is outside. Most likely in the forest, just beyond the gazebo."

"And how long has the king of the dark elves been out there?"

"Three years," he said quickly, backing away ever so slightly. "Only during the night. He is a dark elf, remember?"

I was going to have an aneurysm. Really, I was. "He's been stalking me for three years?"

"Yes," He took another step back, his eyes darting to the potential weapons in the room. "Essentially, it made your mother a prisoner in her home from dusk to dawn. She couldn't risk your safety by being seen by him."

"I'm not going to pretend that doesn't make me feel a little better," I grouched, then realization dawned on me. "Is this because my father ran away? Is that why he's following me? He doesn't think I'll follow through with the bargain, does he?"

"I can only assume he doesn't," Soren said, with a face that clearly indicated he thought there was a more sinister reason.

"Don't feel sorry for me just yet. I intend to get out of this. We already know that the guy is a creepy stalker. There has to be another way to bring about peace without me mating him."

"Let us hope so. Would you like to greet him?"

I considered his shrewd eyes. "I would if it doesn't bother you." Despite feeling violated by Kristian's surveillance, I was determined all the same. I needed to figure out a plan.

"I am resigned to the idea," he answered. "It is inevitable you will meet him. Just be mindful you will feel what seems to be a natural attraction to him. Do not be fooled. That is your mother's magic."

"Okay, I will." I walked toward the front door, stopping when he didn't follow. He still stood beside the couch looking expectantly at me.

"What is it? Aren't you coming?"

"I thought you might want to put on something suitable before you leave the house."

I looked down at my cami and pajama bottoms. "What's wrong with what I'm wearing?"

He stared openly at my breasts. "You might catch a chill. Perhaps you have a nice warm parka you would like to slip on?"

Shivering under his gaze, I said, "Maybe I'll just pull on a jacket."

"Thank you."

I grabbed a hoodie from the closet and tugged it on, trying not to think about his hungry eyes. "Will Kristian be able to read my thoughts?" I knew there were a few high-ranking dark elves that had the ability.

"No. Elves can only earn the gift if they perform a great service to their people. I have met but two with the talent."

"Do Norns have it? Will I have it?"

He smiled. "Yes."

"Good." I sighed. "Show me how to shield my thoughts soon, will you?"

"I will," he promised, taking my hand to escort me outside. "It is quite simple."

"Why not do it now?"

"You know why."

His carnal smile warmed me to my toes. "Anything else I need to know?" I murmured. He was a male that was made for sex, and if he was giving out looks like that, he might need protection from his own stalker—me.

Soren's intense eyes fixed on mine, and I felt another lightning strike of heat move throughout my body. "I have plenty I would like you to know, Emelie, but not at this precise moment. As you say, let's just get this all out in the open."

CHAPTER THREE

"Where is he?" I asked Soren, with a quiver in my voice. I was nearly paralyzed with fear. It wasn't every day you met your future, possibly rapist mate in the woods behind your house.

"The king is just beyond the light of the streetlamp, at the edge of the forest. I will summon him for you." He took a few steps forward and called out, "Come forth. Emelie would like to greet you."

At first, I thought Soren might have been mistaken. Then the mad king materialized into the moonlight from the shadowed tree line like mist turning into flesh. I sucked in a breath. The king was magnificent. That was the only word I could think of that would adequately describe him. His eyes were captivating, sparkling, and as purple as amethysts. His thick, black hair was cut short. And with his straight nose, long eyelashes, and kissable full lips, Kristian was every bit the textbook dark elf. I dragged my gaze down the length of his tan, muscular body and licked my lips. He was nothing short of breathtaking—perfection in elven form. I really hoped I wasn't drooling on my shirt.

Apparently satisfied with my appearance, Kristian smiled as he looked me over and finally broke the silence between us. "You are beautiful, Emelie."

"As are you," I told him, surprising myself. It wasn't like me to be so bold and outspoken, especially with someone who was an alleged rapist and confirmed stalker. Only, he didn't look like a rapist or a stalker. Rapists had trench coats, goatees, and chicken legs, right? And was it really stalking if we were going to be mated soon, was it?

The king took a tentative step closer to me and said, "Son of Odin, I thank you for seeing my beloved to me. You may leave us. I will see her in the house after our visit."

Delighted by his gentle, accented voice and the beloved comment, I gave him a beatific smile and tried to loosen my hand from Soren's. Kristian was so alluring, so … right. I wanted nothing more than to touch him, to be touched by him.

Soren, seeing my fervor to get to Kristian, gripped my hand tightly and tugged me back to his side. "The lady has insisted I remain. Surely you want to ensure her comfort at any cost to your pride." He was unwilling to waver.

Kristian looked supremely angry at his unwillingness to waver for a moment, then he nodded his acquiescence. "Of course. Her happiness is paramount."

Remembering my own anger from earlier, I asked, "Kristian, have you been spying on me?"

His violet eyes drew in as he whispered, "Is that what he told you, my queen?"

I had to cross my arms to keep myself from reaching out. My mother's magic was so potent, it made me desperate to be near him.

"She knows everything," Soren interjected. His voice was cold as he held my resisting form to his side. "Be honest with her, king. She is your intended, remember?"

Kristian's purple eyes flashed to black and back. "I remember, son of Odin. As if I could forget!"

Soren took a menacing step toward him. "Watch your tone, false king."

"Stop!" I snapped at them. They both stopped their glaring to look at me. "Look," I continued, "It's apparent you two can't be civil to one another. So, let me make this easy." I turned to Soren. "Please wait for me at the end of the driveway. Let me have a few private minutes with my future mate." He and I waged a silent war with our eyes for several moments after my demand, before he grudgingly nodded his compliance and walked away without so much as a word. I knew, without a doubt, we would be revisiting this when we were alone.

Once Soren out of sight, I stepped forward, mesmerized by Kristian. Reaching up to graze my knuckles against his smooth cheek, I said, "When you are calm, we can talk more. I want to learn more about you."

He held my hand to his face for a moment then kissed my palm. "I will eagerly await your call, Emelie." His speech was slightly altered as he tried to conceal his emerging eyeteeth.

"Kristian," I purred. "I've never seen anyone else's fangs before." I moved into the warmth of his body, enjoying the sharp breath Kristian drew as his thick erection pressed against my stomach. "Do you mind showing me yours?"

After a moment's hesitation, he flashed his elongated canines in a sinfully seductive smile. "How strange it must be to grow up away from all of your kinsfolk without anyone like yourself to learn from."

"I had my parents, but…" I broke off. I couldn't finish that thought out loud.

Threading his fingers with mine, he pulled me closer. "Emelie, I want you to know that even though the elves are at war because of your father if your parents' murders would have occurred at night when I could have protected them, I would have done everything in my power to save them. It pains me to see you without your family."

"Thank you, Kristian. I appreciate that." And I did appreciate that little bit of kindness. So much it convinced me to take things with my king a step farther. "Kristian?"

"Yes, my queen?"

"My mother once told me a single drop of light elf blood could allow a dark elf to see the sun for a week," I said, my voice slow and relaxed.

He eyes narrowed into an appraising look. "Did she?"

"Yes." I reached up and gently ran my finger across his lip, exposing a sharp white fang.

He sighed and closed his eyes as he wrapped an arm around my waist, wound a fist in my hair, and pulled me tight against him. "Emelie," he whispered.

With nothing to lose, I punctured the pad of my thumb against the point of his tooth and felt him go rigid. We both watched as the blood beaded up and started to drip. "Taste it," I urged. "I want you to."

With reverence, he lifted my hand to his mouth and licked the blood I offered. "My mate, you unravel me," he said, his voice a greedy growl.

"Kristian..." I couldn't finish the thought. My whole body was trembling against his as his tongue rasped my skin. There was a stronger connection between us now—something electric.

Something undeniable.

The moment we locked eyes, we stared at one another as if we were trying to memorize each other's face, neither of us blinking until a twig snapped, indicating Soren's return. Only then were we quick to move to a respectable distance for conversation.

In a hurried voice, Kristian asked, "Will I see you tomorrow, Emelie?"

The longing in his voice spoke to my own loneliness, and I was helpless to deny him. "I hope so, Kristian," I whispered.

After Soren and I let ourselves into the house, I went straight to my bathroom to shower, ignoring his suggestion to rest in favor of picking up my mess and feeling like my usual self. Sure, I knew it was a feeble attempt to forget about what I'd just done with Kristian, but I was trying hard to ignore all of that. Like, all of that. Because what I'd done felt like a colossal mistake.

Examining the situation from every angle, I tried to look for an answer that didn't make me feel like an idiot as I shampooed the smell of the mad king from my hair. I failed to find one. I had been so infatuated with him when I met him, so unbearably enamored, but that white-hot electric connection that was so strong between us outside was now nonexistent, and I felt like a fool. Soren had warned me against my mother's magic. Why couldn't I have just listened?

I was drying my hair when Soren decided to join me in the bathroom. He perched on the vanity, his keen eyes taking in everything. "So, the mad king did not live up to your expectations?"

Lifting the towel, I looked at him. "Is that sarcasm I detect?"

"Possibly," he said through gritted teeth.

I shrugged, trying to make the best of it. "He could've been a lot worse, I guess."

"I do not know how that could be possible," Soren huffed. Stalking to the bedroom, he turned down the sheets and began aggressively punching my pillow, which I assumed was his way of 'fluffing'.

"What do you mean by that?" I asked, following him in my towel.

He threw the pillow into place. "He could be a fucking rapist, Emelie. Who cares if he was a 'nice guy'? Do you not have any self-preservation?"

I pouted in response. He was right, of course, but I wasn't about to say it out loud. His ego was big enough.

He pointed to the bed. "Get some rest. You have an early day tomorrow."

"Why? What's going to happen?"

"Tomorrow, we leave here."

I nodded and climbed into bed. I'd forgotten, in all the excitement, I would have to go to one of the worlds of the Yggdrasil. I couldn't rely on others to supply my magical life-force forever. But leave California? I'd lived here my entire life. My human life was the only one I'd ever known. I had no idea what to expect, or where I would go once I got to the Norselands.

Soren smiled at me in a 'you poor creature' way. "You will be staying with me until your mating … if that is what is to happen. My butler, Cedric, will pick us up from the airport tomorrow. He and I will accompany you to my home in Sweden until your move to Väsen Castle on Svartálfaheim."

"Oh," I said slowly, the realization hitting me that I wouldn't be seeing Kristian tomorrow after all. I snuggled into my blanket and sighed. Sweden? Regardless of it being a good or bad thing, my brilliant idea to see the king the next day had backfired spectacularly.

"As it should," Soren berated from the doorway. "I really do not know what you were thinking."

I threw my hands up. "Where were you with that mind-reading thirty minutes ago, smarty-pants?"

"I endeavor to strengthen my resolve around you." He smiled ruefully. "I find it difficult to tell you no."

"Well, you better learn to fast." I sighed and rolled away from him, pulling the blanket over my head. "I'm kind of a walking disaster right now."

"Yes," he agreed, speaking softly. "But a beautiful disaster."

I awoke to unfamiliar surroundings with a start. Swinging my feet off the edge of the luxurious bed, I noticed a notepad on the nightstand. Milestone Hotel, it read. For a moment, I stupidly wondered how Soren had managed to transport the two of us to London without waking me, but I already knew—magic. My parents teleported using a shifting stone all the time, anyone could, but they would never be able to bring the luggage on the low table across from the bed or my favorite old teddy bear propped up on top of it.

The moonlight spilling through the sheer curtains illuminated the object of my thoughts. His soft breaths lured me closer. I took a moment to admire his peaceful face. One thing was certain, he was beautiful as he slept, not at all like the frowning male I was used to. Impulsively, I leaned forward and caught a lock of his hair between my fingers. It was softer than any fur I had ever felt and so white I could barely distinguish the long strands from the pillowcase. It was as perfect as it ever was in my dreams. He was as perfect as my dreams.

After a few minutes of aimless staring, thinking and worrying, I decided to take a bath to soothe my nerves. However, my attempt, or should I say, attempts, at heaving myself upright proved to be a more significant feat than I'd expected. I wobbled before finding my balance and tottering across the small room to what must be the bathroom door. Closing it behind me as quietly as I could, I turned on the light and wrenched off my clothes, dropping them unceremoniously to the floor. Then I turned on the bathtub's faucet and stuck my hand under it, waiting for it to warm. It felt good to do something routine—something normal for a change. Stoppering the tub once the water was hot, I climbed in, letting the water fill up around me just like I'd done a thousand times before and probably would a million more in my long lifespan. When the tub was full, I turned the faucet off with my feet, sighed contentedly, and immersed myself up to my nose. I floated there for at least a half hour, listening to the drip of the faucet and thinking about what I was going to do. I knew that even if I developed my Norn power today, I couldn't just walk in there, stop my mating, and change Kristian's fate. I had to think of a way to end the war and give his fated mate back to him. I had to do both. It was up to me to fix what my mother had broken. I had to do the right thing. I had to, no matter how afraid I was to do it.

Without the slightest hope left in my heart, I turned over in the water, lamenting my situation as my hair floated around my face, and for the first time in my life, the thought of never breathing again sounded like a welcome change. I'd suffered so long and would continue to if Kristian turned out to be the monster he was rumored to be. I didn't think I could do this. Only a week ago, I was just a typical sophomore in college. My biggest worry was having enough tuition money allotted for a well-deserved Peanut Buster® Parfait at the Dairy Queen every week or so. I had my whole life ahead of me to worry about the big stuff. All of that was gone now. All the innocent frivolity I'd taken for granted, all of it, gone—vanished. And in its place, I had nothing. Nothing but sorrow and heartache. So, why not end it all? Why not stop things before they could even start? It would be so easy.

I screamed as hands closed around my arms and I was roughly jerked out of the water and set on my feet. "Wha-what the hell do you think you're doing?" I coughed out, trying to wipe my waterlogged hair out of my eyes.

"Me?" Soren yelled. "What are you doing? You think because your parents are dead, and you have an arranged mating, that gives you permission to drown yourself? The dark elves depend on you! Thousands of elves, Emelie!"

I furiously swiped the mass of hair out of my face, only to find Soren's red eyes were full of pity. "Don't," I snapped. "Don't look at me like that. I'm sick to death of that look."

"I apologize," he said quickly, no doubt sensing I was about to fall apart.

"No. There's no need," I said, waving away his apology. "It's me, Soren. It's all me." Sinking onto the plush bathmat, I broke into sobs, gasping convulsively as I tried to speak. "I … can't … do this. I … just … can't."

Obviously well practiced in dealing with a hysterical female, Soren joined me on the floor in a fluid movement that was almost too fast to see, covered my naked breasts with a towel, and then took me in his arms, hugging me into his warm chest. "Fear not, little one," he soothed. "You will be all right. You have my vow of protection for as long as you feel it is needed. Indeed, forever, if that is what you ask." He leaned his chin against my wet hair and hummed an odd lullaby, gently rocking me as I soaked his black shirt with wet hair and tears of despair.

After a minute or two, I lifted my eyes to his. I wanted to see them when he promised me his protection. I had to know for sure I could depend on him if I were going to put my life in his hands. "I want to be able to trust you, Soren. Can I?"

His face was heartbreakingly sincere as he stroked my hair back with both hands. "Emelie, I would do anything to protect you—anything at all."

My heart thumped in my chest. "Anything?"

He caressed the side of my face with a thumb and cupped my chin lightly. "You have been a part of my destiny for almost as long as I can remember. Until my death, you will have my constant devotion."

"Soren, I—"

Stopping what was sure to be three years' worth of repressed adoration, he crushed his mouth to mine, effectively taking my breath away, and with it, all my thoughts. I couldn't seem to think of anything but his soft lips on mine, the strong hands pulling me closer, and the slight chafe of his shirt against my bare breasts.

Wait. Bare breasts? A blush crept up into my cheeks as I realized the towel that was between us was now covering my lap and nothing else.

I'd dreamt of this moment for three years. It was the culmination of everything my teenage heart thought it wanted—until it happened when I was naked. I mean, yeah, I liked him, might even love him, but I was still a virgin. I didn't know what I was doing with my clothes on, much less with them off.

Soren broke the kiss and produced another towel from nowhere, never taking his gaze from mine. "I didn't know you were … innocent," he said, getting to his feet. "I will … leave you … to it."

"O-okay," I answered, not moving from my position against the tub. I couldn't make my limbs cooperate or even think coherently now.

He gifted me with a small knowing smile. "So, I'll see you in a few minutes?"

"Okay," I repeated.

He hesitated, looking questionably at my awed, boneless state. "Do you need my assistance?"

I stared at the floor, unbelievingly embarrassed. Of course, the male of my dreams just had to say that to me. Hey, you're still sitting bare-assed on a hotel bathmat is the kind of thing you have to say to crazy people.

Soren reached down to offer me his hand. "You are neither crazy nor a person, Emelie. You are elven, a Norn, and perfect."

"Well, this perfect non-person is going to get in the shower … and possibly die from embarrassment," I told him, self-consciously holding the towels tight against my more sensitive areas as I got up on my own. Any other way and I would've lost my towel again.

Judging by Soren's stricken face, he hadn't thought of that when he offered his help. Without another word, he nodded apologetically and quickly left the room.

As soon as he was gone, I leaned against the nearest wall, dazed. Soren Vidar kissed me. I almost wanted to pinch myself to see if I was really awake. The kiss had been everything I expected it to be, passionate and hungry, just like in the movies. I touched my lips and closed my eyes, reliving the moment. I'd probably relive it a million times. Because that would be all I could do. I wasn't fated to Soren, no matter how much I wanted to be. And damn, I really wanted to be.

CHAPTER FOUR

After my shower, I dried off with a fresh set of white towels Soren must have brought in for me. How he managed to sneak them in unnoticed was a mystery. There was a pair of pajama pants and a cami waiting on the counter next to the towels, but to my relief, no panties. If by some miracle, Soren ever touches my underwear, I want to be in them while he's doing it.

Proving me right about his enigmatic ways, Soren was nowhere to be found when I finally plucked up the courage to tip-toe out of the bathroom. I could still smell his unique scent, a scent I was rapidly falling in love with, so I knew he must be close by, but he was nowhere in sight. Maybe he was outside getting some air? God knows I was driving him crazy with the incessant rambling in my head. I'd be so glad when he taught me to block his telepathy. I had no idea it would be so hard to control what I thought about until I tried doing it.

About a minute later, just as I was snuggling into bed, Soren came back into the room with a tiny teacup of hot chocolate cradled in his pale hands. He handed it to me with a serene smile and asked, "How are you feeling, Emelie?"

I grinned. "Better, thanks. And thanks for the cocoa. It always makes me feel better." I sipped the hot, chocolaty deliciousness while studiously ignoring how gorgeous his hair looked with the lamp reflecting off it. "How did you know?"

"Anders told me how much you loved it once," he admitted. "He said you had an unnatural love for chocolate, actually."

"If the inability to pass up any kind of chocolate counts as an unnatural love, I guess I do."

"I'd say that counts." He smiled that enigmatic half smile of his and watched me in silence until I finished. "Rest now," he said, gently prying the empty cup from my hands.

28

I settled under the covers, though I knew I'd never be able to sleep. "It's so strange, Soren. I'm usually good for a cat nap any time of the day. But since we met, I haven't been tired at all."

He pulled the duvet up to my chin. "Be that as it may, you must try to rest. Tomorrow is sure to be overwhelming for you."

I sat up. "Okay, if I wasn't worried before, I am now."

"There is nothing to fear," he assured me. "Lie back. Close your eyes."

I did as he asked, but sleep was a long time coming. I couldn't stop worrying—about going to Sweden, Soren, Kristian, more Soren, Crazy-Freyr-Guy, even more about Soren … my mind was in overload. And when I finally fell asleep, I dreamt of Soren.

In the dream, he was dressed in the kind of suit a human would wear to church or a business meeting. His hair was down and gleaming in the dusky twilight. Reaching out, he took my hand, and we were transported to a hill that overlooked a massive blue lake. I sat between his knees on the grass, and he held me as we watched the sun go down. There were no words spoken between us, but the way he held me said everything we wanted to say. It was a peaceful bond, full of love and understanding. It wasn't in a way I was experienced with. No, this was something new to me … something that felt scary, but, at the same, time felt right.

I awoke a short time later to find Soren sitting at the desk in the room, clad in jeans and a white V-neck shirt, looking every bit as mouthwatering as he'd been in my dream. I swear, he was so sexy; he could wear a garbage bag, and I'd still want to have my way with him.

I sat up cross-legged on the bed and mumbled, "You've been in my dreams again."

He looked taken aback but delighted. "Have I?"

"Yes," I blushed and looked down at the blanket. "I dream of you almost every night."

He stood and sat on the edge of the bed. "On the rare occasions I do sleep, you are in mine, as well," he confided.

"Really?" I asked skeptically. He was so incredible in every way, not to mention, at least a few zillion years older than me. Why would I be in his dreams?

His face became serious as he heard my thoughts. "I would not lie to you, little one."

I flinched. His glowing red eyes made him appear so severe. They honestly unnerved me as much as they intrigued me. Not able to maintain eye contact, I stared at his lips instead. They were inching their way upward into a slight smile.

"Something on your mind?" he asked.

"Your eyes, they …" I trailed off. I didn't know how to finish that sentence without offending him.

"Are red?" he supplied, shrugging his shoulders.

"I'm so sorry," I said, horrified at my insensitivity. "It's just I've never seen anyone with eyes like yours. They are so … unique."

He gave a weak laugh. "Do not worry, Emelie. You are not the first one to notice their unusual color. They are unusual, yes, but not unheard of in the Yggdrasil. My Father has brought many young into existence with many females. The eye color is a common trait we all share."

"Are you okay, Soren?" His voice sounded normal, but his exhaustion was so palpable, I could feel it from across the room. "Would you like some water, or maybe you'd like to lie down with me for a little while?"

With humor twinkling in those luminescent eyes, he asked, "Inviting me into your bed, Emelie? Just what are these dreams of yours about?"

"Nothing like that!" I screeched, mortified beyond belief. I was a complete liar, of course. I'd had some dreams that would qualify for a triple X rating.

Barely suppressing laughter, he said, "I will gladly accept the invitation to lie with you. I do think I would feel better if I slept for a while. The healing magic I gave you has left me rather tired."

I watched as he stood and exhaled deeply, looking bone-weary. I hurried over to give him room in the small double bed. "Okay, first things first … are you an under the cover or on top of the cover kind of guy?" I lifted the blanket as if that would help him decide.

"Under the covers," he answered, pulling his shirt off and pushing his jeans from his hips.

I blushed and let out an uncharacteristic, high, nervous laugh, trying hard not to stare at his perfection openly. It wasn't easy. I was sure my mouth was hanging open like a lunatic. To me, he looked every bit like the warrior he was—a gorgeous, ancient, and naked warrior. I felt faint just looking at him.

He smirked, apparently amused at my reaction and stretched out, catlike, beside me. "Please, do not fear me," he said in a low voice. "You are safe from my advances tonight." Holding out his arms, he beckoned to me. "Come."

I didn't hesitate to snuggle into Soren's side. He was warm, familiar. When he reached to trace my jaw, I sighed, blissfully relaxed against him with my eyes closed. Being in his arms felt like the most natural thing in any of the worlds. After a lifetime of feeling wrong, feeling different, something finally felt right.

The runes tattooed on his skin in red ink were the only things I noticed when I dared to open my eyes. I lifted my head and followed the strange assortment from the single design over his heart to the line of script leading from his right ribcage to his back. Runes hadn't been used in ages. That meant Soren had been around for a long, long time.

I met his icy gaze. "How old are you, Soren?"

He gave me a dismayed glance before staring past my shoulder. "I am one of the first inhabitants of our worlds. We didn't keep up with such things in the beginning. There was no reason to do so. But if I had to wager a guess, it would be about six or seven-thousand of your human years."

My breath caught. I hadn't expected putting a number on his age would disappoint me so much or make me feel so inconsequential. I couldn't fathom the things he'd seen, the things he'd experienced, or the sheer number of lovers he'd probably had. What would he ever want with an inexperienced, twenty-year-old virgin like me?

Soren tsked. "I do not think you inconsequential, Emelie."

"Stop reading my mind!" I groaned, rolling away from him.

"As if I could or would," he said chuckling. "Permit me to say you have a wickedly imaginative mind."

"And I am so, so sorry about that," I told him, utterly ashamed.

"Don't be, Emelie. I'm flattered you think of me in that light. You are a stunning female."

Eyes widening, I desperately tried to block my latest thoughts, imagining a brick wall in front of my mind.

"It is a pity," he said, laughing again as he gathered me back to his side. "Now, it is time for you to sleep."

Was he crazy? Sleep? In addition to me being cuddled around his very naked body, I'd seen and heard things in the last ten minutes that would keep me up for an eternity.

He chuckled again. "You could try counting sheep over your brick wall. Nice detail, by the way."

"Shut up," I said, yawning.

"If that is what you desire."

"It is," I said, nuzzling into his rib cage. I fell asleep before three sheep made it over the wall.

"I can't do it!" I whined, falling into my seat dramatically. "I give up."

"Again!" Soren said, ignoring my pleading. "Close your eyes, and imagine a barrier between your mind and everything else. Emelie, you did this without even trying last night."

Baring my fangs, I growled at him, making my displeasure clear. His optimism was unrelenting, and at this point, annoying. "I told you. I can't do it." Of that, I was sure.

We'd been practicing shielding for over two hours nonstop with no results. I was mentally exhausted. And totally embarrassed by the things he'd seen in my mind. So far, he'd seen the time I wrote, Mrs. Soren Vidar, fifty times in my notebook, the time I stole one of his pictures from the album and kissed it goodnight, and the time my father sat me down and told me my obsession with Soren had gotten out of control. If he didn't think I was a silly little girl before, he sure did now.

Soren tapped his fingers, looking bored at my dental display. "I'm terrified, little elf. Now, again!"

Giving up my anger with a sigh, I prepared for him to see another embarrassing moment. "Fine. Go ahead."

"I would not see anything if you would kindly prevent me from entering," he reminded me, then lifted a brow. "I must tell you. That is not a very ladylike hand gesture."

I narrowed my eyes. "I hate you."

Soren knelt in front of me. "Use your hatred, imagine it into an impenetrable fortress around you."

I blew out an irritated breath. "I'll try one more time, but that's it. I need a break."

"Do you want Odin to control you, Emelie?

I glared at him. "Are you insane? I mean, really. Are you?"

"Get serious about this," he said reproachfully. "It will take Odin only a moment to get in and find out where and what you are. You can never let my father gain your power. If we are ever to defeat him, we need your magic on our side."

As much as I hated it, he was right. Odin was not to be trifled with. I needed to pull it together.

Drawing in a deep breath, I closed my eyes tightly, imagining a thick, ivy-covered brick wall, throwing in a moat filled with water dragons for good measure. "Okay, do your worst, Soren."

He gripped my forearms. "Show me something else ... something horrifying you would never want me to know."

I gritted my teeth as I felt his mind touch mine. It would be so easy to let him in, to give up. The effort to keep someone with his power out was almost too much for me to maintain.

"Perfect," he declared abruptly. "Do you think you can do that again?"

"I think so."

"Good," he said, pressing me back into my seat to buckle my seatbelt. "We will cross into the portal area within the minute."

"What?" I felt a strong nudge against my mind's barrier almost the instant he finished speaking. "I feel someone," I hissed.

"Yes," he replied coolly. "That is my father. Do not worry. You are doing an excellent job at keeping him out. Just keep thinking of your brick wall, and know that if your shield fails, mine will not."

The fasten seat belts sign dinged to life above our heads, making us both jump. We were making our descent. "How do you know it's Odin?"

He shrugged his shoulders. "I am fortunate to have telepathic powers my father does not possess. I've made use of this weakness many times."

"Will he know we're together?"

"Absolutely not. I have shielded myself from him for over two millennia."

"Good," I said, grateful to have Soren protecting me.

"You have nothing to fear with me at your side," he assured me, just as a searing pain in my shoulder made me buck up against the restraints.

"Soren, help me!" I screamed.

I was in his arms in a flash. "What is it, Emelie? Where is the pain?"

"My right shoulder," I sobbed, tears streaming down my face.

He pulled up my sweater to examine my shoulder, carefully running his cool fingers across the burning flesh. After only a moment, he put the material back in to place with an uncustomary deep sigh.

"What … is … it?" I asked, between gasping breaths. I couldn't seem to get enough air in my lungs.

His eyes held pity when he finally lifted his red gaze to my silver one. "It is the Valknut, my father's mark. Every creature from the Norselands is born with one. I assume, since you were not born here, your mark was created when you crossed into the portal area. He has residual magic here. I promise I did not know it would be so painful."

"What does it mean?" I asked, drying my eyes on the sleeve of my sweater.

He knelt before me, taking my hands in his. "Nothing, Emelie. We will never let him control you. You are not a pawn to be played, not in his game, not in anyone's game—ever."

I frowned. "None of what you're saying is very comforting."

Soren sighed and nodded in agreement. "Comfort in the Norselands is a rare thing."

As soon as we landed, Soren promised me he'd see me in a minute and disappeared into thin air, leaving me to disembark by myself. I might have been nervous about stepping out into the open in a strange place if it wasn't for Soren's butler. Cedric was a human, maybe fifty years old, but he was still in top form. The only giveaways to his age were his salt and pepper hair and the crinkles at the corners of his eyes when he smiled. And he smiled a lot.

"Hi," he said, grinning as he jogged up the plane's stairs to take my carry-on bags from me.

"Hi," I parroted, smiling back at him. "I'm Emelie."

"Cedric." He offered me his arm. "Shall we?"

"Of course."

Once he had me safely ensconced in the backseat of Soren's SUV, he sat in the driver's seat and turned around to face me with a broad grin. "So, Emelie, tell me about yourself."

"Well, I'm from California."

"Really! So am I! What part?"

"The Bay Area. Los Altos, to be exact."

"I know it well," he exclaimed. "I grew up in Palo Alto."

"No kidding? Really?" I was liking Cedric better by the second. "We were practically neighbors."

"Nope, no joke, and we were a lot closer to neighbors than you think. Soren hired me twenty years ago to tend to a residence in Los Altos. We moved to Sweden only a year or so ago. You know, it always seemed like an odd choice for someone from another plane of existence to want to live with the humans on Midgard, but ..." He gestured to me. "I can see why he spent so much time there now. Are you his fated mate?"

Soren chose that moment to join me in the backseat. He took one look at my blush, then asked Cedric, "What did you say to her?"

Cedric held his hands up innocently and winked at me. "Nothing. I swear."

"A likely story," Soren said, shaking his head. "Let us go, Cedric."

"You got it, Soren." He turned around and clicked his seatbelt into place. "Hang on, Emelie. This ride is going to get a little bumpy."

The minute we pulled out of the airport hangar, Cedric began to regale me with stories of Soren's apparently hilarious introduction into the modern world, much to Soren's dismay. I could tell right away that there was a real father-son bond between the two. Although Soren was over a hundred times older than Cedric, he spoke of Soren with the pride of a father.

With embarrassing stories told all around, we continued to chat amicably in Soren's Land Rover for almost an hour before Cedric turned off onto an unmarked trail, the increasingly tricky roads he was forced to navigate down consuming his attention. Without Cedric's easygoing charm to carry the conversation, the usual vaguely sexual awkwardness rose between Soren and me, and he quickly busied himself with staring out the window with his brows furrowed in deep concentration rather than continue talking to me alone.

It was a good thing I didn't give up so easily. "Penny for your thoughts?" I asked, wondering if he would understand the American saying.

"It's a British quote, at least four hundred years old," Soren said. "And to answer your question, you are in my thoughts, Emelie."

He didn't elaborate, and I didn't bother asking any further questions. Some things you didn't need to say out loud to get your meaning across.

Soren's home was hidden deep in the forests of Uppsala. There was nothing but wall-to-wall trees for a half an hour before we finally arrived at his home. Tense, silent ride aside, I was desperate to get out of the vehicle, just to walk on solid ground again. An hour of the bumpy road was somewhat akin to sailing on rough seas, and I was feeling a bit seasick.

Stumbling out of the car, I glanced up at the grey stone mansion blocking out the sun around us. It was more of a monstrosity than a house. "Why is it so big?" I wondered aloud.

"That's what she said," Cedric muttered under his breath, grinning madly.

I leaned toward him and gave him a squeeze around the middle. "We are so going to get along."

He laughed and carried the luggage up the front steps. "That, we are, my dear."

Soren huffed. "I will answer the question if you two jesters are finished."

I smirked. "Go ahead, Professor Vidar. Do tell us."

"It houses the rest of the Ragnarök warriors, smart-ass. The staff lives here in the winter, as well. You must be very careful not to mention the warriors to the staff during your stay. They can't ever know who we are. Any one of them could be loyal to Odin."

"But Cedric is cool though, right?"

"Yes. Cedric is … cool, as you say."

Cedric gasped in mock delight. "Soren, you say the sweetest things."

Soren sighed, feigning aggravation. "Just unlock the door, Cedric." He rounded the car and tucked my hand into the crook of his arm, smiling down at me. "I hope you do not mind sharing my quarters. As far as the staff is concerned, we are newly engaged. That is the only way to avoid talk of a strange newcomer to the house."

Excitement pooled in my belly at the thought of being alone with him. "Not at all. Show me to our room."

CHAPTER FIVE

The staff were lined up along the steps of the grand staircase when Soren and I stepped into the foyer together. No doubt, Cedric rustled them up to meet the master of the house properly. I had to wonder if Cedric did this for my benefit or whether it was a regular occurrence. Sure, this was a fine house that would require an army of humans to take care of it, but Soren didn't seem like the type to want this kind of attention. And this wasn't a Jane Austen movie. Who still does this nowadays?

A portly female with pale blonde hair and a very stern face stepped forward out of the group. "Welcome home, Master Soren. I hope your trip was favorable."

"Thank you, Svetlana. It is good to be home." He looked down at me at his side and smiled. "The trip was very favorable indeed." Turning his attention to the rest of the staff, he said, "This is Emelie, my bride to be. Please make sure she wants for nothing while she is here."

Bride to be. The sour faces of the staff quickly doused the excitement that was ignited in me upon hearing those words. Ignoring the looks of hatred thrown my way was impossible. This was not welcome news to them, by any means.

I squeezed Soren's forearm, and he took the hint. "Cedric, if you would bring our bags to our room? I'm sure Emelie would like to freshen up before supper."

"Of course, sir."

Smiling to the crowd as brightly as I could, I followed Cedric up the stairs, hoping to receive one in return, but was ultimately disappointed. Not one of them looked even remotely friendly. We weren't even out of earshot before we heard the females start speaking in rapid Swedish. The sound of their voices was followed by a sharp, "Stifle it!" from Svetlana to quiet them.

"Well, they hate me," I said unnecessarily.

"They'll come around," Cedric said. "They've had quite a blow to their egos. Soren is ... was a very eligible bachelor."

Soren cast a fervent look behind us. "What?"

Cedric barked out a laugh. "You mean you didn't notice? Oh, I hope they never learn of your ignorance. Their egos would really be bruised."

I smirked. "That explains a lot."

Soren swept me off my feet at that remark, and I squeaked out a weak protest as he carried me bride-style over the threshold of the door Cedric was holding open. I looked around the room from Soren's arms. "Wow!" That was pretty much the only word fitting for Soren's 'quarters'. His chamber was almost a house within a house. The door from the hallway opened into a sitting room, and the kitchen was situated between two of the largest bedrooms I'd ever seen.

He set me on my feet. "I take it you approve."

"Yes! It's gorgeous. I love the French decor."

"I can't believe how huge the bedrooms are. Which one will I be using?"

Soren's roguish grin said it all. "Cedric has the second room. You'll be bunking with me. I hope that will be satisfactory."

I briefly struggled to form a sentence that didn't start with 'Hallelujah'. "Um ... it's fine. We have to keep up appearances, right?"

There was an odd mix of surprise, comprehension, and relief on Soren's face when he answered, "Yes, we do. I'll show you to our room."

Our room. Those two words sent another thrill of excitement through me. I had to snap out of this. This wasn't real. What was real was the dark elf that was probably going to hang outside

Soren's house tonight making sure I didn't ride off into the sunset with my true love.

Soren led me into the bedroom on the right. Gesturing to a highboy in the corner, he said, "I have cleared this for you, and you will find half of the closet has been emptied for the items you need to hang."

"Thanks." Grabbing my garment bag, I walked to the closet, eager to see what Soren wore on a daily basis.

"The switch is on the left," he called after me.

Soren's scent attacked my senses as I closed the door behind me. He was everywhere in here. I groped for the light switch, finding it exactly where he said it would be. "Found it!" I yelled, quickly hanging the few dresses I owned and stowing the bag underneath. I moved to leave, but I couldn't help lingering over Soren's clothes. I'd expected expensive suits and cashmere sweaters to fill his closet. What I found wasn't remotely close to that. His clothes were normal, mostly jeans and sweaters appropriate for the cold weather. I stopped to run my fingers down a coat close to the door, lifting the sleeve to my nose. The smell of his scent was intoxicating.

"Would you like me to leave you two alone?"

Startled, I yelped at Soren's perfectly serious tone and turned to find a questioning expression on his face. I sighed and rolled my eyes. "Don't ask."

His mouth quirked up. "I did not plan on it."

"You know, I think I can see a mortification pattern developing between us, Soren."

He laughed. "Quite, little one. Quite. Now," He nodded to the coat. "If you are ready. I would like to introduce you to the rest of the warriors before supper is called."

Soren showed me where the kitchen, parlor, and garden were while we waited on the others to arrive. I was extremely nervous to meet them. After the frosty reception with the staff (except for Cedric, of course), I really hoped they would be friendly.

"You have me," Soren reminded me, wrapping his arms around me from behind and resting his chin on top of my head.

I sighed and put up my shield for the forty-billionth time. "Thanks for that. I really appreciate you taking me into your home. You didn't have to."

"Nonsense, Anders was a treasured friend. How could the Rebellion not? We will always protect our brother's young in any way we can."

I felt another twinge of bitter disappointment at his choice of words then silently berated myself for it. What was I expecting? A declaration of love? I was reading way too much into his actions. Sure, he kissed the bejeezus out of me and said he dreamt of me, oh, and let's not forget he slept naked with me, but he could sleep naked every day of his life for all I knew. In addition, there was that whole pesky engaged thing in between us. I had to pull it together. How many times was I going to have to tell myself that?

I believe they have arrived," Soren said, leading me out the kitchen door, into the side yard. He stepped to the edge of the tree line, sighing deeply. "Oh, for the love of the Norse. Brace yourself, Emelie."

I got out, "Wha—" before I was bowled over by a large silver and black wolf-like creature. Immediately panicking, I started screaming like a banshee and thrashing wildly on the ground below it. The wolf, noticing my distress, decided to lick my face with his giant tongue as if that would remedy the situation. "Get it off me!" I yelled to Soren, trying to buck the creature off.

"That is enough, Fenrir!" Soren's voice boomed, startling my assailant and me.

I'd never seen Soren truly angry before. With his red eyes glowing and electricity sparking dangerously around him, he was both terrifying and awe-inspiring … and sexy as hell. For a moment, I forgot about the giant killer wolf standing over me. Soren didn't just draw my attention; he demanded it.

The wolf, apparently sensing his immediate demise, stepped to the side, allowing me to stand. I scrambled away from the beast, brushing dirt and leaves from my clothes as I ran to Soren.

"Are you okay?" he asked, looking me over for any obvious injuries.

"I'm okay." I aimed a grimace at the wolf. "But I think I've just realized I'm more of a cat person."

"Accept our apologies," a voice with a familiar accent said. "Our friend got overly excited when he saw you were here. We so rarely get visitors … and he's a bit of an idiot."

The wolf huffed in protest.

I looked up from my filthy sweater to find two tall, dark, and handsome males standing next to the wolf—who was now wagging his tail like a well-behaved retriever and wearing an adorable grin—the mutt. The males looked remarkably like one another. They both were very tan with short-cropped black hair and emerald green eyes. There was no doubt they were dark elf brothers.

The brother on the right stepped forward and shook my hand. "I can't tell you how excited I am to meet you. Your father and I were friends for hundreds of years. My name is Viggo." He gestured to the right. "This is my brother, Jakob."

"It's nice to meet you." I looked around for the third warrior Soren said would be here. "Soren, I thought you said there were three you wanted me to meet?"

"I am starting to regret that decision," he replied then turned to glare at the wolf. "Are you done, Fenrir?"

I gasped as the wolf turned into a male with a pop. He was tall, just like the others, but with ice blue eyes and shaggy light-brown hair. And he was naked. Like, really, really naked.

The wolf extended his hand. "Hi there, beauty. Call me, Nils. That Fenrir stuff wears on my nerves."

For one excruciatingly long moment, I thought I would bite him. I didn't think I'd ever thought of a male as mouthwatering before, but if he was on the menu, I was hungry, and my fangs were letting me know it. Maybe it was the adrenaline still pumping in my veins, but Nils made me hungry, primal. I wanted to taste him. I needed to taste him.

Jakob snorted, distracting me.

With a distressed cry, I slapped a hand over my mouth and took several steps back.

Viggo laughed. "Emelie, the face you're making is hilarious. You look like a starving person who's had a steak put in front of you."

Okay, that was just embarrassing.

Nils laughed and threw his arm around my shoulders to lead me into the house. Leaning against me with a wistful look, he whispered, "I thought you were going to snack on me. I must be losing my charm."

I shook my head. "Oh, I don't think you're in any danger of that."

Humor twinkled in his blue eyes. "Good. Come on, Em. I'm starving myself."

He led me through several doors and seated me at the head of a long rectangular dinner table, sitting so close to me, our legs touched. The others filed in after us. Soren sat on my other side, giving Nils a look that would probably kill an average male. But Nils was far from average. He was intensely male, intensely sexy, with a side of mysterious wildness that was mouthwatering. I was so engrossed in him, I didn't realize I was staring until Soren kicked my shin under the table.

Embarrassed beyond belief, I mumbled, "I'm sorry," to everyone and closed my eyes until I was relaxed enough to will my fangs back into their proper place.

Viggo caught my gaze when I reopened them. "Don't be embarrassed, Emelie. All elves have moments of weakness. With all the magic now coursing through you, I can imagine it is tough to control your new impulses. And he is ... naked. Put some clothes on, Nils!"

Nils smiled suggestively as his nakedness was replaced with a tight black t-shirt and equally tight black jeans. "I won't just hold it against you if you bite me, Em. I prefer a more direct approach."

In a flash, Soren rose, grabbed Nils' head, and slammed it on the tabletop. I shrieked and toppled backward in my chair, graceful as ever.

Soren, Viggo, and Jakob were crouched down beside me with concerned looks in the blink of an eye. "Are you okay?" Soren asked.

With an addled smile, I answered him. "As soon as I pick the mahogany splinters out of my ass, I will be."

After an awkward dinner of not-so-subtle innuendo from Nils and Soren's occasional muttering about him being an imbecile, I noticed Jakob was going outside to smoke. I asked if I could join him and found both Soren and Nils strongly disapproved of the habit. They were shooting chastising glares at me as I walked out of the door Jakob held open.

Once out of earshot, Jakob said, "You've got a couple of ardent admirers in there."

I smirked. "You think so? I'm almost positive Nils is just horny and looking for someone to sleep with, and Soren, well, he keeps himself at such a distance at all times. I hardly think either one of them will be whisking me away for some happily ever after anytime soon."

He raised his brows. "Do you not?"

I looked in the French doors and saw the two finishing a terse conversation that ended with Nils looking pissed. Soren looked … well, like Soren. Damn, that male was cool; nothing fazed him. I shrugged. "It's all moot anyway. I can't mate either one of them. Did Soren tell you whom I have to mate?"

"He did, and it is a damn shame. I want this ridiculous war between the elves to end, but it is unforgivable that you are the one who must pay for your parent's mistake. Honestly, I don't know what they were thinking when they ran off." He offered his cigarette pack to me.

I waved it away. "No thanks. I just wanted some air."

He chuckled. "Are you certain you do not think of them as admirers?"

I sighed. "I don't know what to think. Got any ideas?"

He ground his cigarette butt under his heel then threw the butt into the fire pit. "I do not."

That made two of us.

We walked back inside just as Cedric brought in coffee. I accepted my cup and perched on the edge of a wingback chair next to Soren. He leaned toward me once I had settled. "Emelie, I have to leave for a few days."

Alarmed, I yelled, "Why?" and every eye in the room turned to us. "Sorry," I mumbled to the group, then lowered my voice. "Why?"

"I have to follow up on a lead I received. I think I might have found the doppelgänger."

"Oh." I was glad he was close to getting some answers, but I didn't want him to leave. What if that thing hurt him?

"Awwwww," Jakob and Viggo chorused.

"Should I go pack your Hello Kitty Band-Aids with your daggers?" Viggo asked.

"Stay out of my head, you two," I scolded, though I should have made the connection before. Of course, Viggo and Jakob were the two dark elves with telepathy that Soren had mentioned yesterday. That power was probably pretty useful to the rebellion.

"Try to refrain for the time being, gentle-males," Soren said. He was smiling like the cat that ate the canary.

"What?" I asked him, uncertain at his reaction. He hardly ever smiled. It couldn't be a good thing. Or could it?

"It is nothing. Never mind." Changing the subject, he said, "Emelie, I have invited your mother's friend, Katrine, to stay here while I'm gone. I think she may be able to give you a boost with your Norn magic."

I nodded. "That's good, I guess." Katrine—the name didn't ring a bell. Of course, my parents hadn't mentioned anyone from their old life but Soren, so that was hardly a surprise.

"We should play some cards," Nils piped up, not able to be less than the center of attention for long. "What about strip poker?"

"No!" Everyone answered in unison.

Eventually, we settled on regular poker, which I sucked royally at (no pun intended) because of my inability to shield. I quit after only a few games and spent the rest of the night alternating between listening to the males' good-natured banter with a bemused smile and staring at the fire, lost in thought. It was so different here. There were so many different personalities, so much life. But it was also completely alien to me. Having a card game with friends? That was something I'd only seen on television. My parents didn't have company over—ever.

Soren shook me awake when the sky began to pinken. "Wake up, sleepyhead."

I smiled at my father's nickname for me and managed to make my way out of the parlor half-asleep with Soren's help. I must have curled up on the couch to take a nap at some point, but I didn't remember closing my eyes. Stumbling up the stairs to the bedroom, I went straight to the bed and collapsed face first into it.

A sudden sharp knock on the door brought me to my hands and knees scaredy-cat-like. Soren laughed heartily at my expense. "Emelie, you never cease to amuse me." He was still shaking his head at my silliness when he opened the door and stepped outside.

I could only make out a few of the words Nils was saying to Soren through the door. But Soren's side I heard loud and clear. He seemed to be purposely raising his voice, so I could listen to his side of the argument. That was nice. It kept me from actually having to get off the bed to eavesdrop.

"Fenrir," I heard him say sternly. "You are wasting your time here. She has given you no sign she is interested in you for anything more than friendship. You, of all people, should respect that she is betrothed, and you know damn well, if she were not, I would claim her myself. She was my chosen one before Kristian was born. Indeed, before his grandfather was born. I should not have to tell you this."

My mouth dropped open, but I quickly put on a face that feigned innocence and blocked my mind when I heard the latch open on the door. I didn't want Soren to know what was going on in my mind because the only thing that seemed to be in there now was *Emelie and Soren sitting in a tree K-I-S-S-I-N-G*. And I was pretty sure that wasn't the most appropriate reaction to finding out your crush is your true mate and the son of Odin. Well, unless you're a seven-year-old.

Soren reentered the room as if nothing happened, smiling when he saw I was still awake. "Are you going to take off your boots before bed?" he asked.

"If I must," I grumbled, slinging my legs over the side of the bed. Under the guise of taking them off, I watched my true mate as he walked to the other side of the bed and began to undress, carefully folding his jeans and t-shirt and laying them on a chair. Thankfully, he left his boxers on this time. I took off my own jeans, but I couldn't find a place to put them that didn't involve me traipsing half naked across the room, so I threw them on the floor and climbed under the covers, snuggling right up to Soren and his now familiar warmth. Despite the bombshell I'd just received, sleep came instantly.

In what felt like seconds later, he woke me by reaching to turn off the bedside lamp. Like any mature adult would do in that situation, I protested this annoyance by whining at him. "Soren!"

"Your majesty, I am sorry to disturb you," he joked in a solemn tone.

"That is not funny on so, so many levels," I groused.

He turned to face me, and I mimicked him. I could barely see his lips move in the darkness. "I will miss you terribly when I leave tomorrow," he whispered.

Even though I heard Soren say he was my original intended only minutes ago, I was still surprised by this admission. I'd assumed he thought the kiss we'd shared was a mistake or it that was the whole impending mating thing, but Jakob had been right. Soren was an admirer. I held my breath as his hand snaked up and stroked my cheek. "Soren…"

"Are my attentions unwanted, Emelie?"

That question sparked an internal debate between right and wrong that I knew would never have a real winner. I knew I should say yes. I was fated to Kristian, after all, but I couldn't. There was only one answer I would ever give Soren. "No, I welcome your attention."

What can I say? I was a glutton for punishment.

Soren rolled us until his body was on top of mine and said, "Excellent," before taking my mouth in a blistering kiss.

I didn't remember much after that moment. The second his lips touched mine, his magic bombarded me, causing my own magic to come to life in a great swooping arc that brought me arching off the bed. The connection between us was so intense; I felt like I was drowning in it.

Soren broke the kiss, pushing himself onto his hands and knees to give me room to breathe. His eyes were frantic. "Emelie, I am sorry. I got carried away."

I answered him in a small breathy voice with my eyes still tightly closed. "It's … okay. I wanted … you."

He lay down beside me and pulled me into the crook of his arm. "Sleep, love."

Love. I smiled. I still hadn't opened my eyes. "You say that like I have a choice."

CHAPTER SIX

S oren had already gone when I woke the next afternoon. In his place, I found a beautiful flower, a Lily of the Valley, arranged on his pillow. As I lay staring at it, I racked my brain to remember what the bloom meant. I was almost positive it signified the return of happiness in the Language of the Flowers book my mother used to have, but perhaps that was a little wishful thinking on my part. Still, how often does a gorgeous male kiss you senseless, expect nothing in return, and then leave a flower for you to wake up to in the morning?

I reached over to pick up the bloom and realized it was pinned to a note that read, *Await my return.* I smiled and unpinned the flower to breathe in its scent.

"Morning, sunshine," Nils said, as he walked in the door—without knocking. He stopped in his tracks when he noticed the flower, becoming visibly upset and confirming my suspicions about the flower's meaning.

I was almost on the verge of panic when, strangely, he sniffed the air, then relaxed. I took that as a good sign and asked, "What's up, wolf?"

"I'm supposed to teach you magic 101 today, but if you'd rather stay in bed, I could be coaxed into joining you. You do look like you could use a little breakfast." He sat opposite of me, so his neck was in my direct view.

Against my will, my fangs sprung out. "Nils, I can't."

"It'll be fun," he urged, in a sing-song voice.

"For me, maybe. What would you get out of it?"

He motioned to his raging hard-on. "Maybe you'll help me get rid of this?"

I laughed. "The hell I will."

"It'll be fun," he reiterated.

"Nils take that 'thing' somewhere else. You're trying to plant your proverbial flagpole in virgin territory over here."

He shuddered and looked toward the ceiling. "I think you just gave me an aneurysm, Emelie. Fuck, you're hot."

Nuh uh. He was the hot one. Between his wolfy, manly scent and his sexy, tousled surfer-boy looks, I was about to have a heart attack. It was either that, or I was about to drink him dry. Just being around him made my brain fuzzy. "Look, degenerate," I shoved at his muscled arm. "Go. So, I can get dressed."

He tsked me. "No parting gifts? And here I was willing to be your breakfast, Emelie. Are you not ashamed of yourself? Even just a little bit?"

"Out, Nils."

"Fine," he grumbled. "I'll go find someone who has taste."

He disappeared, and I shook my head. If he actually showed up later for what he called Magic 101, I really, really hoped he would be sans erection.

I didn't know what could be taking Nils so long. I waited under the tree for him for half an hour before I started picturing him lighting candles to set the mood for his masturbation and giggling hysterically to myself. I was probably going to Hell for what I did to him, but damn if he didn't deserve it. After another few minutes, I gave up on him. I didn't have all day. I closed my eyes and tried to remember the steps Soren told me to take to cast enchantments—relax your mind, let the energy surge through you, and release the power built up, thinking of nothing but what you want to accomplish. That sounded simple enough.

"Hello, Emelie," said a familiar voice from behind me.

I shrieked and pivoted around. "Kristian, what are you doing here?"

He held his elegant hands up in surrender. "I am sorry. Frightening you was not my intention."

"It's … okay," I panted, still trying to catch my breath. My heart was racing out of my chest, it was beating so hard. The connection we'd had before was back, and it seemed amplified by a thousand now I had some of my own magic. I kissed his cheek, enjoying the frisson of electricity that raced across my lips when they touched his skin. "I didn't expect you to find me so soon. I thought you would be out enjoying the daylight."

He smiled somberly at me. "I am enjoying it. How would I have been able to have the joy of seeing your beautiful hair in the sunlight, if I were not here? You were made for the light, Emelie."

Beaming, I said, "That may have been the nicest thing anyone has ever said to me. Thank you." He nodded graciously, but I could tell he had something else to get off his chest. "Are you okay? You seem out of sorts."

Hesitantly, he spoke, "It is just you are so … perfect."

I snorted. "You're delusional." He was one of the most perfect, unequaled males I'd ever met, and I was the whore that was already semi-cheating on him.

Smiling, he said, "No, I am lucid at the moment. That is a certainty. You are everything I could have hoped for in a mate—beautiful and pure of heart, and so giving, even to a stranger. You gave me such a marvelous engagement gift, and I did not even think to offer you anything in return. I don't deserve you, Emelie. I will only bring darkness to your life."

"You can't know that." I took his hands in mine. "So far, I really like you, and I'm sure when you spend more time with me, you'll find I'm not so perfect. I only gave you the blood because it felt like it was the right thing to do. I didn't plan it ahead of time. Don't give up on us already." Feeling awkward, I dropped his hands and went back to practicing.

He cocked his head while studying my employment. "What are you doing?"

I gave him a dubious look. "I'm practicing my magic. What does it look like?"

His furrowed brow deepened. "But, why?"

I laughed at his confused face. "So, I can learn to use it."

"But why have you not learned to use it before now?"

I shrugged. "Apparently, when you've never been outside of the human world, you have to glean a little power from another magic user to get your own started. My parents refused to teach me, so I was never able to learn."

He looked down at me with an adorably hopeful expression. "Would you like some of my magic? You could practice with me."

I felt so guilty. I did not deserve this male. I didn't deserve either one of them, really. It was the ultimate fuck you by the universe that I went from having no one in my life to having two genuine, kind, and intelligent males that wanted me at the same time. How could I ever choose between them?

"Emelie?"

"Oh, yes. I would like that very much. I'm sorry for the distraction. I was just thinking of the night we last met."

Kristian pulled me into his embrace and looked into my eyes. "I have thought about it a thousand times. I have not been without an erection for more than an hour since I tasted you." He pressed into me, proving his words true. "It is agony knowing our mating night is so far away."

Whoa. I wasn't sure how to respond to that. What could I say? I liked him, and there was no denying the attraction I felt when we were together, but I wasn't ready for this the way he was. He'd had years to prepare. I've only had a couple of days. "I-I'm sorry to have put you in such distress."

Tucking a stray lock of my hair behind my ear, he said, "Your innocence is charming. As is everything about you." Lifting me with no warning, he spun us around in a circle. He was so full of joy. It was hard not to join in his enthusiasm.

"Kristian, you're crazy!" I squealed and giggled as he lifted me for another turn.

He put me gently on my feet and grinned. "I apologize if my excitement is a tad overzealous, but I do not think I have ever been in such high spirits. You are a shining beacon of light and hope for me—for us. Our world is not a pleasant place. I have had little to brighten my life." He looked away. "It is my greatest fear that you will be unhappy in our mating. You must be aware I am not your intended mate."

Again, I was struck dumb. I was so confused. When I was with Soren yesterday, I had wholly put Kristian out of my mind. I only wanted him. I couldn't possibly mate anyone else. Nevertheless, today, with Kristian standing so close to me, looking so happy, I didn't want him to have to suffer the disappointment I would cause him if I rejected his proposal—assuming he ever offered one.

I finally spoke just as his slight smile began to falter. "I am aware, and it is a very hard thing for me to know my true mate was taken away from me because of my parent's selfishness. However, I also know this war must end and that it is my duty to do it. I can assure you. If you are a kind mate to me, I will be perfectly happy with our arrangement. I won't reject your proposal."

A look of chagrin crossed his features. "I apologize for my stupidity, Emelie. How could I have not offered you a proposal? You are not without emotions—an object to be casually traded away. Of course, you would want a traditional betrothal. I have made such a fool of myself in this."

"No, you haven't. I think you're doing pretty well so far. Neither one of us has done this before."

He looked thoughtful for a moment. "Emelie, will you accompany me to my kingdom this morning?"

"Sure," I said slowly, looking around for Nils. Besides my horny magic instructor, I doubted anyone would miss me here. "But just for a little while, okay?"

"Of course," he agreed, looking happier than I'd ever seen him. Grinning widely, he reached into the front pocket of his jeans and extracted a pale green stone. "Clasp my arm tightly, Emelie. The journey will only take a moment."

I wrapped both hands around Kristian's forearm and immediately felt a floating sensation. For a couple seconds, my surroundings went bright white, and then I was standing on a hillside facing a castle that looked to be both a faerytale and a nightmare. At least five stories high and massive in width, it was one of the most impressive buildings I'd ever seen. It must have taken the elves fifty years just to gather enough stone for its construction.

"Wow," I breathed, staring up at my soon-to-be home in awe. From the spiky, gothic torrents to the intricately patterned granite, it was magnificent. And that was just what I could see in the low light. It was what was considered daytime in Svartálfaheim, I suppose. But instead of blue skies and the sun, the castle was illuminated by an eerie orange glow. Adding to the spooky atmosphere, there was a deep, rumbling vibration that sounded suspiciously like a growl. I chose to ignore that for the moment. I could only have one panic attack at a time.

Kristian smiled at my astonishment. "It does seem a bit much for a male without a family, does it not?

"You could fit a hundred families in there, Kristian."

"And one day, we will," he said, with his voice full of hope. "That is one of the really excellent perks of being immortal. We can watch our young become great-grandparents."

Did he say young? He hadn't even put a ring on my finger yet, and he was already thinking about kids? Wow, I was in way over my head—way over.

Kristian placed his hand at the small of my back and led me toward the side of the castle. "This way, my queen."

The growling I'd noticed before grew louder the farther down we descended. I stopped walking altogether when its source sounded as if it was only a few hundred feet away. "What is that growling, Kristian?"

He gave me a reassuring smile. "Do not fear the dragon. He is very old and snores quite a bit."

I nodded, mute with fear, and jogged a little to catch up with him. A dragon? He had no clue what this was like for someone who had never been to any of the other worlds of the Norselands before. After semi-recovering from the shock of a real live dragon, I asked, "Do you have night, or is it always like this?"

"Why are you whispering?"

I hadn't realized I was. "Maybe because I'm scared my voice will awaken some sleeping sentry, hell-bent on ridding the castle of unwanted pests—pests like petite, blonde light elves?" There was a bizarre look of pity in his eyes, although he seemed amused. "What? No hell-bent sentries?"

He looked down the hill to the left. "Oh, there are those."

"What?" I screeched, starting to panic again.

"They would never hurt you, Emelie. You are my intended, remember?"

I wanted to believe him, but I kept thinking back to what Soren and the males told me about the ones who benefit from the war. All it would take is one traitor to kill me. "Can I see them? I'd feel safer if I knew where they were."

"Of course." He turned back in the direction he had looked and motioned for the hidden guards to come out.

The castle was very well protected indeed. The sheer number of creatures that appeared from the forest was astounding. Their looks were shockingly unexpected, as well. Some were beautiful, tall and dark, like Kristian, but most were short and troll-like—all pleasant-faced with stately noses, full lips, and bright green eyes, but seemingly cursed with some affliction that made them different from their brothers.

"Behold, soldiers," Kristian stepped away and gestured grandly towards me as if to introduce someone important. "Your queen has finally arrived."

As soon as Kristian spoke the word, 'queen', every single one of the legions of soldiers went down on their knees. "Kristian!" I shot daggers at him with my eyes. "Tell them to get up. I don't deserve this."

"No, my beloved. I will not," he refused, begging me to understand with those hypnotizing, amethyst eyes of his. "For twenty years, they have fought against your kinsfolk, always keeping faith that this day would come. Your arrival is cause for celebration, Emelie. Peace will be had at last. You can at least give them this small happiness, can you not?"

Why was it so hard to deny Kristian? My head was screaming at me not to let him make me into their idea of salvation, but I couldn't seem to make myself listen. I mean, Kristian is charismatic and handsome, but not charismatic and handsome enough for me to put his wishes above my own. It almost felt like he was somehow forcing me to bend to his will.

Giving up with a growl, I said, "Fine!" but I wasn't happy about it—at all.

He lifted my knuckles to his lips. "Thank you, my lady."

Hand in hand, we made our way down the hill, and one by one, the soldiers rose to greet us. "Hi," I said, smiling at the crowd of males as we approached. "I'm Emelie."

Kristian tensed as a tall male in a green uniform stepped forward and put my hand to his heart in thanks. "It is our pleasure, my lady. I can scarcely remember a more joyous day than today."

I blushed at the undeserved praise. "I'm sorry it took so long for me to get here."

"Your presence today assures us that our fighting was not in vain, my lady. And to have such a beautiful queen, well, that almost makes the sacrifice worth it."

"Watch yourself, Asgrim," Kristian warned sternly. Looking angrier than I'd ever seen him, he offered me his free hand to lead me away.

"I meant no disrespect, my king," Asgrim called after us.

Without another word to Asgrim or the assembly, Kristian showed me into the castle through the courtyard.

"Where are we going?" I asked him, a little confused. I'd expected us to go through the main doors, instead of the servant's entrance. Maybe I was being a little paranoid, but the way he was rushing me along almost seemed like he was trying to hide me from someone. I didn't understand why he would. Hadn't he just introduced me to a hundred elves outside? I wasn't exactly a secret around here.

Kristian led me up a set of stone stairs to the right of the kitchen we'd entered. "I am showing you to my private chambers. We can talk uninterrupted in there."

"Oh, okay." The kitchen was so quiet and devoid of life, I expected to see tumbleweeds rolling across our path, but I followed him anyway. The temptation to see his chamber was too great not to.

After a brisk walk down a long hallway, he stopped in front of a door that looked exactly like the many doors we'd already passed. "This is it."

Once inside, Kristian settled me into a plush, deep red sofa in the center of the room, then went back to the door to speak into an intercom in a language I'd never heard before. I took the opportunity to look at my surroundings. This room was decorated to match the rest of the castle. There were huge oil paintings, woven tapestries, and expensive rugs scattered over the grey stone walls and floors to give them much needed warmth, and the furniture was luxurious, but it wasn't garish and overdone. Whoever chose the furnishings, picked them for comfort, not for wow factor, which really helped make this cold place cozy instead of intimidating.

"Are you comfortable?" Kristian asked, seconds before the door opened and a butler stepped in with two crystal goblets on a silver tray.

"Yes," I said, surprised by the arrival of the elf with the fancy drinks. The king was living a lot more extravagantly than I'd expected him to with a war raging for the past twenty years.

"That will be all," Kristian said, taking the tray and dismissing the butler. He handed me one of the glasses. "This is juice from a fruit native to Álfheim—your parent's world. There is nothing like it."

I accepted the offering with a polite, "Thank you," and took a tentative sip. It was divine, and he was right; it tasted like nothing I'd ever had before. There was no comparison for it on Midgard. "It's delicious. What's it called?"

"Ambrosia." He moved in closer to me and sat his glass on the coffee table. "Emelie?"

"Yes, Kristian?" I asked, losing myself in eyes that were burning their way into my soul.

"Can I kiss you?"

"Yes," I answered hesitantly, then tried to take a deep breath. I wanted to kiss Kristian. He was sweet, thoughtful, and downright gorgeous, but I was already on the verge of hyperventilation just sitting next to him. I was sure I'd end up in a full-blown panic attack the moment his lips touched mine.

Smiling, Kristian took my glass, put it with his own, and then knelt in front of me. Next, he pulled a delicately filigreed ring with an enormous black stone out of his pocket. "Mate me, Emelie. Trust in my affection for you. It is genuine." He searched my face with his intensely purple eyes and must have seen encouragement. "Beloved, please end my misery and the misery of my people."

I thought I was going to need a paper bag to breathe in. Everything was happening so fast. But really, what other choice did I have? My fate had already been decided. Mind made up, I said, "Yes, Kristian, I will mate you."

He leaned forward and gently kissed me, making my lips tingle where his touched mine. I closed my eyes to savor the moment and was surprised to feel him drag his lips across my cheek and down the column of my throat. A shiver of anticipation ran through me. He was going to bite me, and strangely, I wanted him to.

Groaning, Kristian pulled away at the last moment and took my left hand. Pushing the heavy ring onto my third finger, he tried to smile without showing his fangs.

"It's beautiful, Kristian."

"It was meant to be Viveka's, for her mating to your father, but when that didn't happen, she lost her chance at ruling, and it was entrusted to me for my future mate. It is the Queen's ring. Every reigning queen has worn it since our society began."

"Is Viveka your sister?"

"A step-sister—the daughter of my father's second mate. She is mad."

"Mad?" I asked, bewildered.

"She lost her mind when her fate was changed. She is determined to have vengeance against the Norns for ruining her chances at becoming queen."

I shifted nervously, and he caught the apprehensive movement. "Do not worry, Emelie. Although it is certain she will despise you for taking her place, she will not waste her effort on you. She has me for her whipping post. Sometimes, I believe she lives to torment me."

I took his hands in mine. "I'm sorry."

He turned my hands over and looked at the ring. "Let us not speak of this unpleasantness on our day of engagement." Cupping my face in his hands, he softly kissed my lips. I responded in kind, letting our passion quickly burn out of control. His full lips against mine brought back the memory of the intimacy we'd shared outside of my house, and I couldn't keep my reason anymore. I wanted this. He was meant for me.

Kristian sat on the sofa beside me, and I climbed into his lap. He ran his hands down my sides to my bottom and pulled me tight against him, groaning his pleasure into my mouth.

I growled out a pleasured moan of my own before two hands grabbed me from behind, tore me away from Kristian, and shoved me onto the marble floor. Shocked, I looked up to see a beautiful but crazed-looking female with long trailing hair as black as raven feathers standing over Kristian.

"Kristian, is there not a room in your harem to fuck your females? How dare you sully my father's parlor with your whore!" She turned to me and spat, "Get back into the harem. You can suck his cock in there."

I looked to Kristian and mouthed, "Harem?" How could I have forgotten about the warning Soren gave me so quickly?

He looked away as if he couldn't bear for me to know his secret. "Leave us, Viveka."

She snarled down at me. "If you will not leave, I can take you there myself." She twisted my sleeve in her grasp, dragging me out into the hallway to the doorway of next room. I cried out in pain when she wrenched me off the floor and shoved me into the door frame.

"STOP!" Kristian bellowed, making both of us jump. "You will unhand my future bride. Now."

Viveka grabbed my left hand, then fell to her knees, wailing with grief upon seeing the ring. I took advantage of the distraction and ran to Kristian.

He caught me and held me tight, stroking my hair. "Everything is fine, Emelie. Let us take our leave."

Nodding, I let him lead me back to his chamber, grateful he'd put a stop to her tantrum.

"But my king, don't you want to introduce her to the rest of your guests?" Viveka asked.

Unable to ignore her, I turned to see Kristian's step-sister standing next to the now open door. There were five dark-haired, semi-naked beauties standing together just inside. The tallest one stepped forward to the doorway, her body covered in nothing but clear crystals. They spiraled up, accumulating heavily over her nipples and crotch. "My king, the others are not willing to make love to a female, but I will if it is what you desire. We are all eager to please you, except for Melini, who is still recuperating from your advances last night." She stepped back into the lineup.

"Kristian?" I jerked my hand from his. "Last night? You slept with one of them last night?"

His face said everything I needed to know. Going back the way we'd come, I walked back down the hallway, out of the castle, and past the still sleeping dragon. I didn't stop until I was back on top of the hill, and I realized I didn't know how to get home.

"FUCK!" I screamed to no one. Well, if a hundred guards hiding in the forest is no one. I'm sure I looked like a friggin' idiot.

"I am sorry," Kristian said from behind me.

I wouldn't face him. "Don't talk to me, Kristian."

"There is nowhere for you to go," he reasoned.

I heard a low-pitched growling coming from the other side of the hill and looked frantically at Kristian. Pushing me behind him, he pulled a dagger from his side and had just enough time to face the threat when Nils flew at us from the left. He collided into the king with a thud, sending both of them down the other side of the hill. After mere seconds of intense fighting, Nils escaped the battle with an uppercut that knocked Kristian out. He bounded back up the hill and latched on to me as he ran by. When he increased his speed, I wrapped my legs around his waist and held on for dear life. The trees were whipping by so fast I couldn't focus.

"Hey, Em," Nils said, grinning as he jumped over the low boundary wall that circled the castle grounds. "Did you miss me?"

I looked to the heavens and sighed. "I can't believe I'm going to say this, but, yes, I missed you. Now, please, get me the hell out of here?"

"Absolutely. If you'll just reach into my right front pocket."

Wary, I asked, "Why?"

"To get the shifting stone out." He laughed. "Why else?"

"Hey, you have priors, Nils, and you're not exactly trustworthy in my book yet. I wouldn't put anything past you."

"That is a wise choice," he growled.

"Behave yourself," I told him, carefully clinging onto his neck with my right hand and reaching into his pocket with my left. I straightened myself with nothing to show for my effort but an exasperated expression. "Nils, for the love of all that's holy."

"I never said whose right I was referring to," he said innocently.

Breathing in deeply through my nose, I willed myself not to smack him in the back of the head. "Is it really going to be in there, or is this another trick?"

"There was no trick! I swear!"

"Uh huh." Against my better judgment, I leaned to fish the stone out of his left pocket and, thankfully, found what I went in there for right away.

"It doesn't bite, Emelie. You could've stayed in there a little longer."

I rolled my eyes. "No, I couldn't." I held up the stone. "Now what?"

"We make sweet love on your betrothed's land before he catches up with us?"

"What do I need to do with the stone, pervert!"

"Close your eyes, hold it in your palm, and think of where you want to go." I could feel the rumble of repressed laughter through his chest.

"Are we still talking about the stone?"

"Come on, Em. As much as I am enjoying this, it is hard to run with a hard cock. It chaffs, you know."

"Nils!" I shook my head and held the stone tight. Immediately, I saw the white blindness, then we were back in the field I was practicing in this morning. I unwrapped my legs, climbed down shakily, and hugged him tight around his middle. "Thank you, wolf."

He smiled a cheeky grin. "You were gone a long time. You were going to miss supper."

"I didn't realize I'd been gone so long." It was almost dark, but it seemed like I'd only been gone an hour at most.

"Time moves swiftly in Svartálfaheim." He eyed me with interest. "I have to shower before dinner. You could come with me if you like."

I laughed. His expectant face was so hopeful; it was comical. "Thanks, but no thanks."

"Not even for the sake of water conservation?"

I started to make my way to the house. "No, Nils."

"Okay, then. See ya."

He sprinted past me, bounding toward the house. I watched him until he was out of sight, all the while shaking my head. Despite his brash behavior and the constant seducing, the Fenrir wolf really was a decent guy.

CHAPTER SEVEN

I was sitting with Viggo, Nils, and Jakob, admiring Soren's gold-rimmed tableware when Cedric showed Katrine into the dining room. Viggo and I shared a look as he offered her a chair with a flourish and then lingered after she took it. Anyone who wasn't blind could see Cedric was more than a little interested in her. And who could blame him? Katrine was an exquisite beauty. Between her dark hair and eyes and the fading sparkles she was leaving in her wake, she looked every inch a Greek goddess.

Intrigued, I called out to Cedric just as he was leaving the room. "Cedric, would you join us for dinner? I feel like I haven't seen much of you lately."

Katrine rewarded me with a thousand-watt smile for the gesture, but Cedric glanced around as if nervous about the males' response to the addition. Clearly, dinner with the masters wasn't a common occurrence.

I glanced questioningly to the guys with a 'you better not screw this up' look, and Jakob and Nils both gave me 'who cares' shrugs. Viggo piped up with, "There's an empty chair next to Katrine."

After we were all settled and the first course was served, I watched the pair sneak glances and shy touches, but by the time the soup course was put on the table, it was evident to everyone (judging by the rolled eyes) that Katrine was just as smitten with Cedric as he was with her. I couldn't help but think it was bad fortune that these two couldn't be together because of their fates. It really was terribly unfair. They were made for one another.

I must have been concentrating on them harder than I'd realized because when Viggo tapped me on the shoulder and gestured to Jakob, it was evident he'd been trying to get my attention for some time. "What?" I mouthed.

"Can I see you in the parlor, Emelie?"

His angry face confused me. "Yes, of course."

Jakob yanked me into the doorway as soon as I was around the table. "What the hell do you think you are doing?"

"What?"

"You caused that, Emelie."

"Caused what, Jakob?" I was getting annoyed.

He sighed, exasperated, and spun me in the direction of the dining room. "That."

Looking in, I saw Viggo and Nils laughing hysterically at Cedric and Katrine, who were kissing like they'd never get the chance again. "I did that?"

Jakob looked amused and horrified at the same time. "Yes. It appears your mother's magic has surfaced."

I felt lightheaded. "Do you know how I can stop this? I'm afraid to try, Jakob. What if I do it wrong? I don't know what I'm doing!"

Jakob noticed my pale pallor and eased me into a stiff plaid chair. "Do not worry. We will figure this out. Ask Katrine when she comes up for air. A Dis will know what to do … unless she is happy with your choice for her. Then there might be nothing to do but enjoy the fruits of your labor."

I nodded and frowned as I watched the pair. I was really crossing my fingers for that last scenario.

Resigned to do the right thing, I asked Katrine to come outside with me after dinner. As Jakob predicted, she was reluctant to leave Cedric's side (and their make-out session), but he gave her a little push in my direction, and she finally complied. We stepped outside together, thankful that Viggo had the foresight to start a fire in the pit. It was freezing out. Living in California hadn't exactly prepared me for Sweden's weather. I'm not sure if living in Antarctica could've prepared me.

"Jakob tells me you are a Dis?" I asked her, warming my fingers over the flames.

"The dark one speaks the truth. We help a Norn's vision become a reality if there are impediments." She gave me a contemplative look. "I was your mother's Dis. She was my best friend for hundreds of years, and in all of those years, she never once gave me a gift like you have today."

"A gift?"

"Cedric, silly." She grinned. "I know you are distressed, but please, put your mind at ease. I rather enjoy the time I am spending with him. It has been decades since something of interest has happened to me, and it certainly doesn't hurt that he's hot."

"Hot?" I burst into laughter.

"What? Is that not what they say in modern Midgard?"

"Yes. I just never expected it to be in your vocabulary."

She sighed happily as she looked in at Cedric. "Neither did I."

We both giggled. "Does Cedric know what you are?" I asked, wondering if it would even matter to him.

"He knows we are from different realms. He does not seem to mind."

"I'm glad," I told her, blowing out a relieved breath. At least, there was one thing in my life that wasn't complete shit.

"I take it, you're not excited about your match."

I blushed and studied my jeans. "You heard that?"

She laughed again. "Yes. You are remarkably bad at shielding your thoughts. It is quite amusing for the males." She pointed inside, and even I had to laugh at myself. They were hanging onto our every word.

"Concentrate on blocking them out, Emelie." She paused for a moment. "Now think about kittens."

I giggled again as she looked back inside. The guys were still looking expectantly at the glass. "Okay girl, spill."

I hesitated. Should I tell her? I barely knew her.

Oh, screw it. I was going to explode if I didn't tell someone. "I met Kristian the night Soren came to get me, and we had kind of a moment," I blurted out. "Long story short, I let him drink my blood

Surprise lit her features. "How interesting. And what did he give you in return? A proposal?"

"He didn't give me anything."

She looked thoughtful. "Odd indeed."

"He came to see me today before you arrived."

"Why didn't you say so?"

"I wanted to start at the beginning, with the … um … blood thing."

"I see." She tucked her bare feet under her and got comfortable. "What did he say when he came here today?"

"He asked if I would go to his castle with him. I did, and he proposed."

"You accepted?"

"Yes, I accepted."

She glanced at my barren ring finger. "But, no ring?"

I pulled it out of my pocket and showed her. "I met Viveka while I was there."

She looked up sharply. "Did you?"

I pursed my lips, thinking how distraught Viveka had been when she saw the ring. "I did, and she is not a very nice person."

"Jilted elves rarely are, especially to the offspring of the union that broke her fate."

"I can tell you that statement is one hundred percent true."

"So, tell me why you do not have that gargantuan ring on your finger?"

I sighed. "Because of his harem."

"Pardon?"

"He has a harem. I saw them all lined up for him to choose from. It was revolting."

"I had no idea that rumor was true. Are you sure you are not mistaken? Could they have been the castle staff?"

Shaking my head in the negative, I muttered, "I wish I were mistaken. The only staff they're worried about is the king's."

Katrine pulled me into a hug. "Oh, Emelie, that sucks. You need to call him and tell him to choose between you and the harem. I suspect he will choose you. The fate of his kingdom depends on it."

"Yes, but I can't stand the thought of sex with him after this. Not to mention, I don't know whether the other part of the harem rumor is true. What if he really is a rapist?"

"Did they seem afraid of him?"

"Not one bit. They seemed like they couldn't wait to fuck his brains out."

"I really don't think he's forcing himself on them if that is the case."

It was a relief to hear her say that, but I still didn't feel good about it. "What if he says no? How can I ever compete with the six other experienced females in his life?"

"Six? That many? Shit. Forget I said that. Look, the king is almost a thousand years old, and he's only been waiting on you for the last twenty years. That's a blink of an eye for him, and often old habits die hard. You have to forgive him of this."

"I know, and I will. I like everything else about him."

"He is gorgeous, isn't he?"

"He is so freaking hot, Katrine. I feel like I'm losing my mind when we kiss. The match could have been a lot worse. I'll give my mother that."

Katrine and I went inside after the fire started to die down and challenged Nils and Cedric to a game of billiards, boys against girls. I thought this would be an excellent way to keep Nils at bay, but in typical Nils fashion, he tried to show me the correct position for every shot I took by standing behind me and positioning my hands. Katrine, amused by this, eventually asked if he was planning to hump me right on the table.

I blushed at her comment, but almost melted into the floor when he answered, "If Emelie were game, I would do anything and everything to her on this table, under the table, against the table—anywhere she wants."

"Okay. That's enough of that." I hurried out from under him and sat next to Katrine.

Nils barked out a laugh and racked up the balls for the next game. "Coward."

Katrine nudged me and whispered in my ear. "He is very beautiful, is he not?"

"Who? Cedric?"

"Although he is scrumptious, I meant Nils."

"Yes, he is. They all are. Viggo and Jakob in their tall, dark, and delicious way, Nils in his rugged, Viking warrior way, and Soren in his ..." I trailed off thinking how to describe Soren's beauty best. "Being with Soren is like being immersed in the winter's night."

She arched her brow. "That is a very poetic description, Emelie. Some might say romantic."

"I know what I'm here to do, Katrine. I just wish the circumstances were different. I really like Soren, and I'd like to experience love just once before becoming the light elves' savior."

Katrine nodded. "Cedric is my first, as well."

"Your first?"

"My first love. In over four thousand years, I've never felt this way about anyone. I think he might be my true mate." She took my hand. "Thank you, Emelie, for letting me feel this. I did not think I ever would."

"Katrine …" I started. She hadn't mentioned the obvious problem with their love affair—Cedric's mortality.

"I know," she interrupted. "We have spoken about it. He is ready to become immortal if you are willing to perform the necessary enchantments for him."

"I can do that?"

"Emelie, you can do just about anything. You just need to train up a little first."

"Can I get out of mating the King?" I asked, hopeful for the first time since Soren's arrival.

"No. It is your fate. Above all else, you must fulfill your destiny."

I slumped down into the couch, suddenly bone tired. "Bummer."

"Indeed."

"Well, I guess I'm going to turn in. Will I see you in the morning?"

"I am an extremely bored and retired Dis, and you are an unsanctioned Norn with no Dis. I would say you can count on me being around for a while."

I hugged her tightly. "Thanks. I need all the help I can get. Good night."

Leaving the group, I ambled toward Soren's bedroom, ignoring the many appraising eyes of the staff. I just couldn't deal with that right now. Even though things were looking up, I was feeling depressed. I had never truly understood the saying 'Having the weight of the world on your shoulders' until I actually had the fate of two worlds in my ridiculously incapable hands. Clearly, my mother didn't think this thing through. I bet she didn't even blink an eye when she shoved my father's responsibility into my lap.

With a weary sigh, I twisted the key in the lock of the bedroom door, opened it, and flipped on the light, my eyes instantly going to the place where Soren left me the token of his affection. Just looking at the indent he made in the unmade bed made my chest pang with longing. If I was already missing him like this, after only one day, what would it feel like when I was mated to someone else?

I jolted awake. Someone was in the room with me.

"Who's there?" I asked, shielding my eyes from the sudden brightness as a lamp flicked on.

"Did you miss me?" Soren's deep voice asked.

"Soren!" I jumped out of bed and ran to him, squealing when he caught me and easily lifted me off my feet for a hug. Wrapping my legs around him, I buried my face in his hair to breathe in his scent. "I missed you so much," I whispered into his neck, a second before I pierced the skin with my fangs.

Soren's entire body stiffened when I broke the skin, but he soon groaned my name in satisfaction and relaxed against me. Walking us backward to the bed, he sat down, gripping me so firmly, I thought he would break me in two.

Lost in the smell and taste of him, I took a few draws of his blood before resting my spinning head on his shoulder and lazily licking at his wound. It felt like a natural thing to do, though I'd never bitten anyone before. I didn't even realize I was going to do it until the second before I struck. One moment, I was achingly glad to see him, and the next, I was animalistic, mindless of what I was doing. I just had to taste him. To be closer to him. My mother had warned me about this. She told me when I met the one that is destined for me, it would not matter what Norn cast my fate. Nothing would keep me apart from my true mate. She said I would crave him like nothing else.

"Emelie," Soren said seriously, interrupting my thoughts. I lifted my head weakly to look at him, and the world fell away.

"We have to stop meeting like this," Nils said, straddling me while I lay in the grass accumulating enough leaves in my hair for a suitable squirrel habitat.

"That wasn't funny the first five times you said it," I groaned, pushing him off me.

He helped me to my feet for the billionth time since he (literally) dragged me out of bed this morning. He'd gotten a bare foot to the face and a barrage of scathing, four-letter words for doing that, which was probably why he was so chipper while he was kicking my ass from one end of Soren's side yard to the other.

"Emelie!" he shouted across the lawn. "Concentrate on the vines. Tell them to keep me from attacking. It is the simplest magic you can learn. Toddlers can do this."

"Have you ever thought you might just suck at teaching?" I muttered.

"Oh, was that another comedic gem from the female who can't even use her elven magic? I will have you know I'm practically the wolf version of Yoda."

"Yoda?" I deadpanned.

He cleared his throat. "Told, I am. Better teacher, never find, you will. Yes, hmmm."

Closing my eyes, I concentrated on the vines overhead, hoping they would strangle him to death. "I think I'm ready."

Nils sprinted toward me, and in an instant, I was back on my bruised butt with his smiling face above me. "I need a break," I told him, shoving him off again.

"Okay quitter. I have some errands to run, anyway. See ya."

I watched him energetically run across the grounds, even leaping up to scare the birds in the low hanging branches. Just seeing Nils walking upright made me mumble about the 'stupid wolf bastard' the entire length of time it took me to hobble up to the house. Once inside, I made a beeline for the shower. I was sure I was trailing dirt and leaves everywhere, but I just couldn't wait one more second to get these sweaty clothes off. I'd deal with the mess when I got out of the shower. If I didn't collapse and drown in a puddle of water, that is.

The hot water of the shower felt amazing on my aching body. Of course, it wasn't even close to the caliber of amazing I'd felt with Soren last night. What could compare with that? Just thinking about biting him made my gums ache, though I doubted he'd ever let me bite him again. I hadn't realized how upset he was until he left without speaking to me this morning. I'd have to make amends when I saw him next.

When the water started to go cold, I reluctantly stepped out of the shower and realized that, in my haste, I'd forgotten to bring a towel or any clothes with me. Sighing, I mumbled, "Figures," and made a mad dash out of the bathroom to the linen closet, quickly grabbing a towel to dry my dripping hair before I had another mess to clean up.

"Emelie, you are not alone in the room."

I froze with the towel in my hair, then looked up at Soren, smiling to mask my embarrassment, all while casually pulling the towel down to cover my naked front.

Soren's glance lingered on my now fully lengthened canines, making my bloodlust grow stronger. "Emelie," His voice was tense. "You really are terrible at blocking your thoughts."

"So I hear." I couldn't believe we were having this conversation with my front barely covered.

He half-smiled and pulled me into his arms. I shuddered as his heavy jean-clad erection pressed into my stomach. "You should know I have just as hard of a time talking to you without wanting to kiss you, or touch you, or taste you."

"Why?" I asked, watching his eyes change to a glowing crimson. I shivered from the change in temperature as the heat built up between us.

"There are too many reasons," Soren said wickedly. He walked me backward towards the bed and pushed me to my back, the muscles in his arms bulging as he positioned himself between my legs and locked his hands in my hair. Gently rocking his thick shaft against my most intimate part, he whispered huskily into my ear. "I can see it perfectly in your mind. You want me inside of you. You want me to make you scream out my name. And believe me, Emelie, I want to give you all of me. Everything I have. My cock, my heart, my soul, whatever you will take from me, but I cannot. The lives of hundreds of thousands of elves depend on your mating to Kristian. Their deaths would be on my conscience, should we continue like this. It would make us no better than your parents."

I knew he was telling me something important. I knew it. I just couldn't understand it. Not while he was moving against me the way he was. All I could do was concentrate on the heat of him and the sharp breaths against my neck as I met his subtle thrusts with my own, my nails digging into his back. I was frantic, desperate for him. "Please," I begged. I didn't care if I was engaged to another. Kristian wasn't the one I wanted.

"I can deny you nothing," Soren said hungrily, placing blistering hot kisses to my mouth and along my neck.

Quickly rising to my crescendo, my cries of pleasure echoed off the walls until Soren took my mouth in another ravenous kiss. I could feel him trembling in restraint as I clutched myself to his chest and experienced the most unbelievable orgasm of my life.

"You are so beautiful when you come," he told me, nipping at my neck.

I was breathing so hard and fast, I could barely get out a 'thank you'. The way he still held himself tight against me, with the magic throbbing between us in time to the heartbeat in his erection, was sweet torture.

"I aim to please," he growled out, with a hint of wildness in his eyes. He smiled a broad smile that unveiled his own set of sharpened canines.

"Any more surprises?" I asked, almost afraid of the answer.

"Yes," he said seductively. "Plenty."

He was staring intensely at my neck, and I felt obliged to offer it. Hell, I'd put a bow on it if I could get him to bite me. I wanted him in every way.

"Are you sure?" he asked, examining my face as if looking for doubt.

"Yes," I assured him breathlessly. "I want you."

He placed a gentle kiss on my neck before slicing cleanly into the flesh. I cried out in pleasure, my own fangs throbbing in response. As he took his first strong pull of my blood, his body bucked against mine, causing what little control I had to slip. He only resisted for a few seconds as I unzipped his jeans and pushed them down to wrap my fingers around his length. I wanted him inside me—now.

Breaking the suction on my neck, he lifted away from me. "I cannot take your innocence, Emelie. No matter how much you or I want to. It is forbidden."

Defiant, I continued to use my hands to stroke him. "How could anything be more right? I'm supposed to be yours."

He shuddered. "Please, don't do this. I should not have let this go this far."

Boldly caressing his sex against my slick entrance, I moaned. I was so ready for him. "He doesn't have to know I lost it to you. I could have had sex with a human."

"Emelie," he pleaded hoarsely, his eyes squeezed shut. "Please."

I took this as encouragement and pumped my hips, letting him glide between my hands and my wetness. He groaned his satisfaction and took my mouth in a brutal kiss. It was ecstasy. Leaving the tang of my blood on my tongue, he bit into my shoulder, and I cried out, burying my fangs into his neck. Rocking against me, he met my frenzied thrusts with his own, and in one voice, we cried out our completion.

We lay there, too numb to move or speak for a moment, our magic pulsating against our skin to the beat of our hearts. I broke the silence. "Soren?"

He looked down at me with his red eyes glowing. "Emelie?"

"I love you."

He kissed me fiercely. "If there is any other way, I will make you mine."

CHAPTER EIGHT

I walked up the worn stone stairs slowly, carefully trying to avoid tripping on the many vines growing across them. The light at the opening of the temple grew brighter and brighter as I methodically made my way toward it. I couldn't exactly remember why I'd climbed this far up to get there. All I knew was I had to get to the entrance somehow.

After what seemed like hours, I made it to the top. I rested my palms on my thighs, breathing heavily before looking through the illuminated doorway and was startled to see a male standing there. He walked toward me, hand extended. "Hello, Emelie."

"Who are you?" I asked, ignoring his hand. By his appearance, he was a moderately tall, good-looking male, but my instincts told me it was an illusion.

"I am Freyr."

I took a step back, knowing, without a doubt, he was the doppelgänger. "Why am I here? Why are you wearing a disguise? What are you hiding?"

He tsked. "So many questions for such a little elf. You might be polite to your elders, you know. But, in answer, I will say I am here for you. I cannot seem to find you on Midgard, so I thought I would ask you where you are currently residing. As to what I am hiding and why I am wearing a disguise, I could only explain by showing you." Pausing, he smiled. "I do not think you would like what is under this mask."

"Okay, I'll bite. Why wouldn't I like it?"

With a wink, he said, "You will not be able to leave this place with your virginity intact."

I laughed. "What?"

81

He looked furious. "How dare you mock me!"

I smirked. "Well, if you're going to make ridiculous statements like that, I don't see how I'm going to be able to stop. Did you hear yourself? Virginity intact. How did you even keep a straight face when you said that?"

Sultrily, he answered, "You insolent vixen. I think I shall show you what is hiding under this enchantment just to shut that sweet little mouth of yours."

With a pop, a different male stood in his place. He was mesmerizing, young and blond with a gloriously naked bronze body. I looked him over, just taking in his perfection. He was very, very well endowed. A fact I could not ignore, even if I wanted to. I couldn't take my eyes away from the sight of him fondling his erection as he waited for my perusal of his magnificence to end. I stood mute in awe of the horror that was his beauty.

"I tried to warn you," he reminded me. "But no, you had to push me, and now I will be forced to teach you a valuable lesson." He sounded almost bored. "Never make your master angry."

My eyes widened at his words, but I couldn't make the rest of my body move. He grabbed me roughly by the arms and turned my stone body to face the doorway of the temple. Standing close, he pressed roughly into me and whispered, "Would you like to see what life will be like for your fellow elves when I kill you?"

The bright light faded allowing me to see what was happening inside. There were hundreds of elves, all doing various duties. The males were cleaning, cooking, or building an altar, but all of the elven females were lined up for their turn to service him. I watched as he wrenched the closest female to him out of line and threw her on a bed. Forcing her legs open, he ignored her screams as he rutted her like an animal.

"You're a monster," I said, appalled at his brutality.

He laughed. "And you will bow to me just like the rest."

"Never. I will kill you before this happens to the elves," I said through gritted teeth. I could feel my hair stand on end as my magic built in time with my anger.

He stepped away from me in shock. "You are not an elf."

I smiled sweetly. "No, and you should be very, very afraid."

"Trust that I will not underestimate you again," were the last words I heard before I woke.

"Emelie! Are you okay?" Soren turned on the light. "You were yelling in your sleep … something about killing someone?"

"The doppelgänger," I growled out, sitting up. "He came to me in my dream and showed me a temple full of his elven slaves."

He looked alarmed. "What did he say?"

"He said he couldn't find me. He wanted to know where I was hiding." I didn't bother filling him in on the rape. I knew the fake Freyr's reputation was well known in the Norselands.

Soren smirked. "And did the abomination expect you to tell him where you are?"

"I guess so. We really didn't get into that for long before I made him angry."

He quirked an eyebrow, "You? Make someone angry? No. What did you do?"

"I made fun of him when he said I wouldn't be able to keep my virginity intact if I saw his true form."

He burst into laughter. "I am sure he was infuriated."

"You could say that. He did show his true form to me right before enlightening me to his plans for the elves. He said he wanted me to know what would happen to them after he kills me."

"That is enough," he said, getting out of bed. "I have to find him."

"It gets worse."

"How much worse?"

"He knows I'm not a normal elf."

"You displayed your magic?"

I looked at the blanket, full of guilt. "I was so mad, Soren. I couldn't control it."

He lifted my chin with his finger. "Magic is much more about concentration than talent, Emelie. It will eventually become a natural extension of you without you having to think about controlling it. You shall see."

I smiled. "Good. I'm tired of being the weakling around here."

Nils met us outside for what Soren called 'mandatory' magic practice twenty minutes later. I pulled Soren to the side, while Nils was busy loping around the yard in wolf form and asked him why we needed the smug bastard's help to do it. He would only say, "You'll see," in that cryptic way of his before he called Nils over.

"So, guys, what are we practicing today?" Nils asked, looking every bit the wolf version of Tigger as he bounced on the balls of his feet.

Soren looked away from is nakedness. "After you dress, Emelie will begin where she last left off. Move to the back of the field and run toward her. Emelie, you will stop him from reaching you with the vines overhead." He stepped away from me. "Begin."

Nils taunted me when he reached his starting point. "Couldn't stay away, huh? Can't say I'm surprised. Most females love to have me on top of them."

His teasing had my magic begging to be let loose. Ever since the dream about the Freyr-thing, I had been able to channel my anger into magic. It was almost as if a switch had been flipped inside me. I knew I'd have no problem stopping him this time. "We'll see how smart your mouth is when you're tied up, Nils."

He blew me a dramatic kiss and took off in a blur.

Quickly, I summoned the energy in the trees, telling them what I wanted them to do. They obeyed instantly, first slowing Nils down as he tried to avoid their reaching branches, then stopping him altogether and lifting him four feet off the ground.

Batting my eyes at the restrained male, I called, "Oh, darn. I guess I won't have the big bad wolf on top of me after all."

Soren groaned. "That was probably not the best idea."

There wasn't even enough time for me to ask him why. With a massive surge of strength, Nils burst from the vines and leaped after me. Screaming, I ran, though I was hardly a match for his speed. He caught up to me after only a few steps and pounced, causing me to land with a thud and a mouthful of grass.

Nils spoke softly in my ear as he lifted his weight off me. "Emelie, if you want to play these kinky bondage games, all you have to do is ask."

I spat dirt out of my mouth. "Bite me."

"From this position, I'd like to do more than bite you."

"Emelie?" Soren's unusually loud voice distracted us from our witty banter, and we rose to our feet.

"Yes?"

"Will you please send Nils to the house?"

"Okay. Go fetch, pooch." I was rewarded with a lovely hand gesture for that remark.

Soren tried to keep a straight face and failed. "Will him into the house with your magic, little one."

Closing my eyes, I searched through myself to find the same magic I'd used with Cedric and Katrine. It was extremely hard to pull it together. The magic seemed reluctant to do what I wanted as if it was resisting my orders. "I can't. The magic is refusing to obey me."

"The magic is telling you it is not his path. If something should not be changed, the magic will sometimes give you a warning so you will not make a mistake. Try again."

I closed my eyes and found the hidden power much easier this time. As soon as I thought, Nils needs to go to the house, he disappeared.

"Did I do it?"

The back door opened, and Nils poked his head out. "That was … weird."

Soren smiled. "Excellent, Emelie."

"Thanks, I see why we needed Nils now."

He chuckled. "Katrine was my first choice, but she was a little … um, busy. Now, let us move on to something more difficult. I want you to combine the fates of two people in love."

"What? Already?" My mind was instantly filled with thoughts of potential disasters.

"Yes. This should pose no problem for you. Come inside the house. Our practice subjects are there."

I hesitated. Combining fates this soon felt like a monumentally bad idea to me. I had gotten lucky with Cedric and Katrine. What if I really screwed this up? I could ruin lives.

Soren stopped walking and pulled me into his arms. "Have faith in yourself. I know I do."

"I'll try," I said, leaning forward for a kiss.

He stopped me. "No distractions, Emelie."

I pouted. "Fine."

Soren led me into the kitchen where Hilda and Gunnar, the only daytime staff, were prepping for dinner. They bowed formally and immediately went back to their duties when they saw us arrive. Walking to the cupboard, Soren pulled out two bottles of water and handed me one with a significant look. I shook my head furiously.

He sighed and motioned for me to follow him out. "Come on, Emelie. You will not get easier practice than this."

"I know they already like each other, but what if I ruin the good thing they already have going?" I'll admit, I was whining a bit.

"You will not," he assured me.

"How do you know that? They're practically a couple as it is. How would you know if it was them or me?"

"Gauging by Cedric and Katrine's reaction to their bond, I would say we would know by the number of times they disappear to have sex."

"That's not funny."

"Just get in there and do this, Emelie. You are being ridiculous."

"It's not that easy. I swear, I'm telling you the truth."

He shook his head in aggravation. "I will be in my room, when and if you decide to accept your destiny."

Ashamed of my cowardice, I watched Soren climb the stairs and walk down the hallway until he was out of sight. When he didn't glance back, I was sure we'd just had our first fight. I was also pretty sure he'd won it.

Jakob and Viggo decided to pick up Soren's plea of reason an hour or so after he went upstairs. There was no doubt he put them up to it. Viggo looked like the whole situation was causing him to be late for something and had an annoyed look I'd never seen on his face before, and Jakob just appeared to be holding his breath to keep from yelling at me.

"Emelie," he coaxed. "You have to do it sometime. It is what you were born to do."

I tried to keep the cynicism out of my tone. "I thought I could depend on you to stay neutral about this, Jakob."

He huffed. "I would stay neutral if it was not so glaringly obvious that aligning their particular fates is the perfect undertaking for a first-timer."

Giving him a skeptical brow lift, I asked, "You think so?"

"I would not lie to you," he promised.

"What about you, Viggo? What do you think?"

Viggo moved to sit down on the couch with me. Sighing deeply, he took my hand into his, and with a tender expression in his green eyes and a very calm voice, he said, "Emelie, get your ass in there and do this, you fucking coward. You are not going to make me miss the finale of my favorite vampire show tonight. Understand?"

"What? That's tonight?"

Jakob threw his hands up in exasperation. "Can we focus here? Do I need to remind you two how important Emelie's magic is for the Rebellion?"

"No. I'll do it, but Viggo, can you record the show, so I won't miss anything?"

"Sure thing, kid." He checked his watch. "Got to go. Good luck, Emelie."

"Thanks!" I called after him.

"You two are unbelievable," Jakob said, as impatient as ever. "Are you ready, Emelie?"

"Yep. I'll go find Soren."

I trudged up the stairs to our bedroom, dreading what I had to do, and found Soren sprawled out across the bed, staring at the ceiling in deep contemplation. "Hi," I offered. "Is there a spot in this bed for an infuriating elven female?"

There was a lingering silence between us before he finally spoke without looking at me. "My fate was cast at the moment of my birth. It was cast by one of the greatest Norns that has ever lived, Myrgjöl. She is your grandmother, and before you ask, she lives, but I will tell you more of her later."

"Okay." I nodded my acquiescence and waited on him to continue. How well he knew me already! My mind was reeling from this new information.

"When I was very young, maybe eleven or twelve," he continued, "I asked my mother about my intended. You can never know what torture it was to learn I would not see you for more than seven thousand years and that you would be an elf; the elves were not thought of as equals in that time. As I grew older, I had many chances to learn that elves were indeed as worthy as any of the other creatures of the Norse, and I began to look forward to your arrival. This continued for century upon century, until nearly twenty-one years ago, mere months before you were born, came the news that your parents had bargained my only chance at love to the elven crown. I very nearly killed Kristian. If it were not for the war, I would have killed him that night. I have always detested hearing about his obvious displays of excess and his many females." He turned his burning gaze to me. "The king is the lowest of gentle-males and could never deserve you. I despise the thought of him impregnating you with his offspring."

I shuddered as I settled beside him. "As do I, but what of Kristian's original mate? Won't their fates be realigned if we can find a way around the mating?"

"No, they will not. Not unless the royal family is inclined to give their entire fortune to a Norn that is willing to take the risk of performing an illicit fate bonding. That is the only way."

"I could change his fate back, couldn't I? If I trained up a bit? Do you think the elves would stop fighting if they saw he was fated to his true mate?" Poor Kristian. He was just as much of a pawn in this situation as I was.

"Sadly, no. His people are not interested in his happiness. What matters to them is the unity between the races." He sighed deeply. "There is little time before your mating, and I cannot conceive how I will be able to think of a way out of this. I have tried in vain for two decades."

I kissed him softly on the cheek. "We'll think of something, Soren. I have faith."

He caught my face between his hands as I was moving away. "We have to. I love you, Emelie. I do not think I can let you go."

"And I love you," I said, kissing him a little more firmly. This time on the mouth. "That's why I'm sure we'll figure this out."

"I will never tire of hearing those words from your lips."

"Which ones? I'm sure we'll figure this out?"

Shaking his head, he grinned and grabbed my thigh, pulling me on top of him. "No, smartass. I love you. I have waited an eternity to hear those words come from your perfect mouth." He tucked my hair behind my ear. "Tell me, beauty, how do you fare tonight? I fear I was too hard on you earlier. Sometimes, it is hard to remember you are but a novice when there are so many pressing worries at hand."

"You don't have to apologize, Soren. I get it, and I'm okay, I guess. I actually came up here to tell you I'm ready to take on Hilda and Gunnar's fates."

"That is very good."

"But? What's wrong, Soren?"

"Nothing. I just …" His brows furrowed. "Have you ever felt cooped up?"

"Yes. I'm feeling pretty cooped up myself."

"Would you like to do something about that?" he asked, with a glint of mischief in his eyes.

I clambered off Soren and sat on the end of the bed, bouncing with excitement. "I thought you'd never ask! Where are we going?"

He got to his feet, laughing, and pulled me into his embrace. "You shall see. Hold on to me, tightly."

In a blink, we reappeared in the vestibule of a large apartment. Adorned in a strange modern decor, it was evident we were no longer on Midgard. "Where are we, Soren?"

"Ásgard. This was to be our home after we were mated."

"Our home?"

"Yes," he answered, with a very uncustomary look of nervousness on his face. "What do you think of it?"

Before I answered, I looked around, walking from room to room, admiring the careful consideration of the design. "I like it. Overall, it's pretty great, but ..."

"But?" he pressed.

"Well, if we moved here, I would want to make a few changes."

Relief filled his features for a moment, then he frowned. "What things?"

"Like, the kitchen wall. I really prefer an open floor plan. It wouldn't be any trouble to take that out, would it?"

He looked stunned but shook his head. "No ... I guess not."

Beaming, I said, "Great! Do you think we could have a few more windows installed on the east side of the apartment, as well?"

Warily, he looked down to me. "Yes, Emelie. If that is what you desire. Is there anything else?"

I wrapped my arms around his waist and peered up at him. "Soren?"

"My love?"

"I'm just kidding. I love the apartment."

"Are you in jest?"

Gigging, I admitted, "I don't even know which side the east side is on."

"You little imp," he scolded, before making my knees buckle as he seized my lips in a furious kiss.

I narrowed my eyes. "Speaking of an imp, don't think I haven't noticed you never told me what you learned from your visit to your father."

Soren's face fell. He hadn't expected me to bring it up. "Honestly, I did not mean to vex you," he began slowly. "I did not want to add more to your worries."

"Why? What did you find out?" I asked, feeling the edges of panic closing around me.

"Just what I expected to find; the doppelgänger is completely mad. He has put a price on your head."

"Is that why you brought me here? Are we in hiding?"

"No, we are returning to the compound soon. I just wanted to show you where we will be living after everything is settled. Are you sure you like it?"

I rolled my eyes. "Of course, look at this place. It's like the decorator knew to put in a perfect mix of your style and mine."

He smiled widely. "She did. I asked your grandmother to tell me what your tastes would be, and she was happy to oblige. Myrgjöl is a singular creature. I would like you to meet her as soon as you feel you are ready. She can give you invaluable advice, and more important to the present, we can trust her. She is infamous for her intolerance of changing fates for gain."

"She's my grandmother. I'm pretty much ready to meet her at any time. Where does she live? Can we visit her?" A knock on the door interrupted his answer. "Who could that be?" I whispered.

Alarmed, Soren grabbed me by the arms and yanked me away from the door. "Hide in the kitchen until I call for you. Make haste!"

I ran into the kitchen as fast as I could and crouched down inside the pantry, trying to make myself as small and unnoticeable as possible. Listening intently, I heard another knock on the door, the sound of Soren opening it, and then … nothing, until the locked pantry door sprang open.

"Well, are you going to just sit there, or are you going to give your grandmother a hug?" said the young silver-haired female smiling down at me.

"Myrgjöl?" I asked.

She grinned widely. "Yes child, and you must be my darling, Emelie."

I held onto the shelves on either side of me as I scurried up. "Yes, Ma'am." I was in shock. I couldn't believe she was here or how much she reminded me of my mother.

My grandmother held out her arms. "I've been waiting forever to see you! How are you, baby?"

I choked up with tears as she hugged me, barely able to answer her. "I'm … fine."

She leaned back to look at me, frowning at what she found. "No, you're not." She glanced at Soren who was leaning inside the kitchen doorway. "I hate Wist has done this to both of you—all this undeserved pain." She shook her head and returned her attention to me. "Your mother was a fool. The fate I spun for her was the correct one, but she thought she could do better than the humble merchant that was to be hers. Yes, Anders was a wonderful elf, but he was never meant for her, and neither was Viveka."

I shuddered. "I can't imagine anyone being Viveka's fated. She is so awful."

Myrgjöl laughed. "Viveka is an acquired taste, a fact your father was no stranger to." She wiped away my tears with a handkerchief she pulled out from nowhere. "Don't cry, Emelie. All will be well soon enough. You have a long life ahead of you, after all."

Momentarily hopeful, I asked, "What does that mean, Grandmother?"

"Tsk, tsk, Emelie. You know I cannot interfere. Soren did tell you what a stickler for the rules I am, did he not?"

"Yes." Wow. She did know everything.

"Of course, I know all, my dear one. I spun your mother's and Soren's fate. You were always a great part of their destinies."

"So, basically, what you're saying is, you know what will happen, but you can't tell us?"

"That is the sum of it, yes."

"Well, that just sucks."

She laughed again. "Yes, it does, but both of you will persevere. You shall see."

I could tell Soren and Myrgjöl were old friends when they settled onto the couch in the living room, chatting amicably. They were comfortable around each other in a way I'd never been around anyone, including my parents. Not sure what to contribute to the conversation, I remained standing and paced the floor with my worries heavy on my mind as they caught up with each other. Idly, I wondered if I would ever get used to the reality of the Norselands. The Yggdrasil had always felt so foreign to me, and now that I had to play a significant part in some of its worlds, I didn't think I could cope. If one of the most potent Norns in the worlds couldn't help me get out of this mess, what chance did I have?

Glancing over at my pacing, Myrgjöl said, "Soren, I know you'd like to stretch your wings for a bit. I will see to Emelie's safety whilst you are out."

"That would be welcome, Myrgjöl. Thank you."

I was confused by her words, but even more confused by his answer. What were they talking about? Where was he going?

Soren smiled at my worried expression. "Emelie, do not fear. I will not be long."

"I love you," I said. There was an unmistakable hint of desperation in my voice. I didn't understand what was happening?

He leaned down to kiss me. "And I, you. I promise I will not be long."

I watched him open the balcony doors and take a step out into the night air. A second later, he was enveloped in a bright white flash. When the light faded, a giant white owl stood in his place.

I joined him on the balcony. "Soren?"

The owl turned his head in the direction of my voice and blinked. Amazed at his transformation, I walked toward him, trailing my fingers down the snowy white feathers of his wings. They were as soft as silk. "You are magnificent," I whispered.

The owl dipped his regal head and spread his wings for takeoff. A moment later, he was soaring away into the distance. I watched him until I couldn't see him anymore then sat next to Myrgjöl on the sofa. "Huh," I said to myself, still a bit shaken up.

"You and the son of Odin are adorable together," Myrgjöl said, smiling brightly at me. "True mates are such a rarity these days. It does me good to see you two."

I love him," I said plainly. "I think I've always loved him."

"And you always will," she told me. "But that is not what I want to talk about while Soren is out. No, I would like you to tell me about the dark elf king. Has he promised to rid the castle of his ladies of ill repute yet?"

I sighed. "No. But it doesn't matter if he does. I won't ever sleep with him."

"And he should not expect you to." She paused and pursed her lips. "At least, not right away."

Tears sprang to my eyes. "I don't think he's much of a gentle-male, Myrgjöl. What am I going to do?"

"I think you'll find the dark elves' morals are comparable to the most steadfast of creatures. Every species has its own dark and light. And who knows? This could be Kristian's only darkness."

"I guess that's true. Kristian is nearly perfect in every other way."

She raised a brow. "Is he now?"

I blushed. "Well, he's certainly a better elf than his step-sister. That's for sure."

"Ah, yes. Viveka is quite awful, isn't she?"

"You have no idea."

Myrgjöl snapped her fingers and sat up straight. "That reminds me. Was Soren very upset when he learned you went to Väsen castle?"

Horrified, I asked, "Soren knows I went to Svartálfaheim?" My chest constricted with guilt. I felt awful he had to hear it second-hand. I was beyond embarrassed I'd went in the first place. It had been a huge mistake.

"It wasn't a mistake," she said, responding to my thoughts again. "It is better you learn of Kristian's flaws now. They would have been harder to deal with if you were mated beforehand."

"You're right," I said, absentmindedly toying with the tassel on a throw pillow. "It would've been." I took a deep breath and smiled at her. "Enough about my problems, Grandmother. I'm dying to hear about your life. Tell me how you became a Norn and how you met my grandfather."

Humor crinkled her grey eyes at the corners. "I thought you'd never ask! I was born on Ásgard almost eight thousand years ago. When I was three, I was taken from my parent's home to the council's grounds on Álfheim to be trained as a Norn. I started casting fates full time at fifteen."

"Fifteen?" I interrupted.

She nodded. "Norns begin very early. We have always been in high demand."

"Wow. I have a lot to learn, don't I?"

She patted my hand. "Not as much as you think, my dear. The magic comes naturally when it is time. Most of the training was to teach us not to interfere with the fates we cast. They say there is a fine line between being helpful and meddling. Personally, I don't see the point. If you're meant to be, you're meant to be, right? What does it matter if we give them a little push in the right direction?"

I shrugged. "I don't think there's anything wrong with that."

"Right! What am I supposed to do? Just tell them who their mate is and when they'll be born then set them on their merry way? No. They need direction, or they'll miss the chances that are there for them!"

I raised my eyebrows at her excitement and tried not to laugh. "Okay."

"I'm getting off the subject, aren't I? I do that, sometimes." She thoughtfully tapped her chin "What were we talking about before? Ah, yes … me. Let's see, after about a thousand years of casting, Odin brought me his first son. I could see Soren would be known as a good male, and I was thrilled to find he was fated to join my own family. Overjoyed, not only because seeing his fate allowed me to see what is to be his unyielding love for you, but also because seeing his future gave me the opportunity to see a glimpse of my daughter's future for the first time—her triumphs and her many mistakes. It was terribly hard knowing I could not intervene, but I have remained strong … well, as strong as I can be. As I said, some things need a little push." She grinned. "Anyway, a few thousand years later, I retired and mated a human man named Barnabas. He was a perfect mate to me and a doting father to Wist. We were happy until the day he passed. I still miss his laugh. He had the best one I've ever heard."

"A human?" I jerked my gaze to hers. "Then, that means I'm part human?"

"Yes. I suspect you've always felt at home on Midgard, haven't you?"

"Definitely. When my parents told me I was a light elf, I didn't want to believe them. I felt normal, not magical at all. Honestly, I don't think I really believed I was from the Norselands until my parents died."

"I'm not surprised. You are very much like your grandfather."

She tucked her feet under her, reminding me of Katrine for a moment.

"Too right, I do," she said.

"Pardon?"

"Remind you of Katrine. You did know she is my half-sister, didn't you?"

I shook my head. "No, I didn't know."

"She probably didn't mention our sisterhood because she didn't want to get your hopes up about meeting me. I do not always make myself known. But, for you, my dear Emelie, I will always be around."

"She didn't even tell me we were even related." I shrugged. "Maybe she was just preoccupied."

"Preoccupied?" She looked at me like she was seeing me for the first time. "You changed Katrine's fate?"

Mortified, I stared at my shoes. "Yes."

She nodded sagely. "When I predicted Soren's future, I could not see any of the fates you would cast. I thought nothing of it then, but it is very odd I could not see this coming from you or Katrine. Unbelievable would be a more appropriate word choice. I have to wonder what it means."

"I'm sorry. I didn't mean to. I just thought they made such a wonderful couple. Cedric was so smitten, and she was definitely returning the affection. To me, it seemed like the most natural choice in the worlds ... so natural, I didn't know I'd really done anything until someone pointed it out to me."

"I am simply amazed, Emelie," she said in reply. "I don't think Katrine knows this, but I have tried countless times to find her true mate. To be perfectly truthful, I didn't think she would ever have one. Tell me, what is he like?"

I smiled. Cedric was awesome. She was going to love him. "He's really great. He actually works for Soren, as his ... um, right-hand man."

She pursed her lips. "You are appallingly bad at keeping your thoughts private. Would it not be better to just tell me, instead of letting me pick it out of your mind?"

I cringed. She was relentless with the mind-reading thing. "Yes, Ma'am. Okay, Cedric is Soren's butler ... and a human."

"That is unexpected," she pondered out loud. "And Katrine is fine with letting her human lover go in a few short decades, is she?"

"Uh, no. She told me I could perform the magic to make him immortal." I watched as her face registered shock and then turned murderous.

"Call to Soren now!" she barked.

I didn't know what she was asking me to do, but I closed my eyes and screamed for him in my mind anyway.

In a flash, he stood next to me. "What has happened?"

"Katrine has been possessed, or it may not be her at all. I see it now. This is why I could not find her mate; she is not in her own mind. You must leave here immediately. The imposter cannot be trusted."

I reached to hug her goodbye. "Thank you, Grandmother."

She hurried to the door. "You are welcome, child. I will see you soon."

Soren bent in a funny little bow and said, "Myrgjöl, as always, I am in your debt."

"Yes, yes," she said impatiently. "Now scoot!"

Soren held out his hand to me. I stepped to him, holding tightly to his waist, and in an instant, we were transported back to Midgard.

The acrid smell of smoke was the first thing I noticed. The sound of screaming was the second. Something was terribly wrong. Soren quickly pulled me back into the shadows of the forest. "What's going on?" I whispered.

"We have been attacked." He pointed towards a plume of smoke above the trees that were barely visible against the night sky.

"Wh—" I started before Soren clamped a hand over my mouth and pulled me down to the forest floor.

Seconds later, I heard the rustling of leaves and Katrine's distraught voice. "Why have you done this, Freyr? I asked only for his safety. You could not let me have that?"

The couple came into our view just as he answered her coldly. "No. What consequence was he to me? A human who serves my enemies? You should consider yourself lucky I do not destroy you for your treachery."

She threw herself to her knees. "Please, forgive me. It was through no fault of my own. He was my true mate."

I was sickened by her betrayal, but more disgusted by the sight of the doppelgänger stroking himself through his pants as she knelt prostrate in front of him. Gross. This guy defined the words, 'sexual deviant'.

Freyr released himself and chuckled darkly. "I may have some use for you yet. I do enjoy a female groveling on her knees." He grabbed a fistful of Katrine's hair, pulled her face towards his waiting erection, and they disappeared.

Soren shook his head in disgust and laced his fingers with mine. "Hold on to me, Emelie."

CHAPTER NINE

W hen Soren and I finally arrived at the wreckage of the house, we recoiled in horror at the carnage the doppelgänger had left behind. There were dead humans everywhere, what appeared to be the entire staff. Most of them seemed to have been burnt alive, their faces etched with the agony they had felt as they lay dying; the rest must have been caught in the explosion.

"Cedric!" I cried, shutting out everything around me to try to listen to the grounds, desperate to find some signature or fate I could touch with my power. I pointed toward the front gate. "Cedric. He's there!"

We ran to the gate and found him conscious but barely clinging to life. He was severely burned and bleeding from his left ear and mouth.

Soren dropped to his knees beside him. "Cedric, can you hear me?"

His eyes focused a little as he tried to sit up.

"No, Cedric, lie back and relax," I whispered, trying not to cry as I used the elven magic Nils taught me to thicken the grass under his head.

Slowly, he began to speak. "Soren … it was … Freyr. He has … bewitched … my Katrine. You must save … her."

"Do not worry, Cedric, I will. Do you know where the others are?"

"Myrgjöl … called them … away," he said, closing his eyes.

"No!" I screamed. He was leaving us. I could feel his fate slipping away. "Cedric, don't go to sleep! Please!"

Cedric half-smiled, "Emelie ... you'll do ... what's right. And ... I know ... you ... will ... find a ... way to ... take care ... of Soren." He turned his unseeing eyes over to Soren, and with shallow breaths, he said his last words. "Never let her ... go."

Soren and I locked our gazes on one another after we felt the last of Cedric's energy leave his body, and for the first time since we'd met, he let me into his mind. It was chaos. He was in complete despair, his thoughts an echo of the anguish on his face. He'd lost his best friend in all the worlds, and he couldn't seem to remember what to do with his body. And how would he ever keep his promise to save Katrine? She'd all but caused his death! It was everything he could do not to find her and her kill her right this second.

Standing, I did the only thing I could do to help soothe his mind. "Leave the burial to me," I said, pulling my elven magic to the forefront. Tears were blurring my vision, but I didn't need to see to do what I needed to. Nature would do that for me.

Calling to the vines in the trees, I asked them to pick up Cedric's body and carry him to his favorite reading spot in the garden. Pushing my power out further, I asked the grass to move aside and the roots to open the ground. Slowly, methodically, the vines crawled over themselves to lovingly lower Cedric's body into the impossibly deep crevasse the roots provided then returned them from whence they came. As a final tribute, I arranged his portrait in the trunk of the tallest ash tree in place of a headstone, taking care that the tree's roots protected the newly disturbed ground around his body.

When it was all done, I sat on my knees and wept. I wept for Cedric, I wept for Soren, and I wept for myself. I'd never felt so bereft before. For most of my short life, I'd never known the pain of losing someone. Now, I was feeling the pain so many times in such quick secession, it was driving me to the brink. I couldn't lose anybody else. I didn't think I could take it.

Soren sank to his knees beside me and spoke with his mind. *"He did love the shade of this tree. He always said the faeries in this corner made the most beautiful flowers in the garden. I wish so much that you could have had more time with him. He was a very rare human."*

I took his hand and answered him in the same fashion. *"Me, too. I—"*

"Excuse me. Can you tell me if the fighting is over?" a small voice asked.

I looked to my left and saw a tiny female with delicate wings fluttering around the tree. She was amazing, a miniature of a fair-haired human in every way. I looked at Soren for an explanation. This was a first for me.

Soren stood and bowed. "I am Soren Vidar of Ásgard, and this is Lady Emelie of Midgard."

I stood and curtsied, unsure of what I should say.

"I'm Arlette. Pleased to meet you." She flew to our eye level and hovered. "Will Freyr come back?"

"No, he will not," Soren assured her. "He will have no reason to return. I will not rebuild here."

"Good." She flew back to the tree. "We will watch over his resting place for you, but we will also be watching to see if you keep your promise to him, son of Odin."

"You know Katrine is allied with the evil one," he said, sighing heavily.

"Cedric was one of us," she said sternly. "The promise he asked of you will be kept."

Resigned, Soren nodded. "It shall."

"Thank you … from all of us," she said to me, then she disappeared with a pop.

Soren ran his hands through his hair. "Emelie, we must go somewhere safe. Can you reach Jakob?"

"Maybe." I frowned. "But, why don't you?"

"The Väsens would never let me into their minds. I am the son of Odin. I doubt any of them will ever be able to trust me fully."

I huffed. "It's not your fault Odin is a dick. You can't pick your parents. Believe me, things would be way less complicated if we could."

Soren laughed and put his arm around me, leading me into the forest. "I would love to see my father's face if he ever heard you call him a dick."

I cringed. "I wouldn't. He might smite me or something."

"Yes, I think he might," Soren said thoughtfully. "You have caused quite a bit of trouble to him by being the doppelgängers' obsession. It would serve him well to see to your demise."

I stopped walking. "You're scaring me."

"I mean to scare you, Emelie. Odin does not have the humanity in his heart that you've become accustomed to seeing on Midgard. He considers himself a supreme leader, meaning he would kill you and everyone you love if he ever deemed it necessary."

My eyes widened. "Why would he think that necessary?"

"Let me give you an example. Say you are captured by Odin and asked to change a fate you know should not be altered or asked to make sure of someone's death. You would say no, correct?

I nodded.

"Then he would think of you as opposition. You would be prohibiting him from furthering his reign. That would be unacceptable; thus, your death would come soon after. Promise me you will stay put wherever I decide you must hide. Will you do this for me?"

"Of course," I said quickly, not knowing if I could keep the promise.

"You can. If I must keep my impossible promise to the faeries, the least you can do is keep this one."

"I'll try," I told him, then I reached Jakob. *"Where are you?"* I sent to him.

"Álfheim," he said after a moment's hesitation. *"Soren will know where."*

"They're on Álfheim," I told Soren. "They said you'd know where."

"I do. Come." He held out his arms to embrace me, and we were gone in a blink.

Arriving on Álfheim in seconds, my first thought was that we were standing on the side of a cliff, but a quick glance around proved otherwise. I was standing on an expensive Persian rug in a house that was undoubtedly built on a mountainside. There was no window blocking the view of the enormous castle complete with medieval-style towers and a surrounding village in the far distance. It was picturesque, almost like what I'd always imagined Camelot would look like … and I could barely summon the energy to care.

Shaky, I looked up to Soren. "Did that really just happen?"

He pressed my head into his chest and caressed my hair. "My love, we will heal."

"It's like a nightmare," I said woodenly.

"Yes, one that isn't quite over yet." Soren unclasped his hand from my death grip and looked me in the eye. "I have to leave to alert the human authorities."

"You're leaving me here?"

"You've been through enough today. I do not want you there for the cleanup and questioning."

I nodded, blinded by tears. "How long will you be gone?"

"Not long; one or two days, at most." He smiled reassuringly. "You can handle this, Emelie. You must be brave."

I sighed. "But I don't know how to tell them, Soren."

"You will do fine." He pushed his fingers into my hair and bent to kiss me. "I love you, Emelie."

"I love you, too," I said, barely flinching as he turned away and shifted into his owl form to fly into the afternoon sun. I was too numb to register much of anything now.

Collapsing in on myself, I sank to the floor and stared at the castle in front of me for a few seconds before Viggo's lightly accented voice spoke my name. I smiled without glancing up. "Hi, Viggo."

"It is a breathtaking view of Svartálfaheim, is it not?" He sat next to me and stretched out his legs.

The tears I'd been holding back since the burial started to flow as I answered, "Yes."

He wrapped his thickset arms around me, holding me against his chest until I couldn't cry another tear. When I was finally finished, he asked, "The staff didn't make it, did they?"

"No," I sniffed. "Katrine, she allied with the doppelgänger. We were too late to save them."

Viggo pulled away and looked at the castle again. "This madness must end, Emelie. We lost a great friend and many good people today. I will not stand idly by while my loved ones are put to death, one by one. We must kill this Freyr thing, and you must mate into dark elf royalty." He glanced at me wistfully. "I only wish I would have been chosen as your betrothed instead of my brother."

I was astonished. "You and Jakob are Kristian's brothers? Why didn't you tell me before?"

"Emelie, most of the time, I do not know how Kristian and I can be related. His arrogance and deceitful nature are not the only indications I have seen to mark him as a psychopath. I do not trust him."

"We are in total agreement on that sentiment," I said, watching him closely for any resemblance to the king. I shook my head. "I still can't believe you didn't tell me this from the start."

He smiled his usual cheerful grin. "I didn't want to tarnish your good opinion of us by telling you our brother was your intended. He is much altered."

"Altered?"

"He is a servant of Odin now. The brother we knew is gone."

My stomach plummeted. "No." There was nothing worse than my fiancée being a servant of someone who probably wanted me dead? "Please tell me you're kidding."

Viggo put a reassuring hand on my shoulder. "You will make it through this. Soren will return soon, and we will formulate a plan."

"Okay, but..."

"No buts, Emelie."

Nodding, I glanced ahead and was startled when I began to feel drawn into the illusion. It was almost as if I needed to get up and go there right now. "Is this what the castle looked like before the war?" I asked.

"Yes. When the light elves were a part of our lives, we were able to live in the sun."

"Something is …" I trailed off.

He furrowed his brows, looking concerned. "Emelie, what is it?"

"Nothing. The castle…" I shook my head to clear it. "I'm fine. Is there somewhere else we can go?"

"Of course," he said, taking my hand and leading me toward the next room.

Nils and Jakob were seated on opposite couches when we walked in. They were leaning toward one another and most assuredly in a deep, silent conversation. I sat next to Jakob, and surprisingly, he moved to sit closer to me.

"Emelie, if we cannot find a way around your engagement, you will be my sister, and no matter that you will be mating the worst representation of our bloodline, I promise, I will do my best to protect you. On this, you have my honor."

"As will I," Nils echoed.

"Thank you both so much," I said, getting misty-eyed. "You don't know how much I appreciate this."

After their declarations, Jakob and Nils left me alone with my thoughts, but Viggo stayed curled on the couch with me. As I stared at the happily crackling fireplace, I just couldn't seem to shake the image of the sunlit castle from my mind. I knew there was something significant about it, but my Norn abilities weren't sharpened enough to tell me what I was supposed to see.

"Viggo?"

"Yes, little one?"

I smiled at the familiar endearment. "Can you tell me why the castle is no longer in the sun?"

"It's straightforward. After the light elves departed, we were not able to acquire their blood, so we had a spell cast to protect us from the sun."

I cringed, thinking of my first meeting with Kristian. I hadn't realized, until this moment, what a huge deal it was that I gave him my blood.

Jakob, upon hearing my thoughts, came back into the room. "Emelie, please tell me you didn't."

"I'm sorry, Jakob. I don't know what I was thinking."

"That is so hot," Nils declared, wriggling his eyebrows suggestively as he followed Jakob into the room.

Viggo rolled his eyes. "Keep it in your pants, Nils. Emelie, don't sweat this. It shouldn't be in his system much longer. You aren't a full-blooded elf."

I sighed in relief. "Good."

Nils clapped his hands. "Well, now that that is settled, how about some breakfast?" He held his hand out to me to help me up. When I took it, he added, "You should know, Emelie, I have had nothing but compliments on my sausage."

I rolled my eyes. "Nice, Nils, very gentlemanly." Shaking my head, I followed him into the kitchen and sat at the granite bar, sure if I spent much more time with the wolf, my eyes were going to get permanently stuck in the rolled back position.

After our breakfast (which was really dinner), Jakob and I sat down in the living room to practice shielding. Right off the bat, I could tell he would not be nearly as patient as Soren was while teaching me. It took less than five minutes before a vein started popping out of his forehead. Who would have thought a fifth consecutive failure would push someone to the edge like that?

"Emelie," he said calmly, with the bridge of his nose pinched between his thumb and forefinger. "You will not be given the luxury of time when you face Katrine and the doppelgänger, or Thor, or even Odin himself."

"I understand that," I said, losing my temper. "I'm trying as hard as I can, you know."

"Fine," he placated. But after two more failures, he really lost his cool. "You are the most infuriating female I have ever met! I do not think you are trying at all!"

"Yeah, because I like having someone invade my thoughts, and then proceed to yell at me for only having my magic for a millisecond!"

Smiling nastily, he replied, "I would not have to yell if you would politely pull your head out of your ass and get serious."

I was dumbfounded. I'd never been spoken to like that in my life. "Well, I think—"

Jakob interrupted me. "Do not bother. I can pick your thoughts right out of your head. You think I am an asshole."

"Well, yes, but—"

"And you think I should go fuck myself."

"I never said that!"

"You did not have to." He tapped his chin feigning deep thought. "Let me think. What do I want to see next? Oh, I know. Tell me a little bit about your love life."

If Jakob was trying to humiliate me completely, he was doing a superb job of it. It was hopeless. I couldn't stop myself from thinking of the times Soren and I were together.

"Never mind," Jakob said. "I see everything I need to see, and I would bet my inheritance Kristian will not appreciate what you have been doing behind his back."

"No, I know he won't, but I can't control who I love Jakob. Soren is my true mate."

"How well I know that. I have heard your name from Soren's lips tens of thousands of times. I just do not know whom I pity more out of the three of you." He sighed. "Now, let us not get sidetracked. Your only problem is that you lack focus and self-control. What will I have to extract from your mind before you use your magic to block me?"

I felt sheer panic when I heard those words. No way was he getting back in. As soon as I felt his intention to invade my mind, I struck back, pushing my magic throughout me until it provided an armor of sorts. It was almost too easy to deflect him this time. I could feel his efforts, but the block I hastily threw up was much too strong for him to penetrate. I'd finally figured it out. I just had to stop over-thinking it and let the magic do its thing.

"Perfect, Emelie," Nils said from behind us. "That must be one hell of a secret."

"Thanks!" I preened. "Now can I go watch Viggo play the Xbox?"

Jakob laughed. "You may. You have earned it."

***

My nights and days in Álfheim with the males were monotonous. I slept, ate, watched TV, read, and kicked Viggo's ass on the Xbox, but I was never invited to any of their super-secret rebellion meetings, given any updates on when Soren would return or kept up to date on what was going on outside of the house. I guess they thought ignorance would be bliss.

I couldn't have disagreed more. Ignorance only made the wait worse for me. I spent my days coming up with far-fetched scenarios and wild assumptions on what could be keeping Soren so long. None of which would bring him back to me in the end.

Thankfully, on the fifth miserable day with Soren, I was spared from another night's worth of my vivid imagination. I rose from the couch and walked to the doorway of what I called the 'cliff room' as soon as I recognized his signature. "He's here," I told the males.

Viggo looked up from his game. "What's up, Em?"

"Soren is here."

He shrugged. "I don't think so."

"It's him," I reaffirmed, opening the door and smiling as his familiar scent surrounded me. "Where are you, Soren?"

"I am here." His voice came from a shadowed corner unlit by the candle in the center of the room.

"What's going on? Why didn't you come inside?"

He stepped into the candlelight and gazed out at the burning torches surrounding the castle. "It really is beautiful, is it not?"

"Yes, and so are you," I answered, rushing to wrap my arms around his middle. "I've missed you terribly."

A disbelieving look crossed his features. "Have you?"

His response wasn't exactly the one I'd been expecting. Soren seemed oddly detached, almost angry. And something was definitely different between us.

"What's wrong? You're acting strangely."

"I cannot hear your thoughts," he admitted.

I grinned. "I know. I've been practicing with Jakob."

His congratulatory smile didn't reach his eyes. "I thought I would be happier when you were properly prepared, but I miss experiencing your excitement when you see me."

I dropped my shield instantly, revealing to him how ecstatic I was that he'd returned and the naughty ways I'd like to celebrate.

Nils opened the door, intruding on our reunion. "Damn, Em! And they tell me to keep it in my pants."

"Manners, Fenrir," Soren growled.

"Yeah, yeah. So, what's the word in Midgard?"

"The human authorities have ruled the explosion accidental. We lost eighteen of the staff—Cedric, four maids, eight gardeners, and five in the stables. I think they tried to stop the doppelgänger and Katrine from entering the house. Everything is a total loss."

"Did you locate them?"

Soren focused on the image of the castle in the distance. "There."

I gasped. "No."

Nils laughed. "Em, this mate of yours is sounding better and better."

I shot daggers at him. "Shut it, Nils."

"Wow, already with the bridezilla stuff? You haven't even started planning the wedding yet."

Without even thinking of how it could go sideways, I took off my shoe and whipped it at his head as hard as I could. I was done with his snarky comebacks, done with him not taking my (sure to be) traumatic future seriously.

Chuckling, Nils caught it easily and walked out the door smirking, still holding my shoe.

I looked up at Soren's angry face. "That male is unbalanced."

"I did warn you," Soren reminded me.

"That, you did."

"Is that you, Soren?" Viggo yelled from the next room.

"It is," he called back, his eyes flashing to mine. "Emelie, can you leave us?"

"What? Why?"

His face was empty of emotion as he spoke. "I need to speak to Viggo, privately."

"Okay. Will you find me when you're done?"

Jakob appeared from nowhere and gave Soren a nod. "Follow me, Emelie."

I was confused. "What the hell is going on, Soren?"

Soren didn't respond. He only glanced at Jakob and nodded his head.

"Emelie?" Jakob prompted, offering me an arm.

"Fine, I said, ignoring his chivalry. "Don't tell me, but good fucking luck keeping anything from me once my magic progresses. You will all get payback for this clandestine bullshit." I stormed past Jakob and a surprised Viggo and slammed the door behind me.

Jakob caught up with me in the hallway but didn't say anything until he gestured for me to go to his bedroom instead of my own. "What is going on?" he asked. "Viggo was adamant I come to get you, but he wouldn't say why."

"I don't know. Soren is acting strangely. You don't think he's trying to distance himself from me, do you?"

"I do. And honestly, I would be worried if he didn't. There is not much time before your mating."

"I'm not ready to let him go," I sniffed, wiping at my eyes.

"It is better for him to do it this way. It will ease his pain."

"It doesn't ease mine."

"It will," he assured me. "In time."

I scoffed. "How would you even know, Jakob?"

Annoyed, he said, "Do you really think that in over four thousand years I have not had my share of heartbreak?"

"No, of course not," I said, completely ashamed of my petulant behavior. "I'm just upset. Forgive me?"

He cupped my face and used his thumbs to wipe away the tears. "Eternal life is not always the gift it appears to be."

"No, it isn't," I agreed.

Nodding, he was silent for so long after that I started to worry.

"Are you okay? You're still holding my face."

Dropping his hands to his sides, he stared into my eyes and said, "I believe I have thought of something that could be of great importance in your mating."

"What's that?" I couldn't imagine what would make that much of a difference. Knowing him, he probably wanted to go get his grandmother's mating dress from the castle so I could wear to the wedding. He had never opposed my mating Kristian as much as the others had.

"I have to go," he said hastily. "I'll be back soon."

I shrugged. "Why not? Everyone is leaving me in the dark today. Why not strait-laced Jakob Väsen, too?"

Jakob shook his head, and for the first time, I got a genuine smile out of him. "It's not like that, Emelie. You know it's not."

"If you say so."

He gathered me into his arms and pressed his lips to my forehead. "It's going to be okay. I know it's hard for you to understand right now. You are young. But Emelie, the things we are doing right now are not small. They are not insignificant. We are fighting for an entire race of creatures. We cannot let the actions of a few of us erase the elves' futures. The fighting must end. The deaths must stop. Because at the end of the day, Odin is what both factions of elves need to be concentrating on. Light or dark, he is the real enemy."

"Why aren't you the king, Jakob? You seem to have a much better head on your shoulders than Kristian. I doubt you'd be consorting with the enemy."

He frowned. "What do you mean?"

"Soren said Freyr and Katrine were at the castle with Kristian."

Startled, he jerked away from me and nearly run to the door. "I have to go."

I nodded and stared his closed door for a minute before I went back to sit on the bed in my own room—alone. So. Very. Alone.

"You will be happy to know his grandmother was buried in her mating dress," my grandmother said from beside me.

I yelped and jumped halfway across the room at the surprise of her voice. "You have to start making a noise when you get here, Myrgjöl! You scared the life out of me!"

"I'm sorry, dear one," she said, chagrined. "I just knew you had need of me. So, here I am."

"But how? I thought I was blocking my thoughts."

"Oh, you are, but I am your grandmother. If you need me, I will know."

"I think it's over between Soren and me," I blurted out. I couldn't hold it in another second.

She nodded. "Yes, I think so."

Tears sprung to my eyes. "I thought I'd think of a way before it was too late."

She wrapped me in a hug. "Emelie, yours is not an ideal position to be in, but in time, you will be happy. That I can promise you."

"That will never happen without Soren."

She pulled away and looked at me seriously. "I know you love Soren, and that you'd give anything right now to solve this between you two, however, you can't ever become desperate enough to use your magic to accomplish it. You must take care that your desires, even the ones of revenge you preserve for Freyr's doppelgänger, do not come to fruition. You are a Norn—anything or anyone will bend to your whims if you want it bad enough."

"So, I'm supposed to just forget the love of my life and quietly mate Kristian—an elf that has a room full of whores and an allegiance with Odin?"

"The very one, Emelie. Your life may feel like an unfair game, but you will play it with the hand you have been dealt. No cheating."

No, there would be no cheating. I knew that now. Changing my fate was never the answer. Taking your life into your own hands is foolish. I didn't want to end up like my mother. "I don't know how I'm going to do it, but I promise I will do what's right."

She took my hands in hers. "I am proud of you."

A bittersweet smile crossed my lips. "Well, at least, something good came out of this."

She pursed her lips. "How many days do you have left?"

"Just two more until my birthday."

"I suggest you contact Kristian right away to arrange for your things to be moved to the castle. Make sure you stand your ground with everything. And make sure you request a private ceremony for the mating. That way, you'll survive your mating night. You must avoid being an easy target for the doppelgänger. He will try to kill you before the truce can be struck."

I hugged her again, and this time, I held on tight. "I'm scared."

"I think you're well up for this challenge," she said, stroking my hair back from my forehead. "I have faith you will do everything in your power to do what is right for both elven worlds. You are my granddaughter, after all."

"Yeah, there is that," I said, brightening up for her benefit.

"Good girl. Now, let us call Kristian."

"What?" I asked, starting to panic. "Now?"

"Of course! There's no time like the present."

"How are we going to call him? I don't have his number, and I somehow doubt he's listed in the phonebook."

She pointed at her head. "You have the nearly all-knowing over here."

"Oh … right. What am I going to say to him?"

"You will say you will commit to the mating as promised."

"What if he doesn't want me anymore?"

She sighed. "It matters little in your case. Kristian is desperate to stop this war. Don't forget; he has suffered more than most because of it."

That was true. Not only had he lost his own mate, but he had also seen his world literally turn to darkness. And the deaths he'd seen—how many elves had died in this pointless war only because I wasn't old enough to mate yet?

"So, what you're saying is that there's no way either one of us can afford to back down from the mating even if he has turned to the dark side?"

"Exactly. You know, you are getting quite good at this figuring it out thing."

"Oh, you're hilarious." I sighed. "Do you think Kristian will protect me from the doppelgänger? Soren said he was hiding out there."

"I think you can protect yourself," she huffed. "That 'Freyr' would be wise to never cross any of my family."

"Grandmother, you have a temper—I like it."

"I may not be able to interfere in your life, but this Freyr thing and I have history. No one would be surprised if I made sure he disappeared."

Note to self: Don't piss off grandma.

"All right, sweetie, I have to go. Soren is coming."

"What about the phone call?"

"Later. Love you!" She blew me a kiss and was gone in a blink.

"Love you back," I mumbled, then a tap on the door made me jump.

Soren cracked open the door and peeked in. "Emelie?"

"I'm here." I walked straight into his outstretched arms. I wanted to remember everything about him—his smell, the pulse of his restrained power, the way he held the back of my head when we embraced—everything. "I hate this," I whispered into his chest.

Ignoring what I said, he growled—actually growled and tried to make small talk. "Are your quarters satisfactory?"

"Very. Aren't you sharing them with me?" I asked, already knowing the depressing answer.

Sighing, he closed his eyes, unable to meet my gaze. "Emelie," he started.

"Don't bother, Soren. I know."

He opened his eyes and scrutinized my face. "You know, do you? Then you know how much I still want to share your bed, how much I want to rid you of the only gift you have to give your mate so he will never have the opportunity to take it? Do you know I've been considering killing him?"

"Killing him would be selfish, Soren. Too many elves have died in this war already."

He raised my knuckles to his mouth and pressed his lips against them. "When it comes to you, I will always be selfish. You are everything to me, Emelie. Everything."

"As you are to me," I said, sliding my hands around his waist. Tonight was our last chance to do what we had always been meant to do and my body screaming for him to make it his. I wasn't about to waste the opportunity.

He wound a fist in my hair and pulled me closer. Harshly, he whispered, "Take off your clothes," into my ear, before biting into my neck. I cried out and fumbled with the buttons on my shirt, eventually ripping the fabric open to expose my breasts.

"You are so beautiful," he said, palming his erection. "I am dying to be inside of you."

I slid my panties and skirt to the floor and climbed seductively on the bed. Instantly, Soren was naked and pressed into my body. Turning me on my back, he kissed and nipped his way from my breasts toward my core. I held my breath and gripped the sheets in anxious anticipation, gasping loudly the first time I felt his tongue intimately. Soon, I was screaming out his name in orgasm.

Pulling himself up my body, he laid his massive erection between my thighs. "I cannot wait any longer, Emelie. Are you ready for me?"

Between sharp, pleasured breaths, I answered, "Yes, Soren, please."

He took my mouth and slid against my welcoming wetness to begin the achingly slow push into me, only to withdraw suddenly when a loud bang on the door startled us both.

Soren groaned and muttered, "I am fucking serious. Someone better be dead."

Shouting erupted from outside the door.

"Soren, come out of there, or I am coming in to get you!" It was Jakob.

"Come on out, Soren. You cannot do this. It will hurt you both." And Viggo.

"Fuck them! If you do not do this, I will!" Nils added.

With his eyes full of regret, Soren moved to the edge of the bed and yelled back, "Do not come in. I am coming out."

"No, Soren, please!" I couldn't lose my virginity to Kristian. I just … couldn't.

"I cannot, my love. Forgive me."

With tears blinding my vision, I whispered, "I do, Soren."

And I did. I really did. But I sure as hell didn't have to be happy with the outcome.

Sighing in deep disappointment, I gathered my clothes and locked myself in the bathroom while Soren dressed. I didn't want him to see me break down.

"I am sorry," he said, his voice barely audible through the door.

"Me too," I whispered, mostly to myself.

As soon as I stepped out of the tub, I could feel that Soren had left. Hurrying into my robe, I ran to the living room to find somber and guilty faces. "Where is he?"

Jakob stood, but couldn't look me in the eye. "He has gone. He will not return."

My heart stuttered in my chest. Soren had left me. After the years of dreams and fantasies, it was all gone—he was gone. It was for the best, of course. I knew that, but it still made me wish he had left me to die alone in my house that night. I could never love anyone the way I loved Soren.

Bereft, I turned back the way I'd come and spent the rest of the day and most of the night alternating between crying, screaming, and staring at the number that had magically appeared on my bathroom mirror in the afternoon. Myrgjöl wouldn't even give me a day to wallow in my misery. She was relentless.

The guys weren't too keen on my mourning, either. They had to listen to it first-hand. With my mind in turmoil from having my heart broken, my shield was non-existent.

In desperation, all three of them tried to get me to come out of my room at one time or another. First, Viggo tried to get me to come to breakfast, but I chased him away. Then, Nils knocked on the door at lunchtime. I didn't even answer. I couldn't stomach sexual innuendo from him while I felt like this. Finally, in the early morning, Jakob took his turn. He was the most trustworthy of the bunch, so I decided to answer this time, only to have him slyly put his boot in the door and push his way in, tray in hand.

"Good evening, Emelie. I have brought you dinner."

I politely inclined my head. "Jakob, thanks, but I'm not hungry."

"Are you sure?" he questioned. "You have no idea what it is." With a flourish, he whipped the cover off the tray to reveal my kryptonite—a massive hot fudge sundae.

"You are fucking evil!" I seethed then burst into tears and buried my face in his shirt.

He gently pried me off with an indiscernible face. "Emelie, please eat. You need your strength. Promise me you will."

"I will," I lied.

"Emelie!"

"Fine!" Grabbing the spoon, I dug in, griping to myself about pansy males and bullshit wars between bites until he backed his way out of the room.

CHAPTER TEN

I t took several attempts, but I finally worked up the nerve to use the number Myrgjöl had left behind for me the next evening. Eager to get it over with, I carried the phone outside to avoid Kristian's brothers from eavesdropping and dialed my future mate. The phone rang twice before a female answered—a female who wasn't Viveka.

"Kristian's phone."

"May I speak to Kristian, please," I asked, as politely as my temper allowed me to.

Her voiced hardened. "Just a moment."

I could hear knocking, a door opening, and then Kristian came on the line. "Hello?"

"Hi, Kristian."

"Emelie," he breathed.

"I hope I didn't wake you."

"You did, but it is time I rise. Where are you?"

"Álfheim … will you meet me?"

"Name the place."

I racked my brain for somewhere close but secluded. "Can you be at the Álfheim Cemetery in twenty minutes?"

"I'll be there. Thank you for giving me a second chance."

I barely managed to muzzle the tart reply that was on the end of my tongue. He has some nerve saying that after one of his harem answered his cell phone. No doubt, he left it there last night.

"You're welcome, Kristian. See you in twenty."

Hanging up the phone, I took a deep breath and ran to find Jakob.

When I found him reading in the living room, he asked, "How are you feeling today?"

I smiled. "Well, thank you. And productive."

"Oh?"

Cue the skeptical tone.

"Okay, Jakob. Here's the deal. I need an escort."

"Ah," he said, closing his book.

Jakob stood and walked into the cliff room. I followed, curious. His demeanor was so teacher-like that if I didn't know he was thousands of years old, I'd have said he'd been a professor or scholar in a past life. And what was with these one-word replies?

Glancing out at the image of his brother's castle, he asked, "Kristian?"

"Yes, I told him I'd meet him at Álfheim cemetery in twenty minutes."

"I see." He set the book he held down on the table and fixed his eyes on mine. "Emelie, I will do more than escort you to the meet my brother. I will go to the castle with you to stay."

My jaw dropped. "That's an option?"

"It is an unwelcome option, but I cannot, with a clear conscience, let you go to that castle alone. I am afraid of what Viveka's jealousy will bring. And Kristian's alliance with Odin makes me certain they will try to exploit you somehow, especially if he finds out you are a Norn."

"I appreciate this," I told him, not able to believe he was willing to do this for me. It was the kind of thing I would expect from Viggo, but not from Jakob.

He breathed a very typical impatient sigh, and said, "I hope you do. Going back to the castle will not be easy for me."

"I do, Jakob," I promised. "I'm not half as bad as you think I am."

His expression softened. "I do not think you are bad, Emelie. It is only your lack of self-control with your magic and personal life that I have a difficult time ignoring. It is dangerous. It puts us all at risk."

I was stunned. I hadn't expected him to put it so bluntly. But it wasn't as if I could deny any of it. Tears slipped down my cheeks, and I turned away from him, thoroughly ashamed of myself.

"Emelie, do not cry."

"Everything that's happened is my fault. I killed Cedric and all those humans," I sobbed, finally putting my feelings into words.

"That was not your fault. You are still an innocent. It is your mother I blame. You would not be involved with any of this, if not for her. You could never intentionally do something to hurt someone. It is not in your nature."

"Thank you, Jakob. That means a lot to me—you mean a lot to me. You all do."

"And you are welcome," he assured me, kissing my forehead for the second time in two days. "Now, you had better go fix your makeup, dear sister. You only have fourteen minutes before we must be at the cemetery to meet your betrothed."

I smiled at my soon-to-be brother. "Okay. I'll be right back."

Overjoyed and feeling safer already, I raced back to my room and was surprised to see Nils perched on my vanity table, a broad, devious smile stretched across his handsome face.

"Hi there, Em."

Wary, I asked, "What are you doing in here?"

"Wondering if you are going to invite me to the castle with you."

"Can I even do that?"

"He will be expecting you to bring maids, servants, and friends of the royal family when you move in. It is customary."

"I didn't know."

"So," he growled. "Can I come?"

I laughed nervously. "How do you manage to make me feel safe and in danger at the same time?"

He hopped off the table and glided toward me, looking ready to pounce. "Scared, little elf?"

"Nils! That is enough!" We both jumped at the sound of Jakob's sharp tone. "Yes, you can come to the castle, but you will let her decide who she wants to take on as a lover."

"Uh … guys, I'm not planning to sleep with anyone."

Nils gave me an incredulous look and ignored my statement. "Jakob, you can't let Kristian be her first. You know what he does to those females. Can you honestly subject our Emelie to that?"

"We don't have time to talk about this now. Emelie and I have to go."

I quickly wiped the mascara from below my eyes, gave myself a once-over, and followed Jakob out the door.

"This isn't over," Nils called after us.

Jakob and I materialized to the cemetery at precisely the same time as Kristian. His face was a mixture of shock and confusion when he saw his brother as my escort.

"Jakob, it has been too long. How have you come to find my mate?"

"I happened upon her with Odin's son, Soren, brother. Cursed and not herself, she bit him and almost became unchaste."

"And you stopped her from being unfaithful?" Kristian asked, naturally suspicious.

"Yes. Knowing how long you have waited for your betrothed, I knew you would want her untouched. I have, just today, convinced her to return. She is afraid you will not forgive her. However, I have assured her that you have had many more indiscretions since the two of you have been fated. It would be hypocritical of you to harbor anger for an attraction to her father's best friend."

Inwardly amused, I decided to look appropriately chagrined and let Jakob spin his yarn, though I couldn't believe the lies coming out of his mouth. He was completely full of shit and totally redeeming himself for every irate look he'd ever thrown my way.

Kristian nodded at Jakob's words and said, "You have done well indeed, my brother. You are right. I should have the right to my mate's virtue."

I tried to not get pissed at his statement and failed. "I only wish I could have had yours, Kristian."

His amethyst gaze met mine. "I am weak, Emelie."

"Yeah, and you regard me as an idiot if you think I'll believe that line."

Jakob laughed. "How well she knows you already. And such a strong will! I believe she will be a perfect mother to your young."

Kristian's smile gleamed in the moonlight. "Think of how beautiful our children will be."

Jakob grinned at the thought of our children, and I thought I would throw up. Seriously? Ugh.

Holding out a welcoming arm to his brother, Kristian said, "Come. We will go to the castle and make the necessary arrangements for Emelie's arrival. How many servants will she be bringing?"

"None," I answered. "I can attend to myself." And speak for myself, damn it. "But I will be bringing friends—your brother, Jakob, and the Fenrir Wolf."

Alarmed at my answer, Kristian asked, "Did you say the Fenrir Wolf? He is said to be highly combative, and there is the matter of our fight the other day."

"I know, but I'd like him there. He's my confidant." My big, horny confidant. "I promise to make a concentrated effort to keep him on his best behavior."

"Love, you may bring whomever you wish. I only fear for your safety."

"I'll be fine," I assured him, looking up to Jakob in question. "Should we get going?"

"Yes, of course." Jakob produced the pale blue stone we'd used to get here from his pocket, and he and Kristian linked their arms with mine to transport to the front entryway of the castle— my new home.

Unlike the last time I was at the castle, there was no growling dragon to scare the stuffing out of me. Nope, this time there was screaming.

"You fucking, incompetent half-breed! I will kill you for this!"

We all hurried into the double doors and stopped suddenly when we saw Viveka towering over a cornered maid, an overturned tray on the floor beside them the cause of her rage.

Kristian stalked over to the pair, looking furious. "Viveka, we have guests. Let Minka get on with her duties."

Ignoring her brother, Viveka's eyes fell on me, and she sneered until she spotted Jakob. When she saw him, her disposition changed instantly. Aiming a beauty queen-worthy smile at him, she straightened her posture and purred, "Jakob, you have returned."

I was horrified. She was hitting on her brother, her saintly, too good for her brother. Yuck.

Instead of responding, Jakob offered his hand to the maid. She took it and bolted from the room.

"I have returned as a guest of the future queen, nothing more," Jakob said, finally addressing his step-sister.

Viveka's simpering façade dissolved into a scowl, and I took a step back, remembering all too well what she was like when she was angry. "Uh, Kristian? Can you show me to my room?" I asked. I felt the need to escape before she realized I was still in the here.

He nodded and steered me into the hallway, leaving Jakob to continue his stare-off with Viveka.

As soon as we were out of earshot, I blurted out the question that was burning a hole in my brain. "Do Jakob and Viveka have a history?"

"Yes. A romantic one."

"Really? That is … awkward."

"More awkward than our situation?"

"He's her step-brother. I think sex with step-siblings trumps any situation in awkwardness."

He pretended to give it some thought and shuddered. "Yes. I believe you are right."

"Oh, I know I am."

Grinning, Kristian stopped walking and opened the door on his right. "This is it. I hope you will be comfortable here."

I stepped into the room, looking around in awe. The bedroom Kristian assigned me wasn't as large as his (which was next door), but you could still fit eight regular sized bedrooms into it. "This is more than satisfactory, Kristian. Thank you."

His smile faltered. "I am relieved you like it, Emelie, but I hope you will one day feel comfortable enough to share my bed. I want to make you happy."

"I hope so, too," I told him, believing every word with all my heart. Kristian was so earnest tonight; it was hard to remember he had done unforgivable things. If I were to judge only by the handsome, sweet-natured face smiling down at me, I would never believe him capable of such evil. But still, I had to know. "Kristian, are the stories about you true?" I asked him. "The ones about your females?"

He sat on the foot of my bed and stared at the carpet. "Do you know how many people have asked me that question?"

"No."

"Hundreds," he said, looking up with resolve. "And I can only tell you what I told them—the truth. I do not know. It is the only answer I have to give. Honestly."

He paused to gauge my reaction, but I kept a neutral face and decided to get comfortable as I waited for him to elaborate. Kicking off my shoes, I climbed up onto the bed, stretched out, and sank into heaven. "Kristian, this bed … wow." I rolled over and snuggled in the pillows. "It's awesome."

Kristian chuckled, then kicked off his shoes to lay down beside me. "I am glad you approve."

We lay face to face, both of us taking the opportunity to examine each other again. He'd grown a goatee since I'd seen him last, but it didn't diminish his beauty. He would be gorgeous with any amount of facial hair. I wondered what he thought about me and my smeared makeup.

He answered my thoughts. "You are so beautiful, Emelie. I am the luckiest elf of any world."

I blushed. "Thank—"

Kristian stopped my gratitude by gently pressing his lips against mine. My body ignited instantly, responding to his passion like the traitor it was. Damn my mother's magic! The electric connection between us was more intense than it had ever been before. I moaned my pleasure into his mouth.

131

"Do you feel it," Kristian asked. "Our connection? It has returned!"

"Yes." I laced my fingers with his and smiled at the slight tingling.

"I missed this feeling," Kristian mused. "I have not felt myself as of late."

"Yeah, I heard you housed the ones responsible for the explosion at Soren Vidar's house in Sweden."

"Are you speaking of Freyr and Katrine?"

"The same."

He looked … well, pissed. "I had no idea."

I arched a skeptical brow.

"Oh, make no mistake," he amended. "I knew they were up to something, but they never clued me in to their plans. They are only here as a favor to Odin."

A favor to Odin? My mind exploded with sudden revelations. Now I was certain Odin had was involved in trying to kill me off, which meant we were in a lot of trouble. How long would it be before Odin tried to assassinate Kristian to get to me?

I sat up. "Why do you serve Odin? It makes me feel unsafe."

His expression was one of surprise. "Odin has always helped the dark elves in times of great need. I have no reason to distrust him."

"He put Freyr and Katrine here in your castle, Kristian. They could have killed me in the explosion at Soren's house in Sweden." I paused to let that sink in. "You know, your brothers have a theory that Freyr is trying to prevent our mating to regain control of the elves."

"My brothers? Do you know my brother, Viggo?"

"He's my friend, too."

"Emelie, Viggo has always been somewhat of a conspiracy theorist. There is nothing to fear from Odin."

His words were meant to be reassuring, but the smile he offered didn't reach his eyes. He had doubts. I could work with that.

"I know Viggo can be a bit … imaginative, but Jakob is not. He's a realist." I stroked my fingertips along his handsome face. "I want you to be on the alert. I can't have Freyr kill my mate before I get the chance to have the bonding ceremony, or whatever Jakob called it."

"I promise you. I will be careful."

"Okay." I dropped the subject, wanting to steer away from the Odin talk. "Why don't you tell me about yourself?"

"What would you like to know?"

"Everything? You already know so much about me."

"Everything? Hmmm … let me see … how to condense a thousand years?" He smiled and moved closer to me. "Have I told you how beautiful you are tonight?"

"Not in the last few minutes."

"I could tell you every minute of every night." He tipped my chin back up when I blushed and looked down at the duvet. "Even your shyness is charming."

"Thanks," I said, but what I really wanted to say was, "What are you going to do about the whores next door?"

He picked up on my hidden thoughts right away. "What troubles you, Emelie? What is it you have to say?"

"Just that you are handsome, kind, and smart, all the things that make a good mate, but your perversity makes me want to jump out of a window to escape this crazy ordeal. And I want you to ask the harem to leave," I thought, but what I said was, "Ummm …"

"It is the harem?" he asked with a heavy sigh.

"Yes, of course. I almost hung up when one of them answered your phone earlier. Will you ask them to leave, now that I'm here?"

"No," he answered without hesitation.

Aghast, I asked, "Why? Do you love them?"

"Absolutely not." His voice was adamant. "They are nothing to me but whores."

"Then why?" I couldn't fathom why he'd deny me this. Was it some weird dark elf tradition?

A look of fear and guilt crept onto his face. "First, please understand that my father started the harem, not me. I thought it wrong to stray from your destined mate." He paused and looked me in the eyes. "But, one morning, a little over a hundred years ago, I woke to find I had violently raped one of his females."

I recoiled from him. "Were you drunk?"

He shook his head. "I do not drink."

"Then, how could you?"

"For that, I do not have an answer. I have not remembered a single night since the night of the rape."

"Are you serious?"

With his jaw set, he said, "You have no idea how much I wish I were telling you a lie, Emelie."

"Have you ... done what you did again?" Please, please, please say no.

"Every night, just before midnight, I lose myself. I cannot remember anything the next morning when I wake." Tears sprang to his purple eyes. "The females tell me that as long as they give themselves willingly, I do not hurt them."

I struggled to stay in place as my muscles tensed up. What little common sense I had left had set off the fire alarm in my head, and it was telling me to run. However, because Emelie +

dangerous situations = stupid decisions, I ignored it and decided to hear him out.

"I set up a camera once," he continued.

"In the harem?"

He nodded.

I didn't want to know, but I asked anyway. "What did you find?"

"I could not bear to watch it myself, but the females indicated I would find their words true." Shaking his head, he added, "I raped three of them, Emelie—like an animal. I didn't care if I hurt them. All I wanted was to fuck them until they could not take me inside them anymore. I am a monster."

Holy. Shit. "That's why you have so many females here, isn't it?"

"Yes. I do not wish to hurt anyone, and I could never subject you to this … this curse. You understand now why I cannot ask them to leave. I cannot until I can trust myself with you."

I sighed inwardly, both in relief and pity. I could check losing my virginity via sexual assault off my list of worries, but now I felt so sorry for Kristian. He didn't deserve this fate, just like Cedric hadn't deserved his. Truth be told, if I put those two similarities together and added in the fact he had been sneaking around here lately, it pointed the blame directly at the most likely culprit—Freyr. His villainous stench was all over this 'curse'.

"How long has this been happening to you?"

"By the sun on your world, it would be one hundred and forty-eight years."

"What?" Visions of myself in a nun's habit flashed before my eyes. Over a hundred years? There was no way I could go that long without sex. I may be new to the idea, but I knew I wanted to do it. A lot. And when I was with Soren? A whole lot.

"I completely understand if you want to take a lover," Kristian said. "I just ask that it not be Soren. I do not want to lose our connection again."

Whoa. Now, all that lover talk Nils was going on about earlier was starting to make sense. He could sniff out an opportunity to get laid anywhere. "I don't think I will need a lover, Kristian. Just tell me how I can help you."

He thought for a moment. "Be patient? Help me find a cure? Do not give up on me?"

The crack in his voice as he said those words dissolved any doubt he was anything but a good male. "I'll never leave you, Kristian. Not unless you give me a damn good reason to."

"You are an angel," he sighed, making it obvious the weight of his worry had been lifted.

"An angel with an extremely jealous temper," I added. "I suggest you not flaunt the females in front of me."

"Of course not, Emelie. You need not worry. I moved them into another wing after your visit to avoid you overhearing … anything."

I just nodded. What else could I do? I never thought I'd be agreeing to whores. Who in their right mind would?

"How are these females compensated?" I asked, genuinely curious as to why anyone would volunteer to, uh, service him.

"They live a life of luxury here at the castle and are paid handsomely in riches. They also have the opportunity to bear my young. A connection to the royal bloodline is highly sought after in Svartálfaheim. I am surprised Viggo and Jakob have not told you how many females throw themselves into their paths."

I grimaced. "That's… disgusting."

Looking full of regret, he shook his head. "I apologize for the horrible state of things. I wanted so much for this to be over by the time you were old enough to mate."

"No, I'm sorry. No one deserves what you're going through." And as I looked into his tortured face, I knew I meant every word. My heart felt torn in half. My mother's enchantment made me feel so strongly for Kristian. It would be easy to forget all the bad things and concentrate on the many good things about him.

"Thank you, Emelie."

"You're wel—" I started, then yawned unexpectedly. It had been a long, stressful day. "Sorry. I guess I'm a little tired."

He laughed as I yawned again. "Would you like to rest for a while?"

I checked the clock on the wall. It was only half past eight. I could get in a couple of hours of sleep before Kristian turned into Mr. Hyde. "Maybe just a short nap," I told him.

"Very well. I will leave you to your privacy."

I stopped him from rising by putting a hand to his forearm. "Will you stay? I don't want to be alone."

Smiling at me with a look of pride, he said, "There is nothing I would like to do more."

Kristian shifted to his back, and I laid my head on his chest, trailing my fingertips across the thin layer of black hair displayed behind his open collar. It felt right, being with him like this. I sighed in contentment, closing my eyes. "It will be so easy to fall in love with you, Kristian. I didn't expect that."

"I did not expect you to be so good to me." He kissed the top of my head and whispered, "Sleep well, beloved."

At two in the morning, I awoke groggy, disoriented, and alone. As I lay there on the most comfortable bed in any world, I admired the ornate ceiling and thought of Kristian. He'd probably be in the harem right now. The thought of him being with them in that way disturbed me, but I couldn't help but think the females 'sacrificing' their bodies had an ulterior motive. No female would do that if they had any other choice and these females weren't slaves. They came and went as they pleased.

"For a connection to the royal bloodline, my ass," I said, as I swung my legs off the bed. My spidey-sense was tingling. Something was up, and I was going to find out what.

As I was putting my shoes back on, I felt a presence just outside my room. Tip-toeing over, I grabbed the fireplace poker and tried to identify the signature. It was familiar and didn't feel like Kristian, but I couldn't be sure. With him being in his 'cursed' time, he could have a different imprint.

Through the door, Nils whispered, "Emelie, are you in there?"

I jerked the door open, and Nils nearly fell to the ground. "What the hell are you doing roaming the halls of Väsen castle at two in the morning? How did you get past the guards?"

"Seriously, Emelie?" He sighed, looking exasperated. "I am the Fenrir Wolf. I have fought hundreds of warriors at once. Do you think me incapable of such a simple task?"

I shrugged. "I still don't know how you snuck past the guards. There's a ton of them out there."

"I am very sneaky—like a ninja."

"A ninja?"

"Yeah. I am surprised you missed that about me. But then..." He motioned to himself. "Ninja."

I snorted. "Okay."

"I brought some of your stuff," he said, stepping back through the door to fetch my two suitcases, then busying himself with pacing around the room and looking into the closets, bathroom, and dresser drawers for who knows what.

Satisfied with the inspection, he sat on the end of the bed. "What? What's that look for?"

"Don't you think Kristian will be a little pissed when he finds out you're here?"

He smirked at my worried face "No, oh, ye of little faith and magical prowess. I do not think anyone will realize I am here until tomorrow. Kristian certainly will not. Not anytime soon, anyway."

"Tell me you didn't go down there," I groaned, feigning disappointment with him for snooping. I was secretly dying to know what was happening in the other wing.

"Do I seem like someone who would leave well enough alone?"

I sighed. "No. No, you do not."

"Come on, Emelie," he teased. "You are not the least bit interested in what's going on with your mate-to-be down there?"

"No," I lied. Because I was a big fat liar, and that was what liars do. "I respect Kristian's privacy."

"It really is something to see," he hinted, begging me to ask with his eyes.

"No, Nils. I don't want to know. But speaking of knowing, does Jakob know you're here? Have you seen him yet?"

With a pained expression, he started to speak and then shivered. "You do not want to know who he is doing."

"Who he's doing? Oh, you have to spill! What's going on with him and the Wicked Witch of Svartálfaheim?"

"Just your average, every day one on one time with the demon, Lilith."

"That sounds … ominous?"

He mimed zipping his lips. "Do you really want to know?"

I rolled my eyes toward the ceiling. Nils knew I was dying for details, and he was going to try to make me work for every single one of them. "Yes! For the love of the Norse, tell me!"

He stretched across the end of my bed. "Are you sure? It might offend your virgin sensibilities. There are some gentle-males left in the Norselands, you know."

"Uh, yeah. I'm sure there are, but you aren't one of them."

He clutched at his chest. "You wound me, Emelie."

"Uh huh."

He grinned again. "So, can I sleep in here?"

"Sure, but sleep as a wolf, okay? I don't think Kristian would like finding me in bed with another male."

"After what I heard tonight, that would be the ultimate in hypocrisy."

Hands over ears, I said, "All right. All right. I don't want to hear about it."

He shrugged. "Your choice. I just think you deserve better. Like, a thousand times better."

"Thanks," I told him, honestly surprised. Offering heartfelt sentiments wasn't Nils's usual modus operandi. He was more of a pervy limericks kind of guy.

Inclining his head, he said, "You are most welcome, little one."

Smiling warmly at him, I kicked off my shoes and snuggled under the blankets, hoping to find the comfortable spot I'd left earlier—no such luck. "Good night, wolf."

Nils got up to turn off the overhead light, then climbed back onto the bed, cozying right up to me. His eyes reflected the green flames in the fireplace giving them an eerie glow. "Hey, Em?"

"Yeah?"

"Have you heard this one?"

"What one?"

He cleared his throat and took on an accent I'd never heard him use before.

"On the moors, Kelly walked in a daze.

There she'd bark at the moon and the haze.

140

Still, her friends weren't concerned.

For by now they had learned.

Once a month she would go through this phase."

I laughed. "That's clever. Did you come up with that by yourself?"

"Sure."

"Uh huh. So, if I Google it, I won't find out it's like a super famous limerick?"

"Okay, you got me." He chuckled. "It is a pretty good one, though. And it proves that not all of the limericks I know are about sex."

"That it does," I said, giggling. He was so much more likable when he wasn't hitting on me. I could see us being great friends in the future—if he kept up this kind of good behavior. "Good night, Nils."

He shifted into wolf-form and barked a response I assumed was a good night wish, then he laid down beside me again, whining.

I cuddled up to his huge body and stroked the fur at his neck. "I know, Fenrir. You have no idea how well I know."

CHAPTER ELEVEN

There was an orangish glow peeking through the curtains when I woke, and for a second, I was sure it was the sunrise. I glanced over at the clock—four o'clock. Nope, definitely not morning.

Sitting up, I found Nils curled up on the foot of the bed—my big, bad wolfy protector. I nudged him with a toe, and he yawned, stretched, and shifted all at the same time.

"Poke me with those cold toes again, Emelie, and you're going to lose one," he growled.

I snatched my foot back and stuck it back under the comforter. "You wouldn't."

He raised an eyebrow. "Would I not?

"Okay, you would," I conceded. "Did you sleep well down there?"

"I did. However, I would have slept better if you would have allowed me to sleep as a male. I am a male first, wolf second."

"Well, if you knew how to keep your hands to yourself, I would have."

"Yeah, that is not going to happen." He grinned and sprung up from the bed. "I wonder if there is breakfast."

"I think it's still a little early for breakfast."

"It is never too early to eat. Put your shoes on. I can't go traipsing around here without you."

I huffed out a disbelieving breath. "Isn't that exactly what you did last night?"

"Come on, Em."

I sighed heavily and stomped out of bed. "Fine."

Using Nils' keen senses as a guide, we found the kitchen right away. It was both impressive and comical to see him sniff his way down the hallways to the right door. I almost expected him to point when he found it. Inside, we found Jakob and Kristian already seated at a small round table in the corner, whispering over their tea.

Kristian stood so fast, he nearly toppled his chair when he saw me. "Good evening, dear one. Please, join us."

"Thank you, but first, let me reintroduce you to my friend, Fenrir."

"Call me, Nils." He offered him a handshake. "Sorry about punching you in the face the other day."

"It was deserved," Kristian replied while pulling out a chair for me. "Emelie, you must be starved. Let me call the cook for you. I apologize for not having something ready. I did not know when you would awaken." Pulling out his cell phone, he said, "Evangelina," and then spoke to whoever answered in rapid Elvish. I didn't understand a word. Pocketing the phone, he smiled. "She will be down in just a few minutes. Did you sleep well?"

"Yes, I did." He was adorably concerned, and for a moment, I almost forgot about what he'd had been doing a couple of hours before. "Did you sleep?"

"I did. I woke a few hours ago." He lifted the teapot. "Tea?"

"Please." I glanced at Jakob. "How do you fare this evening?" He had been silent since my arrival and was apparently trying to avoid my eye. There had to be something he didn't want me to know.

"I am well," he said. "Do not trouble yourself with my welfare."

Well, that wasn't unusually evasive of him or anything. Now I was sure something was going on. I looked to Nils, who was eyeing Jakob like he had a second head. He shrugged. He didn't get it either.

I was temporarily distracted from the weirdness that was going on with Jakob when a female who must be Evangelina came in with Viveka hot on her heels. I liked her as soon as I laid eyes on her. Her happy smile was downright infectious. She reminded me of a cherub—pleasantly rounded with curly brown hair and an innocent face.

Kristian stood to greet them. "Good evening, ladies. Evangelina, you have not met my mate-to-be, Emelie, and her companion, the Fenrir Wolf. You remember my brother, Jakob, of course."

She smiled graciously and bowed. "It is nice to meet you. My lady, may I say how ingenious it is of you to have such powerful protectors at your side. These are uncertain times."

With absolute clarity, I understood the warning in her words. She was trying to tell me Freyr and Katrine had been staying at the castle. I knew I liked her! There was no doubt; Evangelina and I were destined to get along famously.

"Thank you for your kind words, Evangelina. I know well that my enemies are both hidden and in plain sight. Uniting the elves is something I take very seriously."

She winked at me. "Very well, miss."

I looked to Kristian and was startled to find he was staring intently at me. I blushed and said, "That reminds me. What do you think about moving the ceremony out of the town square and into a more private venue—immediate friends and family only? I feel like we shouldn't be spending elaborately during a war. It may upset the less fortunate. Don't you agree?"

His expression was dubious. "You do not want a royal mating?"

"Not unless you do. It's your tradition, after all."

Kristian kissed my cheek and squeezed my hand. "You are right as usual, love. We should not flaunt extravagance when so many elves are suffering with hardship and grief. However, we should at least record it, so the elves of Álfheim will have proof our union and mating have taken place."

"I'm perfectly fine with that." Actually, I was more than okay with it. If the fake Freyr could see my ceremony, maybe he would abandon his assassination attempts—fingers crossed.

"Do you have a specific location in mind?"

"No, I don't have a prefer ..."

I lost the ability to speak when I looked up and saw Jakob and Viveka kissing over their teacups. A strong, sudden urge to push him away from her almost overtook me. This was just wrong. Jakob deserved someone sweet and intelligent, normal even. Viveka couldn't be good enough for him on her best day. She was too evil ... and insane ... and psychotic. Hell, you could insert any scary word. They all worked for her.

Nils mouthed, "What the fuck?" then spoke to me with his mind. *"I think we might need Sherlock Holmes for this mystery."*

"Yep," I answered back.

Jakob glanced at us with a raised eyebrow, obviously aware that Nils and I were talking to each other. I gave him a raised eyebrow of my own and opened my mind to both of them.

Jakob spoke first. *"You two are staring at us."*

"Well, it is kind of hard to look away from a train wreck," Nils answered.

"Exactly," I agreed. Seeing Jakob with her was sickeningly fascinating. I couldn't seem to look away.

"How nice it is to see you have overcome your differences with Viveka," Kristian said to his brother. There was no doubt he was trying to smooth her ruffled feathers.

"Our reunion has been overdue for quite some time," Jakob replied, smiling like a simpleton at his ex-lover, who was alternating between basking in his attention like a house cat and shooting hateful glances at Nils and me.

"You were saying, Emelie, about the location?" Kristian asked. He was genuinely interested, bless him.

"I was saying I don't have a preference for a location."

Evangelina spoke up from behind the stove. "My lady, if I may offer a suggestion?"

"Of course, Evangelina, you needn't ask my permission to speak. Treat me as you would any friend. And please, call me Emelie."

She looked at Kristian, who nodded his approval. "Very well, my lady. I mean, Emelie. I was going to suggest the garden. Not only is it beautiful this time of year, but it is also safe. It has been used as a meeting place for decades."

"That is a fantastic idea, Evangelina! Can I call you Lina?"

She beamed as she put pancakes and bacon on the table. "All my friends do."

"Get a room, you two," Nils griped, obviously jealous of my new bosom friend. He grabbed a few slices of bacon, sandwiched them between two pancakes, and left the table. "See ya, later."

I stuck out my tongue at his back, and Lina giggled, causing my wolfy friend to roll his eyes on the way out.

"Wait a moment, Fenrir," Kristian called to him. They walked out of the door together, and after a minute or so, Kristian returned alone and sat down as if he had never left.

I opened my mind to Nils as soon as he brushed against my consciousness. *"Well?"*

"He was just telling me where my room was and that the harem has been alerted to the possibility of having a visitor."

"Gross."

"Jealous?"

"Not even a little bit."

"Your loss, Em."

Evangelina placed a large carafe of coffee in the center of the table. "Will there be anything else?"

"No, thank you," Kristian said, dismissing her with a smile.

"Wait. You're not going to eat with us?" I asked. There was more than enough to feed us all.

Her face lit up with a bright grin. "I eat with the other servants, Emelie, but thank you."

"You may leave," Viveka said coldly, finally breaking her silence.

Evangelina's eyes widened, and she hurried to the door, leaving quickly. I was sure she'd had a taste of Viveka's anger before. But really, who hadn't at this point?

Turning my frown on Viveka, I growled. If I had my Norn powers together, I probably would've sent her straight to Hell— where she belonged.

"What?" she asked, haughtily sneering at me. "Will you have us all associating with the help under your rule?"

I sneered right back at her. "Let me see if I have this right. These elves are good enough to fuck and serve your food, but not good enough to sit at your table?"

Viveka's smile was pure saccharine as she retorted, "Would you like me to call the whores to breakfast, Emelie?"

Enraged, I stood and put my palms on the table. Leaning close to her, I spoke in a harsh voice. "If you don't want to end up a servant yourself, I would watch your mouth."

She looked to Kristian for help but found no pity, only humor. "I warned you, sister."

Folding her napkin, she laid it on the table, disgust plain on her face. "Jakob, I have lost my appetite. I will retire to the drawing room."

Jakob waited until after she left the room to scold me. "Emelie, that was not necessary."

Kristian cut off my snappy comeback before I could even start it. "She has had that coming for a hundred years. I think a little perspective might be exactly what she needs."

Jakob stood and laid his own napkin on the table. "Even so."

I knew he wasn't really mad. I was pretty confident by the look on his face, he was more upset about having to deal with the results of my threatening her than her feelings being hurt. I had totally thrown him under the bus. "Sorry, Jakob."

Kristian faced me, ignoring his brother's plight. "After breakfast, will you accompany me to an impromptu meeting of my hird?"

"What is a hird?" It sounded like he-erd with his accent.

"It is a small battalion of soldiers that accompany me when I am in public. I have known most of them for at least half a millennium. They are very anxious to greet their queen properly."

"They follow you everywhere? Even on the grounds?"

"No, not the grounds. You have seen how well protected the castle is. They protect me outside of the castle walls. I tell them where I will be going, and they meet me there."

"How many of them are there?"

"Twelve, but you will only see a few at a time. The rest could be spying in the trees or concealed amongst the townspeople— whatever is necessary for the situation."

I groaned inwardly. That meant they'd been there when we met in the cemetery, the day at Soren's when I agreed to see his home, and the night we'd first met. Every time I thought we'd been alone, they had been there, lurking. Of course, I could appreciate that they were essential to his safety, and I was thankful for that, but they'd seen our first kiss. They saw my ridiculously over the top flirting to get him to taste my blood. Hell, they'd probably even saw our fight over the harem. I felt like such a fool. He was king for goodness sake. Why did I think he would come alone?

"Are you feeling well?" he asked, a concerned expression making a furrow between his brows.

"I'm well. I just feel a little embarrassed for being so forward with you in front of an audience."

His expression changed to one of amusement. "Do not worry. They like you already. They have not stopped mentioning you storming out of the castle since the day it happened."

Well, that answered that question. "I wish you would have told me we were under surveillance. Had I known, I wouldn't have acted so brazenly." Or slutty … or petulant … or insane.

"I am glad you were unaware. Otherwise, I would have never seen the side of you I saw the night we met. I will never forget how extraordinarily beautiful you were when you offered me your blood."

I blushed again. He was such a smooth talker. I knew if I weren't cautious with my future mate, he would charm the panties right off me. His ability to enamor was effortless.

An awkward pause arose between Kristian and me when we finished eating. Desperate to escape the intimate setting of the kitchen table, I took his plate to the sink and started looking for the dish soap to no avail. Giving up, I asked, "Where can I find the dishwashing detergent, Kristian?"

"Let Evangelina do that, Emelie. It is her job, after all."

"I'm just trying to be a good guest."

Kristian stood and claimed my hand, leading me away from the sink. "But you are not a guest. This is your home to do as you like. I can imagine a great many things in the household will change when you are the mistress, however, for now, try to let things flow as normally as possible until you announce the changes you will be making. It will make the transition to a new regime easier."

"Regime?" I laughed.

He smirked. "Forgive me for not having my thesaurus handy."

I raised an eyebrow. "Is that sarcasm I detect?" Was every single guy in the Norselands a smart ass? Yes. Yes, they were.

"I have no idea what you are referring to," he said, placing a possessive hand on my waist. "Are you ready to go meet the hird?"

I smoothed a hand over my hair and straightened my top. "As ready as I'll ever be."

He pulled me closer. "You are perfection. They will love you."

"I really, really hope so."

"How could anyone not love you? I can hardly keep my hands off you."

Smiling, I wrapped my arms around his neck and whispered seductively, "I don't think that's love, Kristian. That sounds like lust."

"A little of both," he admitted in a husky, hungry voice.

I sensed someone new outside the kitchen door just before the male entered and bowed. Kristian acknowledged him with a nod. He looked much like the others, dark featured and tall, but when he spoke his voice was unlike anyone's I'd ever heard. It was beautiful, lyrical even. It was like a lullaby and a favorite teddy bear, soothing and comforting.

"We are ready to move to the garden, if you are, sire."

I hung on the strange male's every word. He was mesmerizing. It was almost as if he was unintentionally hypnotic.

Kristian nodded. "I am. Emelie, this is Axel. He is the commander of my guard. If you have any security concerns, you should see him about them."

Taking the gloved hand he offered, I smiled. "It's nice to …" My words faltered as I met his eyes. They were cat's eyes. No, not cat eyes. They were yellow reptilian eyes, cold and intelligent, like a snake's. I sucked in a shocked gasp. This male was no dark elf. He was something altogether different.

Kristian tightened the possessive hand around my waist, interrupting my close scrutiny. "We will arrive in the garden momentarily, Axel."

Axel quickly dropped my hand and bowed. "Yes, sire." He turned his intimidating stare back at me. "It has been a great honor, Lady Emelie."

"Thank you. And just call me Emelie. There's no need for the formality."

His answering smile was truly nightmarish, full of fangs and sharpened teeth. "I'll do that," he said, raising an eyebrow at my slight flinch. "Sire, if I might suggest it. It is quite chilly outdoors. The lady might need a shawl to keep warm."

"I'll just run and get something," I volunteered before Kristian could send a servant.

Kristian stopped me as I started for the door. "I have just the thing. Stay and get to know Axel. You will be spending a great amount of time with him."

"Okay, thanks," I said, though I desperately wanted him to stay. Alone time with the scary guy was not something I was looking forward to.

He kissed my forehead. "No thanks are necessary. It is a pleasure attending to you, my love."

I turned my attention back to Axel when Kristian left the room and nearly screamed. Anyone would if they turned around to six-four creature brandishing a knife and looking murderous. Wide-eyed, I pivoted to run, only to be stopped by a hand in my hair and his blade at my throat.

"Who are you, female?" Axel hissed. "You are not a light elf. You could not be the daughter of Anders."

Trembling, I swallowed the dry lump that arose in my throat. "I am a light elf and Ander's daughter. I swear it."

He laughed bitterly. "You lie. Your eyes have gone silver, the color of the most powerful of ancients. I know you saw through my glamour, as well."

I started to cry. "I swear it, Axel. I am a light elf. How can I prove myself?"

His forked tongue flicked out and tasted the air. "You cannot. I can smell you. You are human and ... something unrecognizable."

Spotting a lone houseplant hanging in the window, I pushed my will into it, praying it would respond and breathed a slight sigh of relief when it instantly sprang to attention, ready to assist. Faster than I thought possible, the plant's tendrils inched their way down and wound themselves around his legs, then did the same to his arm until the knife was pulled away from my neck. Once he was restrained, the tiny vines dragged him up to the ceiling by his bound feet.

"Release me," he fumed.

I gaped at his audacity. "You just held a knife to my throat! You can rot up there for all I care. I tried to tell you the truth. Maybe I'm not a full-blooded elf, but so what? You aren't either."

"You did see through my glamour," he spat, triumphant.

"Yeah, so what?"

He disappeared from sight and asked, "Can you see through this?"

Out of my mind with panic, I scrambled back into the corner so he couldn't get his blade against my neck again. It was scary just how untrained I really was. Any other light elf would have stopped him before he could get within arm's reach, but me? I was only here because Axel had restraint. He could've killed me if he wanted to.

"Are you frightened, imposter?"

"Is this really the way you want to start our relationship?" I asked, fixing my attention on him and using my magic to locate his fate. He wasn't invisible, just cloaked against his surroundings, like a chameleon—amazing.

"I will do anything I have to do to protect my king."

I nodded. I knew he meant every word. He wasn't the head of the hird for nothing. He would defend Kristian with his life and kill anyone who set out against him. Even if that someone was his future queen.

Looking up at him with solemn eyes, I hoped to convey my honesty. "Axel, I only hope to bring his and my father's race together once more … and to help him with his curse. I mean him no harm. I promise."

He reappeared, still tightly wrapped in my handiwork. "Who is your mother?"

With a shrug, I told him a half-truth. "I do not know my mother."

Exhaling a black cloud of toxin out of his nose, he poisoned my little savior houseplant. It withered and dropped away from him dead in less than a second. I crouched further down into the corner and covered my head with my arms as he dropped lightly on his feet in front of me. I was one dead elf.

Instead of attacking, he offered me his hand. "We all have our little secrets, do we not, Emelie?"

I smiled and took his peace offering. "We do. Does Kristian know about yours?"

"The royal family knows, but you and Freyr are the only strangers that have had the power to see through my glamour. That fucker had me pegged as soon as he came into the castle."

"I take it you have no allegiance to the Freyr imposter?"

He looked angry with me for even asking. "Absolutely not. What do you mean by imposter?"

I sighed in relief. He was telling the truth. With his fate open to me, it allowed me to see exactly why he hated the male so much. Axel had definite issues with Freyr, he just wasn't strong enough to kill him. "I mean that the Freyr that is with Katrine is the doppelgänger."

"The abomination?"

"Yes."

We both looked up as Kristian walked in the room holding a deep teal shawl. "Has Axel kept you entertained with his battle stories, Emelie?"

"Oh, yes. He is quite the fierce warrior."

He draped the shawl over my shoulders and held out his elbow. "Shall we?"

"Yes. Thank you." I walked away with Kristian, not giving Axel another glance. He wouldn't tell Kristian about our altercation or the doppelgänger being in the castle instead of the real Freyr. I was sure of it. He understood what it was like to have secrets that had to be kept.

With an expression of pure pride, Kristian escorted me outside, past the garden and down a hill to a huge, brightly colored tent erected in front of a dark forest of trees. "The hird is waiting under the canopy," he told me. Noticing the fidgeting I was doing, he added, "Do not be nervous, my dear one. You have nothing to worry about."

"Okay." I squeezed his hand a little tighter and let him lead me into the darkened tent, up a short flight of stairs, and out onto a low stage. I immediately felt out of my element when I saw the number of dark elves assembled there to meet me. There were a lot more than the twelve he'd mentioned.

Kristian stepped to the center of the stage. "My hird, thank you for meeting me on such short notice." He smiled as he looked around. "I see your families would not be deterred from coming to meet my queen."

A female stood up and said, "I would like to see him try to stop me!" Everyone laughed.

He smiled down at the short dark-haired beauty. "As would I, Lady Adria. Now, if you would, please allow me to introduce your future queen, Lady Emelie Andersdotter, formally."

I stepped forward, terrified. "Hello. It's nice to meet you all."

Through the applause, I heard the males exclaim things ranging from, "Look at how small and fair she is. She is like a doll," to "There's no way she's going to survive the mating night. The king will snap her like a twig."

Kristian clearly heard the last remark. He was already looking my way apologetically when I glanced over. "Ignore them. They know nothing but rumors of my personal affairs."

"You shouldn't let them talk about you like that. You're their king. You deserve their respect."

"And I get their respect."

"Obviously, not in your personal life," I countered.

He took my hand and brought it to his lips. "Until yesterday, I did not have a personal life."

How did Kristian manage to make me feel so relaxed? As soon as he took my hand, all of my worries seemed so small, so insignificant. Shaking it off, I said, "Look, Kristian, it's no big deal. I just don't want to hear them talking about me that way."

"As you wish, Emelie. I will reprimand them for their crudeness."

"No, I don't think that's necessary," I answered, distracted as I searched the crowd for my grandmother. She was here. I could feel her familiar signature close by. "But in the future, I'd like them to keep those comments to themselves."

"I will speak to them privately," Kristian promised. "It will not happen again." He waved to Axel, who joined us on the stage.

While the king spoke to Axel, I continued looking for Myrgjöl. She waved when I found her in the crowd, then disappeared, only to speak in my mind a few seconds later.

"You should mate him now, Emelie. There will not be a better time."

"Are you kidding?" I asked. *"Now?"*

"Right now. I will perform the ceremony myself."

"If you think it's best, then I'm ready, but Kristian may not be."

"I know it is best," she asserted. *"And you just tell the king that today is the day. I will appear momentarily. I want to fetch your friends first."*

"Okay, I will." I chewed my lip as I watched Kristian's hushed conversation with Axel. *"Grandmother?"*

"Yes?"

"I'm a little nervous."

"I would be worried if you were not, Emelie. See you in a minute."

Steeling myself with a deep breath, I wrapped a hand around Kristian's forearm to get his attention. I couldn't believe this was happening so soon. How much time had Kristian, and I really spent together? What? Twenty, maybe thirty minutes? "Can I talk to you, my king?"

His eyebrows raised. "My king? Is there any particular reason for the sudden flattery, Emelie?"

156

I grinned. "Why, yes, there is. How do feel about mating me today—right now?"

Wary of my meaning, he dismissed Axel from the stage and answered, "I will mate you at any time. Why do you ask?"

"The official is here to perform the bond," I said, laying my hands on his chest, then standing on my toes to reach his mouth with mine.

We both laughed at the resulting, "Awww!" from the crowd.

"How have you done this, Emelie? This was a spontaneous meeting."

"I have a very good friend of the royal family."

"Who?"

Myrgjöl appeared out of nowhere with perfect timing. "Here she is now. Myrgjöl, please meet my betrothed, King Kristian Väsen of Svartálfaheim.

She curtsied. "It is nice to finally meet you, Kristian."

Kristian bowed deeply in return. "The pleasure is mine, Lady Myrgjöl. My bride has many powerful friends. First, I find she knows my brothers, then she brings the Fenrir Wolf, one of the fiercest warriors in the Norselands to live in the castle, and now the most famous of all the Norns is standing in front of me. How do you know them all, Emelie?"

Myrgjöl answered for me. "Now that she is without her parents, it is up to us to look after her. Her new fate with you is a dangerous one."

"How so?" he asked.

"I cannot interfere, as you well know."

"It's Freyr. He wants control of the elves," I told him.

Myrgjöl nodded emphatically. "Yeah, what she said."

Kristian was outraged. "Then, you were right, Emelie. Odin did try to take you from me."

"Myrgjöl will mate us now. All of this—the war, the threats—they can finally be over."

Kristian smiled broadly, ecstatic at the change of events. "Who will give you away?"

"Did you find Viggo?" I asked my grandmother.

"I did. He'll be here in two seconds."

Exactly two seconds later, Nils, Jakob, Viveka, and Viggo appeared on the opposite end of the stage. They walked to us, ignoring the gasps and whispers from the crowd.

Viggo hugged me. "Hi there, little one! What is going on? The Norn wouldn't say anything."

"I'm getting mated today. Actually, it's happening right now. Can you walk me down the aisle?"

He eyed his brother. "Of course, but are you sure you are ready to do this? You still have a day or so until your birthday."

I laced my fingers with Kristian's. "There's no time like the present. Your brother is an honorable male, and I believe his feelings for me are sincere. I'm ready."

Ignoring his brother's doubts, Kristian kissed me lightly on the lips. He was taking all of this in his usual calm stride. "I will make the announcement while you ready yourself, Emelie."

"Okay. I'll see you soon." Woodenly, I let Myrgjöl and Viggo walk me into the castle and straight to a bathroom. My heart was beating out of my chest.

Once the door was closed, my grandmother said, "I know the perfect style of dress. It is a little risqué, as is most of the dark elf fashion, but it will be lovely on you. Maybe we will change your hair color, too. Just for the night."

In a flash, I was wearing a corseted black dress with a skirt made of layered taffeta and lace. I spun around to admire the dress, watching the layers fall quickly back into place. "It's beautiful, grandmother."

She grinned and held out a small mirror. "I had a feeling you would like it, but how do you feel about the hair?"

I didn't recognize myself when I saw my reflection. My hair was so different. She'd changed the color from white-blond to a rich auburn brown. The flyaway curls I'd once had were replaced by a sleek, straight style. "How … how did you do this?"

"Magic, of course. You look stunning."

"Perfect," Viggo added. "Are you sure you would not wish to mate me instead?"

I sighed. "I wish."

"Me too," he said.

"Oh, hush, Viggo. You will find your mate soon enough," Myrgjöl said, teasing him. "Do not say things you'll regret."

He looked up with a severe intensity in his eyes I'd never seen before. "What do you know of my mate, Norn?"

"Quite a bit, actually." She pursed her lips. "Hold still." Snapping her fingers, she dressed Viggo in formal elven attire. She must have dressed everyone at the same time because there was a loud cheer from the audience. She winked at us. "I guess they approve."

I hugged her tight. "You are amazing, the best grandmother in the world!"

She squeezed me back. "I know."

The cheering crowd was deafening as Myrgjöl delivered Viggo and me to the edge of the forest, just behind the center aisle. I could see Kristian and Jakob waiting for us in the middle of the stage. They were both exceedingly handsome in their formal attire. Kristian, as smooth as ever, didn't look nervous in the least, whereas I was shaking in my high-heeled elven boots and Jakob looked like he wanted to be anywhere else. Like, anywhere … on any world … in any realm.

"Your brothers clean up pretty well," Myrgjöl noted.

Viggo pouted playfully. "What about me? I look better than both of them put together."

"You know damn well you do," I told him, smiling and tucking my arm around his. "Thanks for doing this. That goes for both of you. It means a lot to me. Especially since I'm not sure I could've walked up there on my own."

Myrgjöl gave me a heartfelt squeeze, but Viggo just laughed. "I'm honored to do it, sis. And don't worry, if you pass out, I'll just dump you on the stage."

"Thanks," I deadpanned, then lost my breath when music suddenly erupted from invisible speakers.

Viggo laid his hand on my arm. "Relax, Emelie, this will be over in a few minutes. Then you can go back to charming the pants on my brother."

"Don't you mean, charm his pants off?"

He shook his head. "With my brother, you might be better off with the pants on approach."

Myrgjöl put her hand on my shoulder. "You are doing the right thing, and that already makes you a better Norn than your mother. She was never strong enough to take my place. You are, honey. Though we all have the same abilities as Norns, a Norn with a good heart will be the best at what she does."

More than a little doubtful, I asked, "Do you really think so?"

She winked at me and grinned. "I do, and I will see you up there."

The cheers from the mating party grew as she vanished and reappeared on the stage. Viggo inclined his head. "Ready?"

I blew out a long breath. "Probably not, but let's do it before I lose my nerve," I whispered, and we took our first step down the aisle.

We were almost to the stage when Myrgjöl boomed out, "Welcome to all of you. Tonight, we are fortunate to witness a union unlike any other—the mating of the dark elf king, Kristian Väsen, and Lady Emelie Andersdotter, the hope of the light elves, my successor, and my only granddaughter."

The crowd was silent. Like me, they were all staring at their king, waiting on his reaction.

But the king didn't say a word. He only motioned for me to talk to him in private and walked off the stage.

I silently followed him into the castle, terrified of what he'd say.

"You are Wist's daughter?" he guessed, once we were alone.

"I am. I didn't know she wasn't just an elf until after her death."

He nodded. "Do you have the Norn's abilities?"

I fidgeted a bit before answering. I had no idea how the king of Svartálfaheim would react to his mate having more power than he did. "I do," I said, finally.

"How could I have been so blind?" Kristian asked, starting to pace in front of me. "I never suspected Wist of treachery. We thought Anders had persuaded her to change his fate because he didn't want to mate Viveka. Jakob was so in love with her. Anders would not have been able to take her away from him. He would not do that to a friend." He continued to pace the foyer. "But this explains so much." He stopped in front of me. "It also makes it glaringly obvious your parents did an awful thing to you. Everyone knows Wist's daughter was born to be Soren's destined mate. They have ruined your only chance at happiness for their own selfish reasons. That is … despicable."

"They haven't ruined anything. I have just as much chance at happiness as anyone else does. Not many are fated to their true mate."

"All of the creatures that have been lucky enough to have had their fate examined by Myrgjöl are."

"Really? Is that true?"

"Yes. She is the best. It is considered the ultimate gift to have your future mapped by Myrgjöl. And now she has said she is to name you her successor. Emelie, Norns are strictly trained by the council, starting at a very young age. Her choosing a mated, mixed-blood Norn from Midgard will not be tolerated. I believe your Grandmother is about to shake up our worlds."

"What does that mean? What will happen?"

Kristian took my hand and pulled me into his embrace. "Well, the first thing we shall do is get mated. Next, we will take a trip somewhere unnoticed to celebrate that mating." He tucked a strand of my straight, dark hair behind my ear. "And after that, we will do our damnedest to live happily ever after."

"If you're allied with Odin that will not happen. Odin would love to have the most powerful Norn's granddaughter at his disposal. I'd be a sitting duck."

He nodded in realization. "You are right. We must keep you protected from Odin, however, being the queen of Svartálfaheim puts you in the public's eye. It could be quite dangerous for you. I wonder what Myrgjöl was thinking when she outed you."

Myrgjöl blinked into existence between us. "I was thinking it is time she stopped hiding and learned to take care of her own safety. If she is going to take my place, she will need to be able to protect herself when under attack. It is inevitable that it will happen at some point. And because she tends to overlook faults in favor of good traits, our Emelie will have to be especially careful. It is one of the wonderful human characteristics she inherited from her grandfather."

The surprise was evident on Kristian's face as he repeated her. "Human?"

"Yes, king. My mate was a human from Midgard. He was a good, forgiving man. She is much like him."

"Thank you, grandmother," I said, tearing gathering in my eyes.

"Not at all, dear." She eyeballed Kristian. "What are your thoughts on these revelations?"

"I feel ... lucky. How many others have mates who have the power to stop a fruitless war, predict fates, and see the good in creatures known for their lack of compassion?"

"Not one," Myrgjöl confirmed. "I'm glad to see you appreciate the gift you've been given."

"I would be a fool not to," he admitted.

"Okay, guys. I'm still just me over here. I haven't performed any miracles or anything."

Myrgjöl hugged me. "I know you are overwhelmed, but I think it is better this way. It's like pulling the bandage off in one fell swoop, instead of a little bit at a time. Now, hurry up, you two."

Did she just compare exposing me to the Norselands with pulling off a Band-Aid?

"What is a Band-Aid?" she asked silently.

"Never mind."

He grinned down at me. "I should have told you earlier."

"Told me what?"

"That no one has ever looked as beautiful as you do right now."

I smirked. "I think that opinion might be a tad bit biased."

He came in close, towering over me to caress my cheek. "I can guarantee it is." He straightened and walked to the door. "I will give you a moment to yourself."

"I'm right behind you."

As soon as Kristian left, I called Soren. Even with all the drama, my mind was still filled with my true mate. Now, more than ever, I needed to hear his voice—not that I thought he would answer me, but I had a few things to say if he would listen.

"Soren, are you there?"

To my amazement, he answered right away. *"I am here, little one."*

I took a deep breath to steady myself. *"I understand why you left. I think you did it the best way you could."*

"I couldn't stay. Every moment with you made me more certain I would never let you go. It was the hardest thing I have ever done."

"I need to know something."

"Anything."

"If I can bring peace to the elves and escape my mating, will you wait for me?" I had no hope that he would, but I still held my breath in anticipation of his answer.

"I waited seven-thousand years for you. I will continue to wait until you are mine."

I sighed in relief. Though I realized what I was asking of him was unfair, I couldn't bear a future without him. I had to have something to hold on to. *"Soren?"*

"My love?"

"I'm about to have my bonding ceremony."

He was silent for a long moment. *"Pardon?"*

"I'm about to mate the wrong male in front of the other warriors, all of Kristian's top males, and their mates. Myrgjöl is presiding."

He chuckled. *"And you thought now would be the most appropriate time to call to me?"*

"I guess I'm kind of freaking out. They're all waiting for me to come out, and I don't know if I can physically make myself move. I'm scared."

"Has he hurt you?" His voice was hard.

I started to cry. *"No, he's very nice."*

"Emelie, the sooner you mate him, the sooner you will be in my arms."

"I know." He was right, but fuck, I hated it.

He whispered, *"Be brave, little one. You own my heart,"* and then he was gone.

Numb, I stood there not breathing for a few seconds, then I robotically checked my makeup in the mirror. "Okay, Emelie, you can do this. Harden your heart and walk out that door," I said to my reflection.

"So, are we going to do this?" an impatient Nils asked. "Kristian is starting to look nervous out there."

"I just needed to talk to Soren. I'm coming now. And stop sneaking up on me!"

He held out his elbow. "Come on, Em—before the food gets cold."

"Thanks, Nils. That's just the reality check I needed."

"I do what I can," he quipped, then he got serious. "Now that you've been exposed to the worlds, I think you should make sure to show you are irrefutably the right choice for the queen of Svartálfaheim. When we go out, lightly hold onto the fur at my shoulder and try to look as cool as your grandmother."

"Not a problem. I am as cool as my grandmother."

He shook his head sadly. "Not in a million years. As a matter of fact, you saying that kind of cements that you aren't."

"Shut up, you ass. It's supposed to be the happiest day of my life."

As Nils and I made our way through the crowd to rejoin Kristian, everyone, including Jakob and Viggo, went down to one knee. Nils was as tall as I was on all fours, and judging by the reaction of the crowd, looked just terrifying and regal enough to make them nervous. With a loud huff, he safely deposited me next to my future mate. Thanking him, I looked to Myrgjöl for instructions.

"Tell them to rise."

"Please, rise," I called out.

Myrgjöl stepped between us. "Are there any who oppose this bonding?"

No one stood up, though Soren's name raced around the group in whispers. Everyone expected him to appear.

Myrgjöl frowned as her eyes roamed the crowd. After a few seconds of perusal, she shook her head as if to clear it and continued, "Excellent. Kristian, if you will take Emelie's hand and speak the bonding words."

She spoke quickly in my mind. *"He will puncture his finger and place the blood on your bottom lip. You will do the same. The ceremony is then completed with a kiss. I warn you, there may be a bit of discomfort when your fate with Soren is broken."*

Mesmerized by Kristian's intense gaze, I watched as he pushed his index finger into his canine and dragged his finger down my bottom lip. "I accept you as my fated mate, Emelie. Let us never be parted."

"Do the same," Myrgjöl reminded me.

I lifted my palm toward Kristian. "Would you mind helping me out?"

He gave me a heated smile, no doubt remembering the moment we'd shared on the night we met. "Of course not."

Exposing a fang, he brought my finger to his mouth, gently drawing the blood to the surface.

Smiling, I traced my finger down his full bottom lip. "Kristian, I accept you as my fated mate. Let us never be parted."

Myrgjöl spoke to the crowd. "The bonding words have been spoken. They will now seal their destinies."

Kristian leaned down, and I lifted on my toes to meet his kiss. The instant our lips touched, there was an indescribable pain. Soren's consciousness brushed my mind, and I could hear his screams echoing in time with my own. Miraculously, our bond still seemed to be there. Only now, it was irreparably broken. The ties that held our fates together severed for all eternity.

As abruptly as the assault started, it was over. Glancing up, I saw Kristian watching me as if he'd never seen me properly. The bonding has obviously affected him more than me. I felt the same way I did before I met Soren—empty.

My grandmother quieted the roaring crowd. "Never have I agreed to release a fate I have cast, however, in this situation, I believe the bonding of Emelie and Kristian will be for the better good. The war has separated the elves for too long. It is time for them to unite and the elves to be the great society they once were. The bonding of your sovereigns is now complete. Long live the king and queen of Svartálfaheim."

CHAPTER TWELVE

After hours of smiling until my cheeks hurt and enough polite conversation to put me in a coma, Kristian announced we were to leave our post-wedding celebration. I had never liked him more than I did right that second. I was beyond tired after the day's many events. Being physically attacked, outed, and mated all in the same night was more than exhausting; it was mentally draining. I could barely think, let alone fake being blissfully wedded to my soul-mate.

With our goodbyes said, Kristian took me to a hillside overlooking the front entry of my new home. He'd gone to the trouble of having someone hang paper lanterns in the tree overhead us to light the plaid blanket spread out underneath. It was all very thought out. "Are you hungry?" he asked after we sat.

"I could eat," I said eagerly. At this point, I could've eaten a house, a horse, or even escargot. I hadn't wanted to say anything before, but I was starving.

"I arranged to have a picnic brought to us here last night. I thought we could dine alfresco."

Failing to stifle a laugh, I repeated, "Alfresco?" It sounded as if he'd never said the words before.

"I do not know what to say to you, love. You make me so nervous."

"You? I'm about to jump out of my skin over here."

He leaned in to kiss me. "You do not have to fear me. I will not hurt you."

After kissing him softly, but passionately, I whispered, "Don't make promises you can't keep, King Väsen."

Before he could respond, Axel appeared from nowhere and stepped up to us with an honest to goodness wicker basket in his hands. Without a word, he sat it on the blanket and disappeared.

I smiled at my new mate as he dug into the basket with zeal. Kristian was sweet to have put so much thought and effort into tonight. The fleecy warmness of the blanket was just enough to keep the chill away, and the selections of fruit he insisted on hand feeding me were delicious. I only wished Soren was here with us. Sure, I had a greater bond with Kristian now that we were mated, but the bond was in direct competition with the one I already had with Soren. My heart wanted them both.

"This is perfect," I told him, making the best of the situation. There was nothing else I could do, after all. I'd made my choice.

Kristian spoke softly as he reached over to entwine his fingers with mine. "Thank you for mating me, Emelie. Now that I realize you did have to, it means so much more, and I promise you, I will do my best not to hurt you."

"I'm confident you will," I lied. "But do you think the dark elf population will accept me now that they know I'm not one hundred percent light elf."

"Are you in jest? A Norn for a queen—they are sure to be overjoyed. We couldn't hope for more. Our young are rarely ever given the opportunity to have their future mapped. I believe all wrongdoings by the elves of Álfheim will be forgotten once you begin foreseeing their fates."

"I don't know if I feel comfortable doing that. What if I do it wrong ... again?"

"Again? Whose fates did you align?"

"The butler, Cedric, at Soren's house and Katrine."

"Do you mean Freyr's Katrine?"

"She is not his," I seethed, disgusted by the memory of the two together. "Katrine loved Cedric, and Freyr did not spare him. If I were him, I would not trust a female scorned. On top of that, she is sister to Myrgjöl and my aunt—family trumps Freyr any day. She may have betrayed us, but my intuition tells me she did not mean for anyone to be harmed. Honestly, I think she might be a spy."

Alarmed, he asked, "Freyr killed Soren's butler?"

I nodded. "And seventeen others."

He pursed his lips and called down the hillside to his aide-de-camp. "Axel?"

The elusive male materialized in front of us. "Yes, sire."

"Did you hear?"

"Of course."

"Make sure Freyr knows he is no longer welcome on the castle grounds. Katrine, as well."

"It is done," Axel said. He disappeared as abruptly as he arrived.

"You know," I said. "I wonder if Odin actually sent him here. If we can find Katrine, she will tell us. I'm sure of it." There was this peculiar feeling of right when I thought of Katrine.

Kristian wore a well-pleased expression when he met my gaze. "Emelie, your eyes, they are silver."

"Are they?"

"Yes. How extraordinary your magic must be."

I was caught off guard by his beautiful smile. My heart actually skipped a beat. I blushed and looked down at the blanket.

"What are you thinking, my queen?"

"I'm thinking I really like you."

"I'm relieved to hear it. I think I might love you, Emelie."

There were way too many elves listening to our conversation. I focused on the nearest elf and found his mind completely unguarded. It was easy. Too easy. I could hear everything he was thinking.

The male's thoughts were all very complimentary towards me. And in listening to the rest of the hird's thoughts, they all believed Kristian, and I would make beautiful elves. They even thought that if Kristian were the male he was a hundred years ago, ours would have been a perfect union. But the Kristian they knew today, had been changed too long. They had lost faith in his recovery.

Upon hearing this sad truth from them, I felt compelled to help my new mate and to start mending what I could of his dwindling reputation. "Kristian," I asked, "Is it okay if I move into your room tonight?"

His eyes widened. "Are you serious, Emelie?"

"Yes. I think we need to synchronize our schedules. I don't want to be limited to only seeing you for a couple hours in the evening, and I'd like to sleep in the same bed. It was very lonely last night."

He raised a brow. "Even after the wolf arrived?"

I shrugged. "Nils was just looking for a bed to sleep in. I made him sleep as a wolf."

"Did you?" he asked, laughing at the mental image.

"Oh, yes. If you don't believe me, check the blanket for fur."

Circling my waist with his arm, he grinned. "You are a constant surprise."

"A good one, I hope. Did you really think I slept with Nils?"

"You are the best kind of surprise, and no, I did not. Are you ready to go inside?"

"Yes," I answered, tentatively. It was hard to ignore the hird's panicked thoughts when Kristian pulled the pale blue shifting stone from his pocket. They were afraid for me. Aiming a confident smile at them, I addressed the group. "It was nice to meet all of you. Good night."

Kristian took us to the antechamber of his bedroom, to the exact place he'd proposed. "Would you like me to send someone for your belongings?" he asked, looking excited at the turn of events.

"I can get them tomorrow if you have a shirt I could sleep in for the day."

He walked to the chest of drawers in the bedroom, rejecting twenty perfectly good t-shirts before settling on a gray one he'd already cast aside. "This will match your eyes perfectly."

I took the shirt, feeling awful that I didn't feel as strongly for him as he did for me. The relationship was starting to feel a little one-sided.

Myrgjöl's kind voice filled my head. *"Emelie, you have to let go of Soren for now. Enjoy your time with Kristian. It could be a thousand years until you are able to leave him."*

She was right. I just needed to go with it. He was in love with me. That wasn't going to go away. And if I was being honest with myself, when I was around him, I didn't want it to.

"Thank you, Kristian. You are so thoughtful. Any shirt would have been fine."

Brushing his knuckles along my jaw, he said, "The choice was purely for selfish reasons."

I squinted and poked him in his muscular chest. "You are a bad, bad male."

Black flashed across his amethyst eyes. "Are you certain you want to share my bed? I fear you will not be safe from me."

"I can take care of myself."

"Can you?"

"Try me and find out."

His eyes stayed black. "You really shouldn't tempt me, little elf."

He backed us across the room, and I pushed my palms against his chest to stop him. It was a valiant attempt, but I didn't stand a chance. He didn't stop moving until my back was resting against the giant bedpost of his bed. I gasped as he grabbed my wrists and wrenched them open wide. The borrowed shirt fluttered to the floor forgotten.

Without taking his eyes from me, he laced his fingers with mine, stretching me onto my toes. "I want you," he groaned, sliding his lips along the curve of my neck.

His words were all it took for my control to snap. Biting into the tender spot between his neck and shoulder, I ignored his yell of surprise and the shudders that followed. His blood was spicy, delicious, and intoxicatingly magical. Where Soren's had been like a powerful drug, Kristian's was like a key that unlocked the door to my elemental side. I could feel the energy from the stone walls, from the floor beneath our feet, even the bedpost he had me restrained against. It was heaven ... until I realized what I was doing.

In horror, I quickly moved away from him and looked to the floor, mortified I'd bitten someone without their permission again. Jakob had been right. My self-control was dangerous. "I'm so sorry," I said. "I should have asked first."

He shook his head. "It is I who should apologize. I was ... regrettably overeager." He looked pointedly at my dress, which was wet from his orgasm. "That was the first time I have ever been bitten. I did not expect it to be so ... uh, pleasurable."

Laughing seductively, I kissed his mouth. "Will you help me out of this thing?"

"I could not desire anything more," he growled. "However, time is not on our side. I believe I must go soon."

I glanced at the clock across the room—eleven thirty. I probably wouldn't see him until the morning. Suddenly awkward, I didn't know what to say to him. What was appropriate? Good luck? Have fun?

This was madness. "Stay, Kristian. At least, unzip me and get cleaned up before you go."

"Emelie, you cannot fathom how much I want to stay," he said, moving closer to the door. "But I am afraid of what seeing your naked skin will do to me so close to midnight. I cannot risk it."

With disappointed hopes, I watched him leave, wondering who would be the recipient of his cruel indifference tonight. As terrifying as the situation was and as crazy as it sounded, I'd wanted it to be me. Since the bonding ceremony, the harem bothered me a lot more than it had before. I hated the thought of his hands on those females, especially on our mating night.

I decided to go to bed after a shower, but I was so restless, I couldn't sleep. The thought of what Kristian would be doing right now was driving me crazy. Was he inside of one of them this very minute?

After a half hour of staring at the ceiling, I couldn't take it anymore. I wanted to see what the old harem looked like on the inside so I could have an accurate picture in my head of what he was doing. You know, the whole curiosity and the cat thing.

Opening my bedroom door slowly, I listened for voices—nothing. I crept out in the hallway and put my ear to the harem door—there was no noise. Twisting the knob, I cursed inwardly when the door hinges creaked as if it hadn't been opened in years instead of days, then I gasped.

The room was another monstrosity of extravagance with high ceilings, tapestried walls, and expensive furniture. There were three doors on the back wall of the room, two regular entrances, and one smaller doorway with a gold lock in the middle. I walked to the locked door and examined it. Nope. I wouldn't be getting in there without a key. Feeling a little like Goldilocks, I tried the left door. It revealed the females' luxuriant living quarters. The door on the right was obviously the room Viveka so eloquently referred to as, 'the room where you fuck your females'. I stared at the giant bed in part fascination and part disgust. I didn't see any whips or chains, and a quick search of the furniture didn't turn up any kinky stuff, just lube and condoms. Gross. The condoms did strike me as odd since Kristian told me the females did this because they wanted a chance at a royal heir. If that were true, why would they use condoms? Ugh. I didn't want to think about it.

Revolted, I turned to leave, and that's when I noticed the camera. It wasn't mounted in the ceiling as I thought it might be; it was sitting on a high shelf over the door, just begging for me to investigate. I went back outside the room and dragged a heavy ottoman to the doorway to reach it. Standing on the tips of my toes, I took it off my shelf, examining the strange make of camera. As luck would have it, there was still an SD card inside. I stowed it in my robe pocket and put everything back into its proper place before creeping back over to my room.

As soon as I was safe with the bedroom door closed behind me, I became terrified of being discovered. Panicking, I hid the tiny card under the rug behind the nightstand, promising myself I would find a device to play it on tomorrow, and then I'd put it back where I'd found it. I climbed into bed, feeling a little guilty for prying and a lot like a massive pervert for wanting to see if my mate was actually forcing these females into sex. How did my life turn out like this?

The next morning, I woke to find Kristian's naked form beside me. Sitting up, I boldly perused his nude body. His face truly was only the beginning of his perfection, and that was a huge (if you know what I mean) understatement. He was gorgeous from his dark head to his slender arched feet. Smiling, I eased off of the bed slowly, trying not to wake him. His hair appeared to still be wet. He probably hadn't been asleep for very long. Stripping out of his shirt and grabbing a robe along the way, I tiptoed to the bathroom and held my breath as the door closed with a soft click.

"Emelie?" a voice asked.

I quickly put my robe on and cracked open the door. "Good morning, Kristian."

Glancing to where I was holding my robe closed at my cleavage, he said, "I hope you slept well."

"I did. Did you get enough rest? I didn't mean to wake you."

"Only after my nightly … activities, do I find myself asleep. Is sleep a necessity for you because you are part-human?"

"Not at all, I just feel more refreshed after a good night's sleep, like I've recharged my batteries."

"I see." He looked down to the tile, his forehead creased with worry. "Ah, Emelie … I want to talk to you about something."

I was immediately wary. Did he know I stole the card? "What is it?"

Surprisingly, his next expression was one of victory. "I am asking the harem to leave."

Shock really didn't cover what I was feeling. Wasn't he with them just last night? "I'm happy for us, Kristian, but do you think that that is wise?"

"I didn't go to them last night. I believe our bonding ceremony has cured me."

If that was the truth, I was relieved for him and completely frightened for me. It had been naive to think we'd never have sex. Don't get me wrong. He was smoking hot, a total gentle-male, and I was in definite lust, but I would betray Soren if I slept with him. I didn't think I could do that. Okay, maybe I could. I'd wanted to last night. And was it really even cheating? I was mated to Kristian, after all.

I opened the door wide to give him a congratulatory hug. Thank goodness, he'd put some clothes on. "What did you do all night?"

"I sat alone for a while in the harem until I realized nothing was going to happen, then I ran into Nils. He invited me to play poker with the other males." His eyes traveled down to my chest again. "I've called for a fresh pot of tea. Would you like a cup, Emelie?"

When he spoke, it was almost a growl, deep, sexy, and mesmerizing. The way my name rolled off his tongue had me envisioning myself climbing up his towering frame and sticking a flag in him like he was a newly discovered territory or something. I giggled at the thought and was horrified that I had my very first crazy person episode in front of one of the hottest males in existence. Blushing, I hung my head and pretended to examine the marble floor. What the hell was wrong with me?

"Beloved, are you well?"

I glanced up and managed a mumbled reply. "Um, yeah. I'm okay," I slurred. "I'm sorry. Tea would be lovely."

Turning slightly, he extended his elbow to me. "Shall we?"

If there was any hesitance on my part, it was only a second. Our bond drew me out of the bathroom and toward him as if it were the most natural thing in all of the worlds. He smelled delicious, of exotic spices and musk. It was an utterly intoxicating fragrance. Leaning in, I closed my eyes and breathed his essence in. I couldn't seem to keep my wits about me. "Kristian?"

He stopped walking and smiled wickedly. "Yes?"

I stepped in front of him, effectively blocking his path to the doorway. Closing the distance between us, I slid my hands up to the neckline of his shirt and ripped it apart with an animalistic growl, scarcely giving him time to recover before I started kissing my way across his chiseled chest. He groaned as he pulled me back up to face him. Why was he stopping me? I looked to his face for an answer but found it as empty as his signature. Then, without saying a word, he pressed his fingers to my temples and blackness overtook me.

I awoke buried under layers of plush comforters. Lazily snuggling into them, I tried to remember how I got here. The last thing I remembered was Kristian coming to the bathroom door, but nothing after that. Did I slip and hit my head?

Closing my eyes, I sighed, then jerked upright when everything came racing back to me. I owed Kristian a shirt and an apology. I don't know what had gotten into me. Glancing around at the richly colored tapestries that hung on the walls beyond the canopy of the bed and the seemingly priceless antique furniture that filled the room, I realized I didn't recognize any of it. It was an opulent suite, but not in Väsen Castle. Panic filled me. Where was Kristian? Clenching my eyes shut, I tried to search for him with my magic.

Thankfully, he was close—really close. I opened my eyes to find him watching me as he stood in the doorway. Breathing heavily, with a look of extreme concentration on his face, he took a step in, his amethyst eyes locking onto my grey ones. I couldn't look away. Never had I sensed a creature that exhibited so much restraint and lust. It was unbelievable that it was coming from just one individual. I could actually see his essence fighting against itself. His desire slithered toward me in wispy, spiraling tendrils, only to be pushed back by a thick white cloud of his restraint.

Enraptured with the lust in his aura, my heart sped up. He was inadvertently seducing me without saying a word, and I was more than willing to please him. I climbed out of bed, stepping into the icy white cloud to reach him. There was only a moment of clarity before his lust embraced me. It called to my own, and I was helpless to fight it. Winding around me, it intimately caressed me as I approached him.

Groaning, Kristian adjusted the bulge of the erection that pressed tightly against his jeans. He wanted me.

"Let me take care of that," I purred, reaching for his belt.

"No, Emelie!" he exclaimed, grabbing my wrists.

I would not be deterred. I would have my mate inside of me tonight. Wrapping a leg around his waist and an arm around his neck, I ground myself into him, finally feeling the restraint fade as he fisted my hair in his hand. I found his lips and thrust my tongue into his mouth. He returned the kiss with enthusiasm and slid his hands down to cup my bottom. Quickly turning, he lifted me to the top of a dresser and pressed even harder into me, gasping into my mouth when I began to rock against him slowly.

"Please, Kristian," I begged.

He gave me a look of sheer panic, but I soon felt his resignation and took full advantage. Reaching down, I released his engorged arousal from its confinement and was rewarded with one of the most impressive phalluses I'd ever seen. It jutted out, long and tan, from a thatch of black hair, its broad head just begging to be licked. I wanted to worship it. I wanted it in my mouth, my body—any way he would give it to me.

Taking him into my palms, I smiled as he moaned loudly and tore open my robe. With purposeful hands, he gripped my waist, then moved upward, thumbing my hardened nipples as he made his way to my neck. Tangling one hand in my hair, he forced my head roughly to the side to expose my vein. I closed my eyes and shivered in anticipation as his fangs traced along my neck, and he positioned himself against my entrance. I was so ready for him.

The moment I thought he would push himself into me, I felt him bite sharply into my neck. It was incredible. Rolling my hips toward him, I urged him to take me, but he continued to remain motionless. "Please," I pleaded, as frustration filled me. I needed him to pound into me until I screamed.

Ignoring me, he licked the wounds closed, pulled himself out of my grasp, and backed a step away. "Emelie, cover yourself."

"Kristian, please don't," I responded, trying to coax him closer by slowly stroking him.

Shuddering, he restrained me by holding my arms to my sides. "Now, Emelie."

"Okay," I whispered breathlessly, leering at him as tucked himself back into his jeans, fastened the button, and made a hasty retreat. I briefly considered forcing him to come back with my magic, but ultimately decided against it. After that torrid display, I really didn't think rape would be a great addition to the list of awkward sexual escapades piling up between us.

I hopped down from the dresser after a few minutes, disappointed and frustrated. Yes, I probably should have worried more about me almost losing my virginity, then considering forcing Kristian to have sex with me, but, hell, it was apparent, even to me, that my priorities were way, way out of whack at the moment. What a nightmare this was.

Half walking, half stumbling into the adjacent bathroom, I stared at myself in the mirror. My robe was ripped, my neck was bleeding, and my hair was a rat's nest. I looked like a whore, and worse, I felt like one. Grabbing a silver hairbrush and a washcloth, I straightened myself out the best I could, while I contemplated the bizarre situation. Something was definitely going on with Kristian. Nothing about his actions made any sense. He'd never mentioned any powers, but he and I obviously shared a similar talent for influence. He was using it even now. With every pulse of the bite on my neck, I could feel him calling me, beckoning to me to give myself to him.

Soon after leaving the bedroom, I realized I was right about this not being Väsen castle. My surroundings were beyond extravagant. With all the doors lining the hallway open, and I could see every room I passed contained large marble fireplaces, sumptuous fabrics around the windows, and glittering chandeliers above the beds.

After a few minutes of fruitless searching through the long hallways, I heard the sound of angry voices. I picked up my pace, hoping to overhear the argument.

"You have thirty seconds to produce my true mate, or I will kill you," an angry voice said. It was Soren's voice. I crept to the doorway and looked inside. There Soren stood, the smile on his face downright menacing as he aimed it at Kristian. I couldn't help but think it was the sexiest thing I'd ever seen.

Kristian laughed, no doubt at the thoughts he seemed to now hear and turned to look at me in the doorway. "Here she is, safe and sound. Beloved, Soren believes that I have coerced you into sex. Have I done that?"

An answer burst out of my mouth that was not my own. "No, it was I. He is my mate. I want him to fuck me." I looked away. I hated that there was a kernel of truth in those words.

Soren dismissed my response. "I am taking her with me."

Kristian threw his hands up. "Very well, I grow tired of this argument." He turned to me. "I will let you leave with him to prove my innocence. However, I would like to remind you that while Soren is much too cavalier to give you what you need, I am not. I know your deepest desires and will not hesitate to fulfill them when you return to me." He stalked toward me predatorily, and I noticed his violet irises had been replaced with black. He was terrifyingly beautiful. Stroking his fingers down my face, he continued, "She was quite the tart for me before you arrived, Soren. Were you not, my mate?"

"Yes," I answered, through gritted teeth. He was speaking for me again.

"Did you know I could make you come where you stand, Emelie? Tell me you don't want it. Tell me you do not want what I can give you—that you do not want me."

I shook my head sharply and moved to Soren's side, but couldn't tell Kristian I didn't want him. I wanted whatever he wanted.

Turning to Soren, he boasted. "I almost took her for myself, you know. I was so close to being inside her. All it would have taken was one push of my cock to claim her maidenhood. She was scandalously ready—begging for it. Weren't you, Emelie?"

As intense pulses of pleasure ran through my body, straight to my core, I cried out a humiliating moan of ecstasy, fell to my knees, and prayed he would never stop.

"Look at her, son of Odin. She is ripe for the taking. How could you turn this beauty away? And a true mate, too."

"Leave her alone," Soren growled. "This is your last warning."

Kristian crouched next to me and tipped my chin up. "Tell him how much you wanted me, Emelie."

"I wanted him, Soren. I wanted him to fuck me until I screamed." With tears in my eyes, I looked down at the carpet, mortified beyond belief that he'd made me say that but more turned on than I'd ever been in my life.

Kristian stood. "Take her—if you still want her." He walked to the doorway and looked back at me, pursing his lips. "You have only had a taste of what I can give you Emelie. Come back to me when Soren refuses to satisfy you, and I will finish what we started here tonight." Stepping over of the threshold, he stopped but didn't turn around. "And Emelie? He will refuse you. He is obsessed with doing the right thing."

I couldn't take my eyes off of Kristian as he walked from the castle. Mainly, because the farther he strode away, the more acute my desire for him became. Even from this distance, he was still controlling my every thought. "Soren? I ..."

I meant to tell Soren what he was doing, what was going on in my mind, but the moment I felt Kristian's signature leave entirely, hunger overtook me. Desperate, I crawled to him and tried to unbuckle his belt. I needed to feel him inside of me now.

He stilled my hands and pulled me to my feet. "Emelie, please stop. We have to go."

I shed the ripped robe, pleading with him. "Soren, I want you."

He unsheathed the blade at his waist with clenched teeth. "Emelie, any other time, I would fuck you senseless, but right now, we have to go." Dragging the dagger across his neck, he commanded, "Drink."

I instantly obeyed, climbing into his arms and lapping at his potent blood until I couldn't feel anything but my blissful slip into unconsciousness.

When I woke, the first thing that registered in my brain was that I loved the feel of the fur against my freezing, nearly bare skin. I didn't have to open my eyes to know it was Nils' warmth I was curled under. A groan of satisfaction escaped my lips, and the fur was promptly replaced by warm male skin.

Nils chuckled. "You keep that up, and I'm going to think you want to take this relationship to the next level."

The sound of his throaty, gravelly words sent a flash of heat through me, reminding me of the all-consuming hunger that was eating me from the inside out. Nils would do as well as Soren or Kristian would, and more importantly, he wouldn't say no to sex. He would fuck me until I was sated.

I smiled up at him. "Why not? Fuck me, Nils."

His eyes opened wide. "Are you serious?"

"As a heart attack."

His face was one of bewilderment. "What does that mean?"

Reaching between us, I stroked his hardening length. "It means, I want you, Fenrir."

With the touch of my hands, his puzzled expression instantly morphed to a sharp predatory focus. "Are you sure?" he growled.

I tightened my grip. "Do I need to continue my demonstration?"

He hesitated only a second longer before savagely taking my mouth. His kiss was hard, wild, and almost an attack. I matched his intensity with my own uninhibited desire, crying out and digging my nails in his ass when he thrust blindly against me. That brought his fierceness to a heightened level. He bit into my lip, bringing the taste of blood to our mouths and making my fangs emerge. Breaking the kiss, I sank my teeth into his shoulder, quickly replacing what Kristian had drunk from me with the strength of his invigorating blood. Nils retaliated by ripping my tattered robe from my chest, making me gasp out in delight. Finally, someone who knew what they wanted and weren't afraid to take it.

"Am I interrupting something?" a voice asked.

Following the sound of the deadly calm voice, I found Soren fuming in the doorway, his magic burning like embers in his eyes.

"Leave now!" Nils thundered, his eyes going through their own change to wolf yellow.

Soren smirked and spoke in a voice that was sure to raise Nils's hackles. "Forgive me. I thought this was the living room, not your bedroom."

Nils stood up, gloriously naked and ready to fight. "Are you going to fucking leave, Soren, or shall I show you to the door?"

Soren met his challenge, positively dripping with murderous intent as he stepped forward. "No, I am not going to fucking leave. She is my true mate, idiot."

I stood to flee the argument, letting what was left of my robe fall to the carpet. I wasn't going stay here and listen to them fight over me; they knew what I wanted, and when one of them worked up to the nerve to give it to me, I would let them. "I'll be in my room," I said, brushing past their bodies on the way up to my bedroom.

When I heard Soren mutter, "I will fucking kill you, Fenrir," under his breath, I ascended the stairs, positive that their eyes were glued to my naked form, and a sharp knock only moments after I closed the door filled me with triumph once again. I moved to unlock the door feeling hopeful that Nils had come to finish what we'd started. I desperately needed to release the awful urges that had plagued me since I'd left Kristian, and I couldn't think of a better way than Nils's raw power between my legs.

"Emelie?" a voice asked.

My excited, eager smile fell. Soren's fast-moving stream of consciousness was easy to recognize, even with the door between us. "Save your breath, Soren," I called out, dismissing him.

"You are not in your right mind. You must know that. Open the door. Do not make me destroy Jakob's home to get to you."

I scoffed at his audacity but opened the door. "You know, I'd say I'm exactly in my right mind. In fact, my mind has never been so clear. Leave Soren, I need to take a shower before I go."

Pushing his way past me with contempt in his eyes, he roared, "And where are you going to go, back to Kristian's shell at the doppelgänger's lair? It has possessed him, Emelie. He is no longer your mate, just as you are no longer entirely his."

"I am myself, and he is my king. The doppelgänger has nothing to do with this. I have to leave."

Soren refused to budge. "You have no reason to leave the safety of Álfheim. Kristian has already been reported as kidnapped and the kingdom knows you have been put into hiding. Jakob has taken care of everything in your absence."

"You can't keep me here against my will. I have to leave."

"I can and will," he countered. "Now, take your shower and come down for dinner. Hilda has made your favorite."

I bared my teeth and growled. "I told you. I can't." Turning toward the shower, I left him standing there, mouth agape.

"Emelie!" he bellowed, stopping me in my tracks. "You will obey me!"

That pissed me off. "Look, I've had just about enough of you telling me what to do. Fuck. Off."

Livid really seemed like too tame a word to describe his face upon hearing those words. "Fuck off? No. Fuck you, Emelie. I am trying to help you. You will do what I command, or I will make you do it. Those are your only choices."

Shaking my head, I turned away, ignoring his ultimatum as I let go of the magic that was built up inside of me. Only choices, my ass. I was a Norn. I could do whatever I wanted, and right now, I wanted him gone.

"Do you really believe your magic can best me?" Soren asked in a scathing voice from behind me.

Facing him to retort, I froze. He was beyond furious. His eyes held a hatred for me I'd never seen him portray. I backed away, frightened for the first time since we'd met.

"I am the son of Odin," he continued, letting electricity whip around him in a whirlwind of frenzied magic. "Your talents could never compare to mine. Emelie, you will get dressed and join us for dinner, or I will dress you and drag you there myself."

"Just try it," I mumbled under my breath, defiant.

Instantly, I was frozen. "As you wish."

"Damn it, Soren. Let me go."

With an evil smile, he said, "You brought this on yourself."

"Fine. You've stopped me from leaving. Congratulations. Now, how will you dress me?"

"Very simply." He snapped his fingers, and I was dressed in a sweater, jeans, and a pair of boots.

"Cute," I groused, a little embarrassed by my behavior. "I know you're right, by the way."

He gave me a disbelieving look. "What was that?"

"I said you're right. It would be mad to go back to Kristian now." I touched the still tender spots on my neck.

He walked to me and tipped my head back to look into my eyes. "Is this a trick?"

"No tricks, I promise, but you'll have to help me. It's incredibly hard to stay away from him," I admitted. "He calls to me incessantly."

"Damn it." He sighed and let go of the magic holding me in place.

I stumbled forward as I regained my balance. "Thanks."

"You do understand I am only trying to keep you safe, do you not?"

"Of course. I know you love me."

"I love you more than anyone I have ever known, but it is more than that. I have to keep you safe. Not just for me. It is for everyone. You are a potent weapon in the doppelgänger's hands. We cannot let him control you completely. Even if that means I will have to be your jailer for a lifetime of imprisonment."

"You would imprison me, Soren?"

"If it were necessary, I would do anything—kill anyone—to keep you protected."

I didn't know whether to be flattered or terrified of his statement. "So … chicken parmesan?"

Soren's smile was so genuine, it surprised me. I'd forgotten what he was like when he let his guard down. "With extra mozzarella."

"Hilda, this looks delicious." I took a big bite as soon as she set the plate down. I was starving. It seemed like weeks since I'd last eaten, and it turned out Hilda could make a mean chicken parm.

The guys were unusually quiet as they wolfed down their own huge portions. I didn't pretend to be ignorant of the reason. I'd caused nothing but problem after problem since Soren had brought me into their lives. I was a walking disaster.

"Em," Jakob said firmly. "It is not your fault."

"Sorry guys, I didn't realize I was broadcasting my problems." I thought I'd finally gotten the blocking thing under control—guess not.

"You weren't. I can read the guilt on your face like a book."

"Sorry," I mumbled, staring a hole in the table.

"Yeah, well, fuck sorry," Nils said. "Emelie, this is the doppelgänger's doing. Blame him for this shit, not yourself. Repeat after me: This is the doppelgänger's fault, not mine."

I decided to humor him. "This is the doppelgänger's fault, not mine."

Viggo chuckled sarcastically. "Good job, Emelie. Hey Nils, repeat after me: I will stop trying to bang anything that moves."

Nils cranked up a middle finger in his direction. "Unlike some of the other females at the table, I busted out of my chastity belt about five-thousand years ago."

I rolled my eyes, which felt way too normal. "Busted—nice word choice, Nils."

He preened under my attention. "You know me, Em. I'm a real wordsmith." Wriggling his eyebrows, he added, "Especially with the ladies."

I took a deep, overwhelmed breath and put my hand on top of Soren's. "I need some air. Can you walk me outside?"

He stood and offered me his hand. "It would be my pleasure, Queen Emelie.

I shook my head. "Don't you dare start that!"

"I apologize, your majesty."

"You're just sick," I groaned. I looked over at the rest of the snickering males. "You're all just sick."

CHAPTER THIRTEEN

The panicked feeling that plagued me at the dinner table subsided as we strolled around the grounds of Jakob's house. The night air seemed to have a calming effect on me, but not Soren. Despite his jokes at the dinner table, he was still tense and keeping quiet about his thoughts as we walked.

Are you all right?" I ventured, trying to draw him out.

He sighed heavily. "No. I am not. My true mate is bound to a king possessed by Freyr's doppelgänger, and she is possessed by him herself. I am the very opposite of all right."

I wanted to comfort him, to tell him I was fine, but I knew there was nothing I could say to convince him. I was no more than a stranger to him the way I was now, so instead, I lifted a hand and urged the vines hanging before us to braid themselves into a seat for two. "Sit with me, Soren."

Waiting until he was comfortable, I sat and made sure to keep my distance in the seat. I didn't want a repeat of earlier.

"How can we win against him, Emelie?" Soren asked, interrupting my thoughts of restraint.

"I don't know, I ..." Without warning, I had a vision of Katrine. She was on her knees, crying in a glowing, opaque force field of sorts. I was positive it was in the same room I woke up in yesterday. Soren reappeared in front of me as the vision dried up. "I think we need to rescue Katrine."

Holding my chin lightly, he traced my jaw. "Emelie, your eyes, what have you seen?"

"The doppelgänger has Katrine imprisoned in the same castle we were at before. I know she can help us; I just haven't figured out how yet."

"Are you sure?" he asked skeptically.

"Soren, everything in me is telling me to get her out." I took his hand and was surprised when I didn't feel the unbearable urges. "Soren, the doppelgänger is gone. I can't feel his hold anymore."

He jerked his frantic gaze to me. "Do you think he could know about the magic you are using to see Katrine?

I shook my head. It was the magic I used that helped to clear my mind of his hold. I could see that now. The enchantment to change Soren's fate, the vine swing, the vision of Katrine—all of them contributed to pushing his hold farther away. "No, it's my magic. Every time I use it, my mind clears a little more."

He didn't look convinced. "We cannot be sure. This could be another of his tricks. He may be punishing us for finding out about Katrine's imprisonment."

I didn't know much about my Norn magic, but I was pretty damn sure the doppelgänger would have no chance of finding out I saw Katrine's fate. How could I make him believe me? Throwing caution to the wind, I blurted out, "Let's find out. Kiss me."

His reaction was the one I expected. With a disconsolate but hardened look, he said, "You are still unwell, little one."

"I promise you, Soren, I am well. I mean to prove it by showing restraint. I can't think of a better way to make you believe me."

His frown clearly showed he distrusted me, but he leaned into me and lightly kissed my lips. I kissed him back, showing no forcefulness, only innocence. "See?"

"I do see, Emelie. I see how much I missed your sweet mouth, your taste, everything about you." He kissed me much more thoroughly, then laid his forehead on my shoulder.

"I missed you so much," I whispered into his beautiful hair.

"Every day without you has been agony for me. Not being able to keep you safe has been the hardest part. Kristian is weak. I knew he would never be able to keep you out of the doppelgänger's hands."

Words bubbled out of my mouth as my eyes turned silver again. "Kristian has a secret. He has a great power for influence."

His eyes widened. "What?"

The last thing I wanted to believe was that Kristian was involved in the doppelgänger's plot, but he was. It might as well be circled in permanent marker for as obvious as my magic made it now. I saw it all.

Kristian's talent for influence was what got him in league with the doppelgänger. Desperate to become king and not being able to stomach the idea of a light elf on his father's throne, Freyr helped Kristian find a Norn willing to do his bidding—my mother. She realigned Viveka's fate with Jakob's instead of my father's, and everything was wrapped up in a neat little bow. Adding to his delight, my mother made a plea to save my father from death by agreeing to give him his firstborn daughter. He accepted without a second thought. Why wouldn't he? He would still be able to mate a light elf to stop the war, and it would make him a hero. Kristian had indeed lined up the perfect scenario for himself. There was only one problem. What did the doppelgänger have to gain for his part in Kristian's grand scheme? Did Kristian honestly think he would orchestrate all this for him with no payment? No. What he wanted was a puppet, and he found one in Kristian. The doppelgänger didn't do anything for free.

I clutched Soren's arm in my grip. "Holy shit."

"Emelie, tell me what you have seen!"

I quickly told him everything and started to pace. How were we going to fix this?

After a few moments of silence, he finally spoke. "I am not surprised by his treachery. I have told you my opinion of Kristian before."

"I mean sure, Soren, he's a shit, but how much of this do you think is the doppelgänger's doing? I'm definitely seeing Kristian is an opportunist, but I feel like he is only a pawn in the doppelgänger's master plan. He's not a major player in this.

"I do not believe the doppelgänger would still be involved with Kristian if he was not awaiting his own prize. I wish you could see what that might be."

"I have seen it. It's me. If he controls me, he controls the elves. Soren, he hopes to use my power to control everyone."

Though he was alarmed, he tried to play it cool. "I want you to promise me you will use your magic as much as you can until we capture him."

"I promise."

"Hilda and Gunnar are here," he suggested. "Would you like to join them together now?"

I smiled. "That would be perfect. Their fates are already calling me to them. I can actually see where they are. Hilda is in the laundry. Gunnar is watching her from outside of the window."

His eyes widened. "Are you sure? That doesn't sound like Gunnar."

I tapped my head. "I'm right on this one."

Soren laughed and pulled me to my feet. "Let us go bring these two together before Hilda discovers him and decides to press harassment charges."

Walking hand in hand around the corner of the building, we found Gunnar exactly where I predicted he'd be. He was understandably embarrassed and sporting an extremely noticeable erection. I tried not to laugh at the absurdity of the moment.

"My Lord, Lady Emelie, I am sorry. I know what I do is wrong." Gunnar hung his head in shame. "I cannot help myself. I love her so much, but she doesn't know I exist."

I gave him a knowing smile. "I wouldn't be so sure. May I see your hand?"

He looked nervously at Soren, complying when he nodded his head enthusiastically. "Are you going to read my palm?"

"Not exactly." I closed my eyes and pushed the magic that was begging me to join them into Gunnar. He stiffened and stood straighter, his eyes drawn back to the window where his true mate stood. I kept pushing until the magic connected the two.

Hilda looked outside to the three of us. Confused, she stepped to the doorway and curtseyed to Soren and me, before glancing sheepishly at Gunnar. Oh, yes. This was a love match.

"Good evening, Hilda," Soren chirped.

"Good evening, Sir. Madam. Gunnar."

Soren made a show of glancing into the window at her work. "You know, Hilda, I believe the laundry can wait. Actually, I think the two of you should take the next few days off. You have not had a proper vacation in a while. I will supply you both with full pay, of course."

I beamed at Soren. "That's an excellent idea. You know what? I know just the thing to start out your vacation. I saw a bottle of champagne in the kitchen cabinet. Why don't you two take it and pack a few things for an impromptu picnic? It's a gorgeous night— magical even."

Hilda looked stunned. "Are you sure, my lady?"

Soren waved off her worries. "We are sure."

Gunnar finally found his voice. "Thank you both. This is most generous."

Soren put a companionable arm around them and walked them toward the kitchen. "You are welcome. Thank you for excelling at your duties amid all the happenings at the house in Sweden."

Shocked, but happy, the couple made their way inside together, not sparing their employer a glance. They only had eyes for each other.

Expectantly, I looked at Soren. "Do you think it worked?"

"It better have. You just gave them a ten thousand crown bottle of champagne."

"Oh, my goodness! I'm so sorry."

"It is perfectly fine," he assured me, looking everywhere but my face. "I do not think it could be put to better use than this."

Smiling shyly, I said, "Good," and began to walk back to the front yard. Things were different between Soren and me now. He'd distanced himself, and though I knew he did it for self-preservation, it still hurt—a lot. Stopping under the guise of admiring a flowerbed full of moonflowers, I took my true mate's hand. "Thanks for all of this, Soren, I mean it. Thanks for saving me, for helping me, and even for pushing me around—which you're really good at, by the way. I couldn't have escaped from Kristian by myself."

He shook his head and grinned. "You would have eventually. With your temper, you would not have been able to put up with him for very long."

I laughed at his painfully accurate assumption. "You're probably right."

He cupped my face, almost as if he would kiss me, but then dropped his hands. "I just could not leave you there with him."

"I'm glad you didn't. How did you find me?"

It was his turn to look shy. "In a moment of desperation, I called to you, and you did not answer. I could touch your mind, but it was obvious something other than yourself was blocking my entry. I had your blood before, so I simply followed your signature until I found you."

"You followed my signature from Álfheim? Where was I?"

"Jötunheim."

Pouting playfully, I groused. "What? And I didn't get to see any giants?"

He laughed. "Is that all that worries you? I can introduce you to my mother if you would like."

I smacked my forehead. "How could I have forgotten you're half-giant?"

Pretending to ponder the question, he said, "Well, I do take after my father's side."

"Only in looks, thank goodness."

In a blink, his pretense of light, carefree conversation was over. "Speaking of my father, is his friend's doppelgänger still lingering in your mind?"

I smiled, relieved I could tell him some good news for a change. "Not a bit."

"Are you sure?" he asked, searching for clues in my face.

"I am, I..." I stopped talking to listen to someone's thoughts coming from the forest. "There's someone here."

Alarmed, Soren took a fighting stance, blade in hand. "Where, Emelie?"

I pointed to the grove of spruce trees just to the east of us and tensed. "It's Kristian's right hand. He doesn't mean us any harm. He's just trying to figure out a way to speak to us without you attacking him. Axel, come out. Soren won't hurt you … well, unless you attack us."

Axel stepped out slowly with his hands above his head. "I do not seek to injure either one of you. I have come because—"

Interrupting him, I read his mind out loud. "He owes Kristian a life-debt. He is required to attempt a rescue, no matter who he is in allegiance with, or face being a disgrace." Axel's horrible past on his home world was laid out for me in all of its devastating sadness. "I'm so sorry, Axel."

He dismissed my sympathy by ignoring it. "I do not truly believe the king is a servant of the doppelgänger. I believe him to be enchanted," he explained quickly, keeping a wary eye on Soren.

"We believe the same, though he is partly to blame," I said. "Do you know where he is being held?"

"I do. He is at the doppelgänger's castle in Jötunheim. I did a bit of reconnaissance this morning and found him in the west wing, locked in a small closet. He was alive, but unconscious, when I left him."

I nodded at Soren. "He's telling the truth."

Soren sheathed his saber. "The doppelgänger leaves every morning for an hour or two. Do you know where he goes?"

Axel shook his head.

"I think that is the best time for us to rescue your king. However, it is imperative we find out where he goes. We do not want any surprises."

Axel breathed a huge sigh of relief. "Agreed."

"Great! What's the plan?" I asked.

"There is no plan for you, Emelie. You need to stay here."

Axel nodded. "He is right. It is much too dangerous for you to be there."

I didn't like where this was headed. "I can take care of myself, you two."

"I know you can," Soren appeased. "But it is better if you do not. Axel and I can shift without detection. He will not know we are following him."

What he really meant to say was I wasn't that long out of the control of the enemy, and I couldn't be trusted yet. That didn't make me too happy, but annoyingly, I had to agree with him. A scenario where I was unknowingly under the doppelgänger's control was too dangerous for all of us.

"I understand," I assured him. "You should get going if you're going to catch him before he leaves. Thank you for aiding my mate, Axel." I offered him my hand though I was the tiniest bit afraid of him. That poison action he'd pulled in the castle before had a very lasting impression.

He bowed low before taking my offering. "It is my honor, Queen Emelie."

His gloved touch triggered a vision of a series of events in his future. "Oh …"

Soren snatched me out of his grasp and whirled me to his side. "Are you okay?"

I didn't answer him. Instead, I negotiated myself around to speak to Axel. Smiling goofily, I said, "Would you like to know about your fated? She's lovely."

The four hours I waited for Soren and Axel to return were some of the longest hours of my life. I kept myself occupied by doing small amounts of magic with Jakob and Viggo, but the worry never left the back of my mind. I'd never experienced a rush of relief like I felt when they blinked back into existence in the garden. Running outside to meet them, I was thrilled to see triumphant faces. "I can tell by the cat ate the canary expressions on your faces that it went well."

Soren dropped a kiss on my lips. "It did, love."

Axel turned away from us, muttering, "No, my king, fear not. I did not see my queen kissing someone other than you."

I giggled. He was so much like his intended. I couldn't wait for them to meet. "So, when do we rescue Kristian and Katrine?"

"Tomorrow afternoon."

"I'll be ready," I said, determined to end this thing once and for all.

The next afternoon, we crept onto the doppelgänger's land just as he faded away. By Soren's estimation, we only had a guaranteed thirty minutes before he returned. Running full out, we ducked behind the hedge surrounding the castle and waited for the first patrol to pass by. When they were out of sight, I dashed to the front doors and tried the knob.

"It's open," I called out silently.

Axel breathed a massive sigh of relief and joined me at the door with Soren, Viggo, and Nils following close behind. Viggo had been reluctant to come with us. He didn't want to be a liability. His eyes would be sensitive, not having seen the sun in over twenty years … and he'd have to drink my blood, which was just icky because of our brother-sister kind of friendship. In the end, he agreed, but it had been more than awkward while he was at my wrist.

I opened the door slowly and tiptoed quickly through the halls on high alert. "I sense Katrine in the fifth room on the left. Kristian is at the end of the hall in a broom closet."

The males fanned out, Axel and Viggo going down the hallway to check for movement and locate Kristian, Soren, and Nils following me into the room where Katrine was held.

Katrine was restrained in a translucent bubble of magic, but it hardly mattered where she was at physically. In her mind, she was in her own personal hell. It was devastatingly painful for her to be without Cedric, her heart was exuding an agonized keening only she and I could hear. She was beyond hope.

"Aunt," I spoke softly, trying not to frighten her.

Her tears were immediate. "Emelie, I didn't mean for Cedric to die. I am so sorry."

"You didn't do anything to be sorry for, Katrine. The doppelgänger is to blame for all of this."

Her eyes pleaded with me. "Please help me hide from him." I'd seen that empty-eyed look before. She had been through unspeakable things in the time she spent with him.

"Don't worry. We're here to save you."

Relief filled her features. "Thank you."

Okay, now the hard part. "Soren, how do we get her out of that thing?"

He walked closer to the shield and held out his palm.

"You cannot get through this way. It is a trap!" Katrine yelled.

Soren jumped back, and we all enjoyed yet another huge sigh of relief.

"Just a minute. I think I have it." He disappeared into thin air, sending me into panic mode.

"Soren!"

"Have no fear, my love," said his muffled voice from the next room. "The magic prison does not extend into the other room. I am going to try to go through the wall. Stand back, Katrine."

Katrine pushed herself against her glass-like prison as far as she could and crouched down, hands over ears.

A loud, sudden crack coaxed a yelp from my throat, then I held my breath, watching the wall intensely. Seconds later, the wall seemed to fall away like ash, revealing Soren behind it. He quickly helped Katrine to her feet and accepted the desperately grateful embrace she bestowed upon him.

"Such a touching moment, isn't it, Emelie?"

Shrieking, I pivoted around to find the doppelgänger's horribly beautiful face mere inches from my own. He smiled placidly as if we were on a summer stroll through the garden. "To what do I owe the pleasure of your company, my dear?"

My jaw dropped. Was he seriously going to pretend to be ignorant? "I'm here for my aunt. As you can see."

Nils stepped in front of me protectively, with Katrine and Soren following his lead and moving on either side.

I peeked around Nils and finished, "I've come to collect my mate, as well."

He laughed giddily. "Silly elf, I do not have your king hidden here. He arrived last night and only stayed for a moment. I did not question his traveling intentions."

I arched a brow. "So, you're telling me if I walk down this hallway and open the closet at the end, I won't find him gagged, bound, and bleeding on the floor?"

His face fell, and I laughed viciously, the building magic in me making my fear vanish. Viggo and Axel chose that moment to make their grand entrance, blades drawn and pointing into his back. Amusement filled me as his eyes bulged and sweat beaded on his forehead. His sick game was finally over.

Nils laughed along with me. "You heard the lady, we can do this the easy way or the hard way; your choice, but we will be leaving here with the king." He leaned toward the Freyr look-a-like and stage-whispered, "I'm secretly hoping for the hard way myself."

Changing tactics, the doppelgänger sneered and feigned nonchalance. "Soren, you cannot believe your little band of misfits will defeat me?"

Soren's livid face at his comment said precisely what he believed, but he obliged him with an answer I thought was more than satisfactory. "The faith we have in each other is only one of the many powerful weapons we have at our disposal. You would do well to realize you have met your match in any one of us. Decide carefully whether you will resist or not. Your death could be tonight."

The doppelgänger smirked. "Pretty words, son of Odin. It is a pity to see you so deluded."

I felt the static in the room rise and yelled the first thing that popped into my head. "Now!"

There was no plan, so I didn't know what outcome to expect in the melee. I was hoping for the guys to tackle him and run him through with their blades—at the least, to put him in a magical headlock or something. But the result? It was beyond anything I could have imagined. Everyone in front of me, good guys and bad, were frozen. They were awake and blinking but held immobile by my magic.

"Oh, for the love of the Norse!" I cried.

Katrine's weak voice sounded behind me. "You will have to reanimate them one by one if you hope to hold Freyr captive this way."

"I didn't even mean to do this," I complained.

She nodded sympathetically and half-smiled. "Nevertheless, it is a very effective method."

"How do I do the unfreeze?"

"Don't overthink it. Simply concentrate on it as you did for Cedric and me."

The crack in her voice at the end of her sentence undid me. The doppelgänger had done this. He'd ruined so many lives, so much happiness. I would make him pay for his evil doings, and I would make sure all of his victims got the chance to get their revenge. Justice demanded it.

I raised my hand to touch Soren, only to have Katrine grab my arm.

"Wait."

"What is it?" I asked her, a second before she kicked the doppelgänger where it counts.

"Katrine! What the hell?" Freyr didn't move or even blink, but I could feel the pain radiating off his body. Katrine had hit her mark.

"He deserves it. You have no idea what he is like."

I didn't want to know. "Don't waste another second of energy hating this asshole. He's going to get what's coming to him."

She nodded. "I will try."

Giving her a reassuring smile, I closed my eyes, concentrating on freeing all but the doppelgänger. One by one, they came to life, first blinking then falling into a fighting stance as soon as their eyes found the enemy.

"Sorry, guys. My bad."

"I'm used to it," Viggo and Nils said together.

Axel gave them an incredulous look. "Emelie, I don't want to ever get used to that."

"Hey! I'm getting better," I said, indignant. "I unfroze you, didn't I?"

"My queen, I meant no disrespect."

"Then stop disrespecting the talent, buddy."

Soren cleared his throat. "Children, if you are done, we still have the little problem of transporting the prisoner and retrieving the dark elf king."

There was no way I'd be winning an award for mate of the year anytime soon. In all the excitement, I'd forgotten all about Kristian. Walking at a fast clip down the hallway, I opened the closet space to find him curled up asleep on his side, looking no worse for the wear, except for a bloodied bottom lip.

I let out a breath I hadn't realized I'd been holding, knelt, and shook his shoulder lightly. "Kristian, wake up."

His amethyst eyes sprang open. "Emelie?"

"That's me. Are you okay?"

He sat up gingerly, wincing. "I am sore."

"I'm not surprised. You've been folded up in this closet for who knows how long."

Understanding crossed his handsome face. "Freyr ... where is he?"

Soren answered for me. "The one you call Freyr is in the parlor, subdued by the hands of time. However, he is not who you think he is. He is the doppelgänger."

His eyes widened. "The creature that was created?"

Soren nodded in the affirmative.

Kristian's smile was one of furious satisfaction. "I want him in my dungeon. He is a prisoner of the dark elves forevermore."

Viggo stepped forward to help him up. "It shall be done, brother."

Standing on unsteady legs, Kristian touched my cheek with the back of his knuckles. "I am a servant at your feet, Emelie. You have saved the elves and countless others from a similar fate. Axel?"

"Sire?"

I yelped, not realizing Axel was behind me until he spoke.

"Transport the prisoner to the castle and alert the council that I will be calling an emergency meeting. Tell them nothing of what has happened."

"Yes, my king. Right away."

When Axel left, Viggo took his place. "Brother?"

"I am well enough, Viggo. I am thinking clearly for the first time in many years. Let us return to the castle and straighten this catastrophe out. There is much to set to right."

His eyes found mine, and I smiled encouragingly. His returning smile was a tight and distant one. Not exactly the reaction I'd been expecting from my new mate, especially since I'd just saved him from the clutches of a madman, but whatever. At least, all of this was finally over.

CHAPTER FOURTEEN

Myrgjöl was waiting with the dragon when we arrived at Väsen Castle. She smiled and waved to us from where she sat rubbing the shiny blue scales of the beast's belly. Nils was right. I could never be as cool as her.

Kristian seemed confused at her presence, but he bowed in her direction before he went up the steps, then turned around to face Soren. "I would like a moment alone with Emelie—if it would not offend."

Soren smiled tightly. "Of course, you have much to discuss. We will take the prisoner to his new home."

I curtseyed to my grandmother, who laughed and waved, before allowing Kristian to lead me through the heavy front doors and into the eerily quiet castle. Once inside his chamber, I took my usual place on the settee and waited for him to start. No doubt, he would have a lot of questions.

He paced for a few moments, looking at objects around the room as if they were foreign to him. Finally sitting next to me. "Things are changed in the castle. It is almost unrecognizable."

Taken aback, I asked, "You don't remember any of this?"

"I remember you—your eyes and the smell of your hair. Are we mated?"

Well, that was unexpected. I hadn't realized he had lost some of his memories. "Um … yes, for a couple of days."

He nodded. "Have we consummated the mating?"

"No! I mean, what?"

He seemed surprised. "Are you unwilling to bear my young?"

"What?" I asked again. "No. You didn't want to mate until you were able to ask the harem to leave. You really don't remember any of this?"

"I only remember pieces of it," he said impatiently. "Are you saying I used the harem here in the castle?"

"Yes. I haven't seen it for myself, but you mentioned it quite often."

I watched him warily as he walked out of the door and went into the next room, only to return seconds later. "Where are they?"

"You moved them to another wing for me."

He ran a hand through his short, dark hair. "What did I become?"

I took his hand, and he looked worriedly into my eyes. "You were always very kind to me. I don't know how much of it was the doppelgänger, but you did everything you could to make me happy."

Momentarily satisfied, he looked around, examining my things scattered throughout his chamber. "We share a bed?"

"You kept odd hours. I suggested we share a room. I wanted to see you more often."

"And you did this without anything in return?" he asked skeptically.

It was so hard not to get angry with him for saying that after everything I'd been through today. "If you are wondering if I can be trusted, I can. I could have done any number of things to you while you were under his control, but I didn't."

"I am sorry. I do not feel I know you at all. Just your face. I recognized you right away."

"I'm new at this, but I can show you everything I've experienced with you through my eyes if you put down your shield. I'm half-Norn."

"Are you with Lady Myrgjöl? I was surprised to see her outside. I am surprised to see the son of Odin, as well."

"I'm her granddaughter," I said, smiling reassuringly at him. "Will you let me show you?"

He hesitated. "Yes."

"Relax for me." After what he'd been through, I knew it would be hard.

He rested his head against the sofa. "I will try."

As I started to flood the memories into him, I watched his expressions closely. His eyes widened when I showed him the moment we met then became hooded as he saw me share my blood with him.

"You were beautiful," he whispered.

"Thank you," I told him, while I revealed the day Viveka dragged me from the room and made sure I saw the harem.

He grabbed my hand with apologetic eyes. "I am sorry for that, Emelie." He was utterly disgusted with himself.

"Don't worry. That was one of the worst of the memories. Things got much better after that."

He smiled slightly and nodded for me to continue.

At the memory of our unplanned mating, he actually grinned—until I got to the mating night, then he had to put a pillow in his lap. Flushing with embarrassment, I stared at the carpet between my feet. I was still mortified by my behavior that night.

He reached up to feel his neck where I'd bitten him. "I have never been bitten before. It felt ... good."

I savored that particular memory myself. "It was more than good, Kristian. Your blood still flows through my veins. My elemental magic is stronger than ever." Pausing the rush of memories, I was almost afraid to show him what was up next.

"Is that all you have to show me?"

"No."

He took my hand this time. "I can handle whatever it may be."

Taking a deep breath, I reluctantly revealed the moments leading up to where we almost had sex, hoping he wouldn't think badly of me for the way I'd begged for it.

"We almost did," he said quietly, almost to himself.

"Yes."

I continued the vision, disclosing the argument with Soren to him and awaited his response, which was a long time coming.

"My lady, I am sorry for what I have done. I do not know how I could have done all that I have. It is not within my power."

"No, but it was within Freyrs' doppelgänger's power." There was nothing left to show him other than when we rescued Katrine and woke him in the closet, so I did it quickly and hoped for the best.

After a long moment, he said, "I owe you everything."

I shook my head. "You owe me nothing. You didn't mean for this to happen. You only wanted a dark elf on your father's throne. The creature is the one to blame. He took advantage of a desperate situation."

"You were forced into this. I will not make you stay. You deserve a better male than me. You deserve your fated and your freedom."

"You are my fated now."

"You can change that, can you not?"

"I don't know." Could I? I had no idea.

"Myrgjöl will set things to right if the elders approve it. We will request an audience as soon as they will meet with us."

"That, I will," she said from behind us.

"Grandmother?"

She ignored me. "Kristian, though your alliance with the abomination caused countless deaths and strife, the kindness you showed my blood, even when you were possessed by such an evil creature, proves that you, too, deserve happiness." She winked. "And your freedom."

I grinned at her. "Eavesdropper."

She feigned innocence. "Who? Me?"

"No, the other eavesdropper in the room," I said sarcastically.

"Well, there are so many others listening, I could not be sure."

Kristian and I glanced around, searching for whom she could be referring to. I didn't sense anyone. "Who do you mean?"

She pointed to the corner of the room, near the ceiling. "The electronic eyes. They are ever vigilant in their sentry."

Kristian looked confused.

I stood up to look at the camera, pushed the embroidered stool I'd used to reach the other camera underneath it, and climbed up with Kristian's protective hand at my back. "It's a closed-circuit type," I told them. "It's sending the feed somewhere else. We need to find out where the viewing room is. Myrgjöl, do you know where the camera leads?"

"Yes, but I only know it because I saw it in your mind a few minutes ago."

"What?" Why did Myrgjöl have to say everything in riddles? Wouldn't it be easier if she just told me where it is?

"It would be easier, but I want you to figure it out yourself. It is the only way you will learn, you know."

I was flustered. I'd only been to a few rooms in the castle. Where could it possibly be? "Wait a minute. The old harem had a locked door."

"That didn't take long." She clapped her hands. "This is exciting. I feel just like Sherlock Holmes."

"Who?" Kristian asked, bewildered.

Laughing at her excitement, I explained. "It's a character in a series of mystery novels. Follow me, Kristian."

Once in the adjoining room, I caught Kristian out of the corner of my eye shaking with an involuntary shudder. What had happened to him in here? He had the same dead-eyed look Katrine had when we found her.

Myrgjöl popped her head in the doorway. "I will leave you two now. Kristian, I will rouse the council and have them available for you when you want to speak your suggestions of punishment, as is your right. A more deserved retribution there has never been, in my opinion."

The second she disappeared, Kristian began to crumble. "My apologies, Emelie. I cannot be in this room. I feel … I have to leave here."

He stepped out into the hallway, and I followed him, looking for others who might overhear. "I know this must be hard. How can I help you?"

He struggled to speak for a moment, tears springing to his eyes. "The chamber returns horrible memories. I cannot go in there again. At least, not yet."

I pulled him into my arms and held him. I didn't know what else to do. He didn't recoil as I thought he would. He just buried his face in my hair and let go of everything he'd been holding in. Thank goodness the castle had been abandoned. He wouldn't want anyone to see him like this.

My hair was wet with his tears when he finished, and I couldn't bring myself to give a damn. He hadn't shielded his thoughts while I held him, and the things he was remembering were atrocious. If anyone deserved a good cry, it was Kristian. The doppelgänger would be very lucky if he didn't die by my own hand the next time I saw him.

After a few minutes, Kristian wiped his eyes with the back of his hand and smiled weakly. "Thank you."

"There's really no need for thanks, Kristian. You're my mate. Any female would be there for her mate in his time of need."

"That is a falsehood. Not all females are as nurturing as you are."

He was right. After what the females of the harem did to him, I knew elven females could be every bit as vicious as the males could.

"You are my mate," he continued warily. "If you would … extend your kindness a bit further, I would ask you to view the recordings for me. I find I cannot bear to view them myself. I can ask no other."

Disgust and shame consumed me. How strange it was that only a few days ago, I'd wanted to see what was on the card I'd stolen. Now, no way in hell did I want to watch it. I'd seen enough horrible acts in his head to last me an eternity.

"I will do this for you, but first, I must confess something."

His jaw clenched and unclenched before he said, "As you wish."

"I have acted disgracefully, Kristian. I was so intrigued— okay, jealous of the time you spent with the harem on our first night as a mated pair, that I crept into the harem and stole the memory card that was left in the room's camera. It's hidden under the carpet behind the nightstand."

Surprise lit his face. "Truly?"

"Yes, I'll show you." I made a beeline to the nightstand in my previous room, retrieved the card, and handed it to him. "I'm sorry."

He looked at what he held and spoke in his native tongue.

"Pardon? I don't speak Elvish."

"It says, *CARD TO SHOW KRISTIAN.*"

I figured it would say something of the sort. As soon as I picked it up, I knew it was the recording Kristian had mentioned to me before, the one that showed him as the aggressor.

He handed the card back to me. "I believe I have … seen this one."

Myrgjöl spoke into my mind. *"Destroy it, Emelie."*

"How?"

"Change its fate, silly girl."

Inanimate objects have fates? Weird. *"Thanks, grandmother."*

"Anytime, my dear."

I held the card tightly between my palms and watched in awe as my magic grew blindingly bright, before reaching its zenith, rending the card into particles so fine they'd never even dirty the rug beneath our feet.

Noticing Kristian's uncomfortable posture, I decided to give him some alone time to come to grips with the situation. "I'll go see what's behind the door. I may be a while. Why don't you shower, and get Viggo to find Lina? She'll make you something to eat."

"I will do that. Thank you, Emelie."

I hugged him tightly. "No thanks from you, remember?"

He smiled nervously. "I will endeavor to remember."

I watched him until he was out of sight, and then grudgingly dragged myself into the harem room. I hated being in here. Seriously, if these walls could talk, I really hoped it was in a dead language.

Unlocking the door proved to be as simple as a thought. Getting into the computer? Not so much. I tried every combination of words and numbers I could think of and still couldn't figure out the password. Okay, it was time to flex my new mind reading ability. I scanned the castle for signatures. The females of the harem were still here and still very much ignorant of Kristian's reawakening. I scanned their minds with my handy new Norn magic and found they all knew the password. It was *Longlivetheking.*

Those. Fucking. Bitches. Soren needed to know about them now. I'd already seen some of what they'd done to Kristian. Not one of those traitors would ever know freedom again. I would make sure of it. I concentrated and found him on the grounds with the rest of the warriors. *"Soren, is the doppelgänger safely stowed?"*

"He is," he answered quietly.

Instant relief filled me. *"That's great. Can you please see that the harem, all six of them, are arrested immediately?"*

"It shall be done with haste. Is everything okay?" His voice seemed strained. He was worried.

"I'm fine. However, Kristian is not. I believe he will be terribly scarred from this ordeal. I sent him to shower and eat while I take care of some 'evidence'. I'll be with you soon."

"See you then, love. Be careful."

"Always." I hoped that would appease him enough to keep him from checking on me for a while. I didn't know how long this would take. Typing in the password, I waited for the computer to boot up. It took forever—so long I thought the machine was broken, but just when I was about to give up hope, it came to life with a chime of the Windows logo. I threw my fist in the air. Victory!

With just one click, I was rewarded with a meticulously detailed documents folder, full of damning confirmation that was conveniently dated and labeled. How nice of them to make it so easy for me. I'd make a point to thank them for it later. I didn't bother clicking on any of the various icons, the video snapshots serving as icon pictures were bad enough. Nope, I went straight to the folder labeled financial. That folder would yield who was really behind the treason going on in this castle.

Not surprisingly, I was proved correct. The whole group of them were listed alphabetically with their bank account information right beside their names. Huh. I didn't know elves even used banks. Soren would definitely need help with this one.

"Soren?"

"Yes?"

"Can you get the guards from the grounds to help you round up the hird? All of them, except for Axel, are to be arrested. It seems the doppelgänger is not the only one with an agenda for Kristian's future."

"I see. This will take some time. I will call to you when it is done."

"Okay, be careful."

He laughed. *"Again, with the doubt?"*

"You know I have no doubt in your strength. I know you are a lot stronger than you're letting on."

"Maybe."

"Well, then go get those assholes."

"I am already on my way."

Without a doubt, I knew that something, or rather, someone, important was missing from the computer files, an intricate key—Viveka. She, for sure, would play a huge role in this. After all, she's the perfect accomplice. She is a means of entry into the castle, she has an ax to grind with Kristian, and she is a total bitch. There wouldn't be much to gain for her, just money and the satisfaction of seeing Kristian humiliated every night, but honestly, she'd probably have done that to him without any incentives at all.

I clicked around for the better part of an hour. It was fruitless. Viveka was squeaky clean. There was no trace of her ever doing anything. Which probably meant she was the one who maintained the computer. It also meant she'd try to cover her ass when she found out Kristian's lucidity was back. We just had to catch her in the act.

Soren's mind brushed against mine. *"Emelie?"*

"Hi, how's it going?"

He laughed. *"Oh, you know, just relaxing by the poolside."*

"Funny. Did you capture all of the hird?"

"They are all imprisoned, except for one. The exception gave Nils a black eye, and he went wolf on him. The elf was taken to the infirmary. I do not know if he will be able to walk right after today."

Okaaay. *"That's ... lovely. Guess what?"*

"What, little one?"

"Viveka is involved."

There was a long pause. *"How?"*

"The doppelgänger's right hand."

"Shit."

My sentiments exactly. *"Jakob is not going to take this well."*

"No. How long will you be?"

"I may be another hour. I'm finishing up here, and then I'm going to go find Kristian. He's pretty fragile right now."

"I will be in the drawing room with the others. We will need to talk to him about a permanent solution to house the inmates."

"I'll tell him."

"Be careful. Viveka is still about."

"Not for long. I'm going to change her fate to trap her in the room I'm in. She'll come back to it. I'm sure of it."

"Do it safely."

"Yes, sir."

Soren left my mind, and I straightened in my chair. It was time to take care of business.

CHAPTER FIFTEEN

With a little help from Myrgjöl, casting the enchantment to trap Viveka in the viewing room only took a few seconds to set up. When she got caught, she could thank her Freyr for the idea. Now, all that was left to clean up this mess was to destroy the computer. I put my hands on the desktop tower and pushed a surge of magic into it. It glowed, sparkling brightly for a split second, and then suffered the same fate as the SD card had earlier. No one else would ever know what happened to Kristian in this castle—ever.

After taking one last glance around the room for evidence, I hurried out, relocked the door and went to find Kristian. I found him lying in his bed, wide-awake. I sat down and gave him a cheerful, "Hi."

He shifted to his side, propping his head up with his arm. "Hello. Did you have any luck?"

"I did."

He closed his eyes. "Who can I trust?"

"You can trust your brothers, Axel, the castle guards, and the castle staff. They are innocent. The rest of your hird and the harem have been imprisoned. Viveka will be captured soon. She was the mastermind, along with the doppelgänger. I have no doubt she will return to the locked room soon after she finds you have returned. I set a trap to keep her in there."

He sighed, looking exhausted. "Has Jakob been informed?"

"I'm sure Soren has told him by now."

"I find that Soren's name across your lips fills me with a jealousy I have never experienced before. I have no real right to be your mate. I know this. But I find I want you more each time I see you." He took my hand and tugged me down to him, brushing back the hair that fell in my face with an expression that was part-fascination and part-possessiveness. "You are beautiful, pure, and sexy—perfection."

I could feel my face flush with color. "It's my grandmother's magic. I have strong feelings for you, as well."

His expression turned hopeful. "Can I kiss you? I would like a memory of my mate without the creature's taint on it."

If I were to say to him that I didn't want the same thing, I'd be lying. Even after finding out he was the one that brought all of this into our lives, I still wanted him as much as I ever did. There was just something irresistible about him. Leaning forward, I pressed a chaste kiss against his lips. Only, it didn't feel chaste once our lips met. It felt right—really right, so I didn't protest when he deepened the kiss and lifted himself on top of me, or when he seized handfuls of my hair in his palms and kissed me until we were both breathless. It was only when he started unbuttoning my top that I stopped him.

"Kristian?" I shivered as he dragged his sharpened teeth down my neck.

"Yes?"

"We have to stop." My words sounded slurred around my fangs.

He nipped at my collarbone. "Do you want me to stop?"

Did I? Hell no. I felt like I would die if he left right now.

He gazed into my half-closed eyes. "Emelie?"

I shook my head. "No."

Smiling seductively, he asked, "What do you want, Emelie?"

"I want you to taste me."

Surprise lit his features, then hunger. Pushing my hair back to expose my neck, he pierced the tender flesh, and I moaned out his name in complete ecstasy, clutching myself to him, desperate to find his vein—until Soren burst in the door.

"Kristian!" Soren's loud voice reverberated in the vast room.

Standing quickly, Kristian wiped my blood off his mouth with the back of his hand. Judging by the look on his face, he and I agreed. He was a dead elf.

Soren's face was contorted with rage. However, to our surprise, gentle words came from his lips. "Long-term measures need to be taken for your prisoners. There are too many to hold in the dungeon. We are awaiting your direction in the drawing room."

"I will direct them now," Kristian said, then he left the room without even so much as another glance at me—figures.

I thought Soren would berate me. Hell, I wanted him to, but he didn't. He only said, "You are still bleeding."

Dizzily, I reached to touch my neck and pulled back bloody fingers. "Oh."

Sighing, he scooped me up off the bloodstained bed, carried me to the sofa in the sitting room, and knelt beside me. He didn't have to tell me how much it hurt him to have to heal Kristian's bites. I could hear it in his head. He was heart-broken and worried that when all of this was over, I wouldn't pick him.

Ashamed, I whispered, "I'm sorry, Soren."

He put his hand on my neck and closed his eyes. "Why did you do this now?"

Tears dampened the hair at my temples as I stared at the ceiling. I couldn't look at his agonized face. "It's the bond, I think. I know it's no excuse, but when he's around me, it's hard to have any self-control."

He pulled me into his embrace. "I am not angry at you, but Myrgjöl needs to remove your bond—now. If that is what you still want."

"I swear. I only truly want you. I always have."

Giving me a weak smile, he muttered, "And I swear to you, if I find out Kristian has used his talent for influence in any way, I will kill him."

A shrill, enraged scream sounded from the next room, making both of us jump. Soren drew his dagger and stood. "What the hell was that?"

I smiled smugly. "That would be Viveka realizing her charade is over. Shall we go see if she needs our assistance?"

He helped me to my feet and tucked my arm into his. "Let us go finish this—finally."

***

Exhausted after five hours of testimony with Odin's council, I threw myself onto a bench outside the council building and pouted. "They hated me."

Myrgjöl laughed. "They sure did. I have been on the receiving end of some of those looks myself. Not a great feeling, I know, but the council's opinions have never meant much to me. You should follow your grandmother's excellent example."

"She speaks the truth," Soren affirmed. "She has made her sentiments abundantly clear over the last five thousand years."

She winked at him. "Okay, maybe I would like to keep one council member's good opinion. The rest of them—not so much."

He bowed. "Thank you, Myrgjöl. Emelie, remember they are afraid of you. She has named you her successor, but you are an unknown and an untrained stranger to them. They do not know what to expect."

"He is right. They wonder what your motives are and what you would gain if you were to assume the role."

I huffed and stood up to pace. "Why do I have to gain anything? How about just doing it because it's the right thing to do?"

They both burst out laughing.

"Are you laughing at me? Because you know that's rude, don't you?"

They both sobered.

"Little one, no one would undertake that position without payment of some sort—no one."

"Well, I would. If whoever's asking me to cast is willing to pay travel expenses. Mom and Dad left me more money than I'll ever use in my long lifetime, and when I'm mated to Soren, I know I won't even use it."

Soren shook his head. "No. You will not."

"See, I don't need it."

Myrgjöl looked skeptical. "Think about this, Emelie. I don't want to see you become unsatisfied like your mother. After a while, she became bored. She started to resent her chosen path, telling me on many occasions she felt like a servant."

"Uh, no offense, but Mom was selfish, and I'm nothing like her. I'm always going to be interested in finding the right path for others. I found mine, and it's perfect. How could I not want that for everyone?"

Her silver brows lifted. "Indeed? What then of Kristian?"

I glared at her for bringing him up. She knew mentioning him would ruffle Soren's feathers—so to speak. "What do you mean?"

"I mean, would you wish the same for Kristian?"

"Well, yes, I meant everyone, except for the doppelgänger. He doesn't deserve anyone. Or rather, no one deserves him."

"What if there was no other for Kristian?"

"Just get it out into the open," Soren said.

I smiled at him, bemused. "Yeah. What are you getting at?"

With a cheerless voice, she murmured, "I can see no other for him."

Soren's jaw clenched. "You mean, no other than my mate, do you not?"

"Yes."

"Oh, come on!" I exclaimed. "No one has ever had two true mates. It's impossible. You just haven't found her. I haven't tried. Maybe I can find her."

She considered me for a moment. "Maybe."

"Besides," I added. "He's got something a little more important than finding a mate going on today. When will he face the tribunal?"

Myrgjöl glanced up at the three moons on the horizon. "It should be over soon. It is a waste of time as it is. A change in king would cast fear in the hearts of the dark elves. Faith in their leader is compulsory for a happy realm. The council remembers this well."

"They also know Jakob is the rightful king," Soren muttered.

"Look," I reasoned, "Kristian may have made a mistake that ultimately led to the destruction of his personal life, a war, and thousands of deaths, but you cannot deny he was always a good leader to his subjects. The elves have suffered enough. They need stability in their lives."

Soren threw his hands up. "How can you say that? You are one of his subjects, Emelie. Did he treat you well?"

"Emelie's right," Myrgjöl interrupted. "Kristian is a good male. He is only guilty of his desperation to be king and using his influence on Emelie, nothing more."

Thunderstruck, I asked, "How do you know he used his influence?"

"He has been using it since the moment you met him. I wish I could have told you sooner, but you know I am not allowed to interfere."

That explained a lot. Like, how I was tempted to give him my blood and go with him to his castle after I promised Soren I wouldn't, and even why I was so eager to share a bed with him. "That's sad."

Soren's eyebrows shot up in disbelief. "Sad? Try psychotic."

"Well, yeah, but really, all he ever tried to do was have control over the ones he loved, and now he has nothing except his title to console him."

Myrgjöl pinched my cheeks. "You remind me so much of my Barnabas. He would have said much the same."

"I think you two are giving him more credit than he deserves," Jakob said from behind us. He looked somber.

"How did the tribunal go?" I asked with a hopeful note in my voice.

"Their decisions were just. Viveka will serve a century of imprisonment on Niflheim, as will the others involved. Separately, of course. Kristian will remain king, and the doppelgänger will be put to death for offenses previous to the one he committed against Kristian. Those only added to a long list of misdeeds."

"Have you said your goodbyes to Viveka?" I asked. It must be excruciating for him to lose his mate for a hundred years.

"I have. It was painful to say goodbye, but I will soon recover. In what I assume is a test of your honesty and willingness to serve, the council has ordered your first sanctioned fate prediction to be my own."

His smile was telling. Jakob was beyond ready for his true mate. "Are you sure you trust me to do that?"

"I do, indeed, Emelie."

"I am relieved," Soren said. "I despised her."

Jakob nodded. "As did I."

"What about all that lovey-dovey stuff at the castle?"

"It was an act. She hasn't been the female I fell in love with for a thousand years."

"Oh, wow. You're a pretty convincing actor, Jakob."

My grandmother nodded. "He is. You should have seen him play in Macbeth in 1653. You were breathtaking, Jakob."

Color rose in his cheeks. "Uh … thank you, my lady."

I had to laugh. For the first time, I was witnessing Jakob look less than his usual reserved self. "So, what's next?" I asked Soren.

"We find out if they will give their permission to have your fate with Kristian broken."

My stomach twisted in knots. What if Kristian wasn't willing to let me go? What if he had used his influence on the council to keep our bond intact? I closed my eyes and took a deep breath, praying I wouldn't start hyperventilating right here on the sidewalk. It wouldn't be fair to have gone through everything we did and still not be able to be together.

Myrgjöl took my hand, and we walked up the stone steps leading to the doors. "Come on, Emelie. There is only one way to find out what they have decided."

"See you soon," Jakob called after us.

My shoes made small tapping noises as we walked to the reception desk. Self-conscious, I tried to step lighter. No need to bring unwanted attention to me, not when we were about to ask for something that just isn't done—ever.

We lined up along the desk waiting to be acknowledged for a few moments, but the receptionist never looked up. Tired of waiting, I finally said, "Excuse me," but she interrupted.

"The Council is expecting you." She motioned to the bank of elevators to our right. "If you will take one to the fifth floor, you will find they are already in session."

Soren bowed to her. "Thank you."

"What was that?" I asked once we were on our way up.

"Little one, when you are as old as we are, patience is no longer a virtue; it is a way of life."

"On Midgard, we call that rude," I huffed.

Soren laced his fingers with mine. "Calm yourself, Emelie. Do not give them cause to doubt your strength by showing anger."

"I'll try." I was pretty sure anything else would be easier to do. Like, anything else on any world.

Smiling at me in reassurance, Myrgjöl led me out of the elevator, opened a set of double doors, and announced, "We have returned!"

A collective sigh circled the room.

Soren stepped forward and inclined his head to the group. "What is your decision?"

A small-wizened male hurried over with two chairs. Tsking, he said, "Where are our manners? Be seated, ladies."

I obliged and quietly gave my thanks, while my grandmother made a total spectacle of herself, flirting outrageously with the much older looking male.

A sharp female voice sounded from the last row of the council members. "Enough of this frivolity. Let us announce our decision."

"Very well," answered a dark-haired male that stood up tall in the front row. I could feel the exact moment his eyes leveled on my face. Almost unwillingly, I glanced up, and we locked eyes, staring at each other intently for several seconds. He was trying to read me—like I would give him the satisfaction. Clearing his throat, he said, "The council hereby agrees to the dissolution of the bond between the king and queen of Svartálfaheim."

The joy that filled me at his words quickly dissipated when he didn't sit right away. Something else was coming.

"In the matter of Lady Emelie Andersdotter taking the place of Myrgjöl the Great, it has been decided that barring any impediments; she will be an acceptable replacement. We will, of course, need a demonstration to assure her powers are comparable with yours, Myrgjöl."

My grandmother inclined her head. "Of course, you do."

"Prince Jakob Väsen has volunteered his fate to be the first approved prediction. Will someone retrieve him?"

I didn't like the way he stressed the word, 'approved'. Apparently, he knew about Katrine and Cedric or Hilda and Gunnar. Which begged the question—who had told him?

The kind, old male that brought us the chairs walked to a side door and ushered in Jakob, who appeared calm, but was rambling to me in my mind. "Why did I agree to this? Do not fuck this up, Emelie! I do not want to end up mated to a frost giant."

He probably thought I would be offended by his lack of faith. I wasn't. I had the same doubts he did.

"Emelie?"

I coughed to cover up the startled noise I made when Myrgjöl spoke in my head unexpectedly. *"Yes, Grandmother?"*

"We will not be giving a demonstration today—or ever. We are shifting out of here on my command. You have to. Else, you'll have to wait to mate Soren until your service is over. We do this on our terms from here on out. Understand?"

"Yes, but I haven't mastered the art of shifting yet. I'll need someone's help to leave."

"Tell them both we will meet in Álfheim, and have Soren help you get there."

"Okay."

I quickly reiterated the plan to Jakob and Soren. Both gave me barely imperceptible nods of agreement.

Myrgjöl stood. "Lord Councilman, I have decided the Norns will no longer labor under the council's demands and wants. You serve no one, nor shall we. Good day to you."

Her words caused an uproar. Soren threw his arms around me, pulling me tight against him, and then he drew his dagger. The last thing I saw before disappearing were the guards extracting their swords from their sides and running toward us. I was still screaming when we appeared in Jakob's house on Álfheim.

My grandmother clapped her hands together in excitement when she saw us. "I've wanted to do that for at least four millennia."

"I think I'm still struggling not to have a heart attack because of that!" I snarled. My heart felt like it was beating out of my chest.

She laughed. "Don't be silly. Our kind cannot have a heart attack."

Huh, learn something every day, I guess. "You still could have told me you were planning to do that."

Pursing her lips, she said, "I thought you would appreciate it. You and Soren are free to mate now."

Shit. She was right. And, seriously, what Norn forgets they aren't allowed to mate until their service is over? The idiot kind, like me. That's who.

"I'm sorry. I forgot about the stipulations. Wait a minute. You were able to mate. How did you get away with it?"

"I mated a human. It was a mere vacation in the eyes of the council."

"They equated my grandfather to a vacation?"

"You will soon learn the ways of our society, and that will be a sad day, indeed. It had such promise before the council. That is why I find that rebellion is nigh upon us."

"Will they look for us here?"

She looked thoughtful. "I do not believe so. We are infinitely more powerful than they are. They will have to come up with more of a plan than just trying to grab us off the street."

"Or maybe, that is what they want you to believe," Soren said.

"They? Are you not part of the council?"

He shook his head, eyes aglow. "After that, Myrgjöl? I wonder if I am not a wanted male."

Twenty minutes later, Myrgjöl left Álfheim, but not before she congratulated us on a job well done and promised to keep us updated with any happenings we should know about. She, Soren, and Jakob, along with Nils and Viggo had spent the last hour discussing various ideas for my protection, but now that the males were speculating on the ways we all might die at the hands of the council, she was taking her leave. I couldn't blame her. I was tired of hearing death scenarios myself.

Interrupting Viggo's story, in which we were hypothetically dropped into a volcano by a half-male, half-hawk creature that secretly takes care of the council's potential problems, I asked, "Soren, can we go home?"

"Home?"

"I mean, to our apartment on Ásgard."

Nils crowed with laughter. "Holy shit, Soren. You actually showed her that pathetic monument, built for someone who was not expected to arrive for decades to come."

"Shut up, Nils," I said, surprised so many in the room echoed it.

Soren smirked and stood. "Let us go, my love."

We said our goodbyes to everyone but Nils, who refused to talk to us and shifted to the front door of our home. Once there, Soren insisted he make a quick sweep of the rooms before he let me enter. I waited, nervously, with my back to the wall in between the elevator and stairwell, imagining the worst. But he was back in less than a minute to show me inside.

"I had some of your things sent over," he said, pointing to the bedroom. "You should have everything you need to be comfortable for the day."

"Thanks."

"You are welcome. I want to go over the security tapes to see if anyone has been here besides the cleaning crew. No one knows I own this building. However, we cannot be too careful."

"Okay. Hurry?" I was jumpy from all of the events of the day. I didn't want to be alone for long.

He arched a brow. "I promise."

"Good. Is the bathroom still at the end of the hall?"

He smiled. "Last I checked."

Making my way to the bedroom, I lovingly eyeballed the mountain of fluffy pillows on the way to the shower. Sleep sounded so good, but first, I wanted to bathe. I still had dried blood on my neck from last night. Yuck.

Both of us fresh from the shower, I found Soren waiting for me atop the wooden trunk at the foot of the bed. He grinned as he took in my damp hair and pink kitten pajamas. "Feel better?"

"Tons." I sighed, cozying up to him by standing between his knees. "And I'll thank you very much not to make fun of my jammies while you are still wearing Christmas ones."

"I would not dream of it," he said, his eyes twinkling. "Are you ready to dive into this monstrosity of feathers?"

"I thought you'd never ask," I told him, then dove headfirst onto the bed, laughing hysterically when I barely made a dent. "Uh … did you ever stop to think this might be a ridiculous number of pillows?"

He picked a pathway to me through them and lay down on his side. "You don't like my pillows?"

I burst out in horrified laughter. "You like all these?"

"No. That is what is called a joke, Emelie. I know you are young, but surely, you have heard of them by now."

Feigning an expression of shock, I gasped. "A joke? You can do that?"

He kissed me roughly, making my heart palpitate in triple time. "If you have asked all your questions, I have one of my own."

"Yes, I will mate you."

"I believe you are supposed to wait until I ask, Emelie."

"Sorry, go ahead."

He rolled his eyes. "Will you take me as your mate?"

I didn't even take a second to think it over. "Yes."

Without preamble, he took my hand and bit lightly into my palm, only taking enough blood to coat his lip. "I accept you as my fated mate. Let us never be parted."

I lifted his palm to my mouth and bit down, swallowing a mouthful of his potent blood before coating my lip. Soren's eyes opened wide with surprise as my eyes glazed over in a sheen of silver, and I spoke the bonding words in a voice that wasn't my own. "I accept you as my fated mate. Let us never be parted."

It was almost too easy to push the magic that would connect us through him and back into me. Though it was a strange sensation, it was one that felt more than right. It was as if the magic was asking, "What took so long?"

Leaning forward, I pressed my lips to Soren's and waited on the pain that had accompanied my last bonding. Thankfully, no pain came—until a moment later when Kristian's screams filled my head. Opening my eyes, I found Soren's questioning crimson ones trained on me. "It is done."

He didn't speak in words, but in actions, pushing me to my back and slowly taking my mouth with his. I returned the kiss, yearning for him to deepen it, but he was in no rush. He would savor every moment of his mating night.

Dipping a searching fingertip into my cleavage, he gave me a wicked, fanged smile that made me melt. "Emelie, your beauty is only complimented by the clothing you choose to wear. However, I think it is time to lose the kittens."

I trailed my own curious fingertip down his chest and into his pants, snapping the elastic waistband. "You're one to talk, Rudolph."

In an instant, we were both unclothed, and he was kissing his way across my breasts. "Have you anything else to say, sweeting?"

"Yay?"

With a devious expression, he said, "Hmmm … we'll have to do better than that," then started kissing his way down my stomach.

Ten seconds later, I was way past, "Yay!" and fast approaching "Oh, Lord, please let me survive this night so that I can do it again and again for the next million years or so." He was a master with that tongue.

Giving me time to catch my nonexistent breath, he knelt up to sit on his knees and slid his caressing hands lightly over my nipples and then to either side of my waist, pulling me closer and opening my legs for him to enter me. I clutched the sheet on either side of me, waiting.

Leaning forward on all fours above me, he pressed his sex against mine and whispered, "You are so beautiful, Emelie."

I writhed against him, moaning a low cry of pleasure. He made me feel beautiful—sexy even. Everywhere his hungry eyes roamed, his hands and tongue would soon follow. He made me feel like a goddess. "Take me as your mate, Soren."

He savagely took my mouth, before breaking the kiss and positioning himself at my core. "I will be gentle. It will only hurt for a minute."

I nodded, mute with a mixture of arousal, fear, and excitement.

Tensing, I gritted my teeth as he began to push into me. It wasn't anything like I'd imagined it would be. I'd always been told having sex for the first time hurt, but that it was a delicious intrusion. This wasn't like that at all. It was awful, the most excruciating agony I'd ever experienced. With tears leaking from my eyes, I cried out, unable to continue. He felt too big, too hard— and then, in between one deep breath and the next, the pain seemed to evaporate, evolving into something that far surpassed my limited experience in pleasure. There wasn't a word that described what he felt like inside me.

Soren scrutinized my face. "Emelie, I will withdraw."

"No," I gasped. "Please, don't stop."

He blew out a shaky, alleviated breath and kissed me. "If you insist."

"I …" My sassy reply escaped me and turned to moans as he gently pulled out and pushed back in. I raised my hips to meet his thrusts, encouraging him to speed up his rhythm.

The impenetrable control Soren had on his mind seemed to slip as he neared his orgasm, allowing me to hear his frantic thoughts. *"She's so tight, so hot … so perfect. Don't. Fucking. Come."* And those thoughts were all it took to push me over the edge. I cried out incoherent words as I reached my screaming completion and collapsed into the pillows, hoarse and panting beneath him.

My own words came out husky and slurred by fangs. "So, you think I'm perfect?"

He stilled within me and smiled, though it seemed to take considerable effort. "Stop reading my mind, Lady Vidar."

I laughed. "I honestly don't think I can."

His eyes flashed with heat. "On second thought, maybe you shouldn't stop. It could be very interesting."

He moved in me again, making me catch my breath. Exhaling a very feminine sigh, I wrapped my legs around him and luxuriated in the heavenly feeling of his broad sex filling me.

"I love that sound—love the feel of you around my cock," he growled, through clenched teeth

I dug my fingernails into his back as his thrusts became harder, wilder. "Then come for me, Soren."

With a reckless abandon that was utterly out of character, he pounded into me as he lifted my neck to his mouth, first tracing the vein with his tongue, then biting down firmly.

For a second time, I came apart, scoring his back and rocking my hips, answering his every brutal thrust with my own until he spilled into me with a forceful yell of my name.

Several seconds passed before either of us moved. In my blissful state, I wasn't sure I could even remember how. "Wow," I whispered.

Soren lifted his head and gingerly pulled out of me with a look of concern. "Are you okay?"

'Okay' seemed like such a paltry word for the way I felt right now. Fantastic, spectacular, or even just really, really, really good would be a better description than okay. What I felt was ecstasy. "I'm great," I assured him.

He kissed me slowly, nipping at my bottom lip with his teeth—the taste of my blood on his tongue an aphrodisiac. I desperately wanted him to make love to me again.

With a lift of his eyebrows, he asked, "Emelie?"

"Soren?" I answered, completely breathless.

He pushed his still hard sex into me. "I could never deny you. You are my mate."

"Stay out ... of ... my head," I scolded him, between his thrusts.

He chuckled and kissed me again. "I honestly do not think I can."

THE NEXT CHAPTER

Freyr paced in his small metal cell. They were smart. He'd give them that. Iron always did dull his magic. Though he was not a patient male, even he had to admit it would take an enormous stroke of luck, along with all his magic to escape his prison. If there were ever to be any hope, he would have to make sure every potential for error was discovered. That could take time. Thankfully, he had plenty of that. Time would be his only companion in his captor's unyielding cage.

The solitude over the last few weeks had given him the hope he was no longer a concern to them. For days, they turned their scrutiny upon his plans, and for days, he resisted their efforts, relinquishing no information. With his level of magic, there were very few that would gain any knowledge. It was insulting to him that they'd sent the lowliest, common creatures to question him. Was he not a God? Did they think so little of his power?

He shook his head to rid himself of the memory. Just thinking of how the inferior beings treated him as if he were garbage enraged him. Combined with the raw nerve that was exposed by him being bested by one of his slaves, even if she was half-Norn, did not make the wound to his pride any shallower. The elves were his to master.

As the nights spread out behind him, he had little to do but lay in his confinement and plan his revenge. Common sense told him the Norn could not hold him with her magic forever, and when his freedom was finally gained, he would take her as the first of his many returning slaves. She would die when he got tired of her, of that, he was certain. He'd never found one that interested him for very long. Of course, it would all have to be done in secret. There was no need to make her a martyr for the elves. Her death would surely give them a cause for unity, and that was an unnecessary distraction.

Yes, it was time his slaves return to the way of the past, where humans, elves, and all creatures alike worshipped him. It was the only fitting position for a God of his magnitude. The hardest part would be earning their trust. Promises of fertility and peace had been enough in the past, but today's creatures wouldn't be as easy to fool. Most had lived half as long as he. That made the only fitting solution an easy one. He would start with the mortals on Midgard. Humans had always been his easiest targets. In the past, he'd been able to manipulate them into almost anything. It shouldn't pose a problem now. If it did, they could join the thousands of creatures who had allied against him in their eternal slumber.

Freyr continued to pace. Tonight, he felt restless, on edge, like he did before a battle. Someone or something was coming.

A rattle from the antechamber's doors confirmed his suspicions. He had a visitor. Something told him this serendipitous opportunity was the one he had been waiting on. Did he dare attempt an escape? There would only be one chance at freedom. If he failed, he wouldn't need a Norn to predict his future. There was only one fate for a murderer who could not be caged—death.

As footsteps neared the door, he was relieved to recognize Viveka's signature.

"Freyr, it is Katrine." She laughed huskily at her favorite deceptive appearance.

He stood and peered cautiously through the eye-level slot. Katrine was indeed there. She looked exactly as she had when he last saw her, a ravishing, dark-haired beauty with eyes that revealed the madness that plagued her mind.

"Have I been freed?"

Viveka laughed again, this time with her usual maniacal lilt in her voice. "Of course not, I grow tired of the solitude. I will stay no longer."

With a mechanical click, the door swung open.

"How have you incapacitated the guards?"

She smiled serenely. "I did not have to. Let us say that Katrine has a very persuasive mouth."

Freyr pulled her into his arms and kissed her hard, leaving her breathless. "A lovely mouth it is."

She stood unspeaking, ready to obey any command. She would not be difficult to direct. Persuasive mouth or not, she was only an elf.

"Come elf. I have a world to conquer."

THE END

Also by J.D. Nelson

Wicked Ways Series

A Night of Wickedness
All I Want For Christmas Are My Two Front Fangs: A Wicked
Ways Companion Novel
Wolves Will Be Wolves
Too Cute To Spook: A Wicked Ways Companion Novel

Night Aberrations Series

Night Aberrations
The Fire within the Night

Stand Alone Novels

Control: A Tale of Desire

About the Author

JD NELSON BOOKS

JD Nelson is a Bestselling Author of Fantasy Romance and Adult Paranormal Romance. An avid time-waster, JD enjoys watching TV and listening to audiobooks when she really should be writing. JD loves to hear from her readers. You can contact her through her website, AuthorJDNelson.com, or on Facebook, where she spends an alarming amount of time chatting with her many Author and reader friends, much to the dismay of her continually neglected manuscripts.

JD Nelson's Facebook
www.facebook.com/NightAberrations
JD Nelson's Twitter
https://twitter.com/authorjdnelson
JD Nelson's Facebook Fan Page
www.facebook.com/JDNelsonsNightAberrations
JD Nelson's Fan Club
http://www.facebook.com/groups/269730583130725/

www.ingramcontent.com/pod-product-compliance
Lightning Source LLC
Chambersburg PA
CBHW060152180626
46813CB00007B/2715